IT ONLY TAKES
A MOMENT

ALSO BY MARY JANE CLARK

When Day Breaks

Lights Out Tonight

Dancing in the Dark

Hide Yourself Away

Nowhere to Run

Nobody Knows

Close to You

Let Me Whisper in Your Ear

Do You Promise Not to Tell?

Do You Want to Know a Secret?

MARY JANE CLARK

IT ONLY TAKES A MOMENT

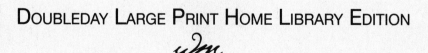

DOUBLEDAY LARGE PRINT HOME LIBRARY EDITION

wm

WILLIAM MORROW

An Imprint of HarperCollinsPublishers

This Large Print Edition, prepared especially
for Doubleday Large Print Home Library,
contains the complete, unabridged text of
the original Publisher's Edition.

Library of Congress Cataloging-in-Publication
Data has been applied for.

ISBN 978-0-7394-9764-7

This Large Print Book carries the
Seal of Approval of N.A.V.H.

For Elizabeth and David

And for all the families who struggle with Fragile X Syndrome, the most common cause of inherited mental impairment. Hang in there. A treatment should be coming soon.

PROLOGUE

Several days from now . . .

Overflowing baskets and tall vases of flowers lined the dimly lit room and people with grim faces stood watching as she approached the small casket. The little coffin was covered with a spray of roses and lilies of the valley arranged in the shape of an angel.

With every bit of strength she had, Eliza forced herself to go forward. She knelt before the casket, her fists clenched, her eyes shut tight. She felt excruciating pressure. Everyone was looking at her, waiting for her reaction, relieved that they were watching *her* life and not theirs. Nothing would go forward without her doing what she had to do.

You have to look. You have to look. You have to see what's inside.

Eliza bent her head down and opened her eyes. The first thing she saw was a cascading shower of white tulle spilling from the casket walls. Her hand shook violently as she reached out to pull back the bridal veil.

MONDAY
JULY 21

CHAPTER 1

"Look!" Janie called out. "She's wearing it, Mrs. Garcia. Mommy's wearing the bracelet."

Carmen Garcia glanced up from gathering the child's shiny brown hair in a ponytail. The middle-aged woman leaned forward to get a better look at the image on the television screen. Eliza Blake, clad in a cornflower-colored blouse that complemented her blue eyes, was smiling from the set of *KEY to America* as she and a cookbook author demonstrated how to organize a summer barbecue. As the camera cut to a close-up of her hand rubbing a mixture of spices on the meat, the red, yellow, and blue plastic beads that encircled her wrist came into clear view.

"*Sí.*" Mrs. Garcia smiled. "Your *mamá* likes the bracelet you made at camp very much."

"How do you say 'bracelet' in Spanish?" Janie asked.

"*Pulsera,*" Mrs. Garcia answered. "Now, hurry. Eat your breakfast. The bus will be here soon."

Janie, wearing navy blue shorts and a white Camp Musquapsink T-shirt, took a seat at the kitchen table while Daisy, the yellow Labrador retriever, positioned herself at the child's feet. Janie dutifully ate the cereal and chunks of cantaloupe that Mrs. Garcia had put out for her while the housekeeper consulted the calendar hanging on the refrigerator door.

"It's Native American Day," Mrs. Garcia announced. "You have archery and horseback riding."

"I know," said Janie, making a face. "I hate archery. It's too hard."

"The more you practice, the easier it will get. Do your best, *mi hija*. Just do the best you can. That makes your *mamá* happy."

"Bows and arrows are dumb," declared Janie. "But we're going to have our faces painted. That will be fun." The little girl's eyes widened with pride. "And you know what else? Musquapsink is a Native American name."

"It is?"

"So is Ho-Ho-Kus," Janie reported, proud that she could teach Mrs. Garcia something. "There are lots of Native American names around here. Pascack and Hackensack and Kinderkamack. My counselor told us."

Mrs. Garcia watched proprietarily as Janie tackled her bowl of cereal. She was such a healthy-looking child. A light suntan and a sprinkling of freckles covered her cheeks and straight little nose. Her blue eyes sparkled, just like her mother's did. Her permanent teeth seemed to be coming in white and, so far, straight. Her legs and arms, which protruded from the day camp uniform, were well-toned and sturdy.

Feeling Mrs. Garcia's eyes on her, Janie looked up. "What are you staring at?" she asked.

"You, *mi hija.* I'm staring at you, *tesoro.*"

"What does that mean?" asked Janie, not familiar with the Spanish word.

"It means 'treasure,'" Mrs. Garcia explained. "You are your *mamá*'s *tesoro*. She loves you more than anything."

The black van cruised slowly on the gently winding road that rimmed the pond. Passing stately colonials and sprawling ranch-style homes separated by acres of rolling lawns and lush landscaping, the driver pulled over to a carefully chosen spot between two houses, confident that the van would not be visible from inside either dwelling. He turned off the engine.

"How ya doin'?" the driver called out his open window, lifting his paper coffee cup in salute to the workman who drove past in a red truck.

In the weeks he'd been staking out this neighborhood, the driver knew the last thing that would ever look out of place here was a service vehicle. Every morning, landscapers, painters, electricians, and carpenters traveled through the quiet streets on their way to their jobs of maintaining the homes of the wealthy.

The homeowners worked on Wall Street or were officers of major corporations or had successful companies of their own. They didn't have the inclination to mow their grass or the desire to spend their weekends making home improvements. They hired people to do those things. His van wouldn't be noted as out of the ordinary at all. In fact, in all the days he had been canvassing the neighborhood, not once had any of the patrolling police cars stopped him.

The driver glanced at his watch. *Anytime now.* He sipped his lukewarm coffee and waited, keeping his eyes trained straight ahead at the brick Federal-style colonial way down at the end of the road.

"They're late this morning," he muttered. "Wouldn't you know they'd be late this morning?"

Finally, the yellow minibus came into view. "There it is," he said, crushing the empty cup in his hand. "There's the bus."

The driver reached out to turn the key in the ignition.

"Hold on," said a voice from the back

of the van. "Don't rush it. We've got plenty of time. We've planned this carefully and we want to do this thing right."

The horn of the camp bus sounded.

Janie took a last swallow of milk, wiped her mouth with the back of her hand, and wrapped her arms around her dog's neck for one more hug. She ran to the front door and waited for Mrs. Garcia to enter the code to disarm the home-security system. Mrs. Garcia stood guard in the open doorway until Janie had safely boarded and the bus drove away.

The housekeeper went back to the kitchen, cleared the bowls, cups, and silverware from the table and put them in the dishwasher. As she stood at the sink and washed her hands, Mrs. Garcia looked out the window, noticing that the geraniums were sorely in need of deadheading. She unlocked the French doors, slid back the screen, and walked out onto the slate patio. After she had separated the brownish buds from the white, healthy ones, Mrs. Garcia returned to the kitchen to drop the spent flowers in the trash.

"Come on, Daisy," Mrs. Garcia said, filling the dog's bowl with water. "Let's get you outside."

The yellow Lab followed the house-keeper out to the rear of the property where a shingled doghouse was positioned under a canopy of leaves. Mrs. Garcia put the bowl of water on the ground and hooked a long leash, designed to provide a wide range of movement, to the dog's collar.

Then, Mrs. Garcia went back into the house, pulling the screen door shut but leaving the French doors open to let in some fresh summer-morning air.

The black van pulled directly into the driveway, coming to rest at the side of the house. Two figures dressed in overalls and work boots emerged. They walked purposefully around to the backyard, pausing to pull latex masks over their heads.

"All set?" hissed the smaller of the two from behind an Olive Oyl mask that sported beady eyes and jet black hair pulled back in a bun.

The other, as Popeye the sailor, stuck up his thumb. "Yep," he said firmly. "We aren't leaving anything to chance. I've been watching her for weeks and, on nice days, she leaves the back door open in the morning."

A dog started barking from the rear of the property. The yellow Lab ran toward them but was pulled back as the leash became taut.

"Don't worry. That damned dog is always barking," said Popeye. "The housekeeper isn't going to think anything of it."

Silently, Olive Oyl slid back the screen door. From inside the house, the telephone rang. Carefully and quietly, they followed in the direction of the voice that answered.

"Sí, Mrs. Blake. Janie got off to camp all right." Mrs. Garcia's voice could be heard coming from upstairs.

The intruders made their way to the staircase.

"Everything is fine here." The housekeeper's voice sounded louder.

They climbed to the second floor.

"Okay, I will see you when you get home, Mrs. Blake."

Mrs. Garcia put the phone back in its cradle. She finished making the bed, fluffing the pillows and smoothing the coverlet. As she straightened up, she glanced in the mirror over the double dresser and saw two masked figures approaching her from behind.

Mrs. Garcia lunged for the table at the side of the bed, but before she could reach the security button designed to summon help, Popeye pulled her back and threw her onto the mattress. Olive Oyl joined in, helping to pin her down. Together, they flipped Mrs. Garcia over so that she was lying with her face pressed against the coverlet, her air supply blocked. Using all her strength, the housekeeper struggled to free herself.

"Don't fight me, lady," said Popeye as he tied Mrs. Garcia's arms behind her back. "Save your energy. You've got a long day ahead of you."

CHAPTER 2

Eliza hung up the phone, unclipped the microphone from her blouse, and got up from the sofa in the *KEY to America* "living room." Today, it was Harry Granger's turn to hang around in case there was any updating needed for the West Coast stations. She was free to go to her office and get organized before the reporter for *People* magazine arrived for an interview scheduled at ten o'clock.

As she walked across the studio, she saw *KTA* producer Annabelle Murphy. "That's some tan you've got there," said Eliza.

Annabelle smiled. "A benefit of working these early hours," she said. "I get to take the twins to the pool almost every afternoon."

"You and Mike and the kids should come out to the 'burbs some weekend soon and hang out at the pool," said Eliza. "Janie loves Tara and Thomas. They can swim and we can relax."

Annabelle rolled her eyes. "Relax? What's that? When I'm at the pool with those two, I never even get a chance to sit down. I'm always breaking up water fights or smearing them with more sunscreen. When I come home from all that *relaxing,* I'm exhausted."

"So you don't want to come?" asked Eliza.

"Are you kidding? We'd love to. When?"

"How about this weekend? Are you and Mike free on Sunday, maybe two o'clock?"

"Great," said Annabelle. "We'll be there." Her eyes traveled to the beads around Eliza's wrist. "Nice bracelet. Bendel's?" she asked.

"Try Camp Musquapsink." Eliza laughed, extending her arm. "Janie made it for me in arts and crafts."

"Well, she should go into business," said Annabelle, examining the beads more closely. "I saw some bracelets, not as nice as this one, selling for fifty bucks apiece. Come to think of it, why don't I get the twins and we can form an assembly line, make these things, sell them at high-end stores, and retire?"

"Sure," said Eliza. "I'm up for flouting child labor laws, if you are."

Annabelle smiled. "Where are you off to?"

"My office. I've got yet another interview this morning. But, to tell you the truth, I think the exposure has gotten a little ridiculous. At some point, nobody cares anymore."

"Who's the interview with this time?" asked Annabelle.

People," answered Eliza. "So, if there is anyone left in America who doesn't know that I'm a widow with a seven-year-old daughter who lives in Ho-Ho-Kus, New Jersey, and relishes an occasional Butterfinger, this interview should take care of that."

As they began to part company, Eliza turned back. "By the way, Margo and I are having lunch today. Want to join us? We can hash over old times."

"What old times?" asked Annabelle. "We haven't known Margo for very long at all. She's just been with KEY News for a few months."

"True," said Eliza, "but it's the quality of the time we've had that counts. There's been some pretty intense stuff packed in there."

"Rain check," said Annabelle. "I've got a piece about compulsive shopping airing tomorrow and it's nowhere near ready. But let's all get together another time soon. We'll get B.J. and have a little reunion of our Sunrise Suspense Society."

Walking the rest of the way across the studio, Annabelle recalled the way the four of them, Eliza, Margo Gonzalez, B.J. D'Elia, and herself, had come together to figure out who had killed Constance Young, the former cohost of *KEY to America*. Those were circumstances that almost cost Eliza her life. Then Annabelle reflected on what it must be like to be the public figure that Eliza Blake was. The idea of having so many of the personal details of one's life displayed for anyone and everyone to see caused Annabelle to shiver involuntarily. She felt all of those media stories could be leaving Eliza open and vulnerable.

CHAPTER 3

"Here's what you're gonna do," said Popeye after he had tied Mrs. Garcia's arms behind her back. He pointed a gun at her. "You are going to call the camp and tell them that you're driving over to pick up Janie. Tell them that something has come up and her mother wants her to come home early."

Mrs. Garcia shook her head. "No. I cannot do that."

"Oh yes, you can, because, if you don't, we are going to make sure that Janie has an accident at camp today. If you choose not to make the call and don't get Janie, then we'll have no other choice than to have our people at the camp hurt her, badly. You know how freak accidents can happen to little kids. A lifeguard looks the other way and a child drowns. Or a counselor doesn't pay attention and a kid wanders into the woods and God knows what the kid will find out there. You wouldn't want that, would you?"

Mrs. Garcia stared into the man's dark eyes, peering out from the eyeholes in the mask. She tried to assess the truthfulness of his words. Were there really people at the day camp working with these awful creatures? Was Janie in danger there?

Carmen Garcia had known fear in her life. The fear of poverty, the fear of not having enough to eat or a dry, safe place to sleep in her native village in Guatemala. She had been scared when she came to America, knowing almost no one, unfamiliar with the new country and its ways. She'd been apprehensive with each job she had taken and every new boss she had tried to please. But not until now, she realized, had she ever experienced abject terror. *What are these people capable of doing?*

"How do I know that you won't hurt Janie if I get her?" she asked, fighting to keep her voice steady.

"You don't. But all I can tell you is, the kid is worth more to us alive than dead. We don't want to hurt Janie. We want her healthy and in one piece."

Mrs. Garcia's mind raced. If the man was bluffing and there were no accomplices at Camp Musquapsink, then Janie was safer right where she was. But if the man was telling the truth, Janie might be in more danger at camp than she would be if Mrs. Garcia went and got her. At least that way, Mrs. Garcia could try to take care of her.

"Don't you think that your boss would want you to be with Janie to protect her?" said Olive Oyl, speaking for the first time. "How do you think Eliza Blake will react when she finds out you had a chance to save her little girl but you decided not to?" It was a woman's voice, but it was raspy. Mrs. Garcia got the impression that the speaker was trying to disguise her voice. But the woman's question helped Mrs. Garcia make up her mind.

"All right," she said. "I make the call."

CHAPTER 4

The reporter from *People* asked all the usual questions.

"How are you finding getting up so early in the morning again?" he inquired.

Eliza smiled. "Obviously, it's not the high point of the job, but that's about the only negative to being back on the show."

"There's been lots of shuffling and trading places among TV news personalities. Katie Couric leaving *Today* for the *CBS Evening News,* Meredith Vieira leaving *The View* to take Katie's place, Charles Gibson switching from *Good Morning America* to *World News Tonight.*

What made you make the change from the evening news back to the morning?" he asked.

"Well, as you know I spent several years hosting *KEY to America* before I began anchoring the *KEY Evening Headlines.* I loved the time I spent on the show back then, but when the opportunity arose to take the anchor spot at night, it was something I felt, professionally, I couldn't, shouldn't, turn down. On a personal level, I thought the hours would be better, perhaps enabling me to spend more time with my daughter." Eliza laughed. "But that clearly isn't the case. Both jobs require an intense time commitment."

"So if both jobs take such a huge time investment, why not stay at the *Evening Headlines*?" the reporter asked.

Eliza tucked some of her shoulder-length brown hair behind her ear. "I know most people view the evening-news anchor job as the pinnacle in network news, and I suppose it is. But I missed the variety of the morning program. I can be interviewing politicians and heads of state about truly important issues, issues that affect the lives of millions of people and, in the same show, learn how to skateboard or chat about the latest fashion trends."

"So would you say that you have a shallow side?" asked the reporter.

Eliza ignored the zinger. "I'd say that life is multifaceted and that I'm interested in all of it," she said.

The reporter flipped over a page of his notebook. "What about your daughter, Janie?"

"What about her?"

"She's seven years old, right?"

"That's right."

"How does she feel about your return to morning television?"

"Janie is at an age where she's just beginning to understand about the notoriety of the job, but it doesn't really interest her much. She's more concerned with her sports teams and her dog, Daisy, and the fact that she wants me there when she comes home from school or camp. When I was anchoring the *Evening Headlines*, I could be there to get her off to school in the morning, but you know how rushed that time always is."

The reporter looked at her with a blank expression on his face.

"Anyway," Eliza continued, "now I'm home at the end of her day, when things are a little more relaxed and we can spend more time together, so it seems to be working out much better. Take today, for instance. When she gets home from day camp, I'll be there and we can take a swim together before dinner and she can tell me about her day. I treasure being able to have that time with her."

"I suppose that must be especially important for a child who doesn't have a father."

Eliza found herself irritated by the observation. Her daughter was not a victim.

"Janie does have a father," Eliza answered evenly. "A father who wanted her very much. Tragically, he died before he could ever hold her in his arms. But Janie is just like every other little kid, with one parent or two or none. She needs attention and love and she gets a lot of both. Janie is my top priority."

CHAPTER 5

The late-model Volvo station wagon pulled in through the stone-pillared entrance to Camp Musquapsink. As Mrs. Garcia parked the car, she was keenly aware of the gun pointed at the back of her head.

"Remember," said the sailor, who lay on the backseat. "We have you wired. We can hear everything you say, so don't try anything funny."

"Funny?" said Mrs. Garcia, her voice trembling. "This is not funny."

"I mean, don't try to show them that something is wrong," said Popeye with exasperation in his voice. "Go inside, get

Janie, and come right out again. No stalling. And when you drive out of here, turn the car in the opposite direction from the way we came."

Mrs. Garcia reached for the door handle.

"And remember," he warned. "We know where your daughter and grandchild live. Westwood is such a nice little town. Think how a town like that would be shaken if something fatal happened to a mother and her baby."

Mrs. Garcia panicked at the thought of the monster's new, terrifying threat. She was shaking as she got out of the car.

Mrs. Garcia thought of pulling off the electronic gadgetry that had been attached to the rear of the waistband of her skirt and beneath the collar of her cotton blouse. If these bad people couldn't hear her, she could get help from the camp staff. But if the microphone didn't transmit any sound, they'd figure out that she was betraying them. Mrs. Garcia didn't know if the man was only making an empty threat against her daughter and baby granddaughter to scare her, but if that was his aim, he had succeeded.

She couldn't take the chance of having something violent and horrible happening to the ones she loved most.

Her heart pounded while she listened to the crunch of her footsteps as she walked across the crushed stone that covered the parking lot. When she entered the camp office, Janie was waiting in a chair at the side of the room. She wore a construction-paper headband, a yellow feather in it, and her face was decorated with the green paint her camp counselor had applied to resemble a Native American in ceremonial dress.

The child jumped out of her seat. "Where are we going? What are we doing?" The excitement and trust on the little girl's painted face caused Mrs. Garcia to swallow hard.

"It's a surprise, *hija*. Your *mamá* is going to meet us at home with a surprise for you."

"Tell me," said Janie. "Tell me."

"You have to wait, *chiquita*. You have to wait."

Mrs. Garcia turned and went to the main desk. The camp staff member who was running the desk pushed a leather ledger across the counter.

"Just sign your name and the time," she said.

Mrs. Garcia paused and stared hard in the direction of the young woman, but she was busy collating sheets of paper.

"What are you doing there?" Mrs. Garcia asked, trying to get the staffer to look up at her so she could mouth or gesture her distress.

"Just putting together copies of the lyrics for the sing-along." The staffer stayed focused on her task.

"Oh? When is the sing-along?" asked Mrs. Garcia as she silently prayed that the woman's eyes would meet hers. *Por favor, Señor, por favor,* she prayed. *Let the girl look up.*

"Friday afternoon," answered the woman, keeping her head down.

Mrs. Garcia was acutely aware that the man in the car was waiting and listening. She couldn't risk any more time trying to get the attention of this *tonta* girl. Mrs. Garcia picked up a pen and wrote in shaky script, *"Call police."*

Taking Janie by the hand, Mrs. Garcia walked out to the parking lot. Her breathing was rapid, her face was hot, and beads of perspiration were scattered across her brow.

The young woman staffing the desk never looked up.

CHAPTER 6

When the interview was finished, Eliza posed for some pictures at her desk and then on the *KTA* set. Doris Brice stood by, stepping in from time to time to powder Eliza's nose or fix an errant strand of hair. By eleven o'clock the photo session for the magazine spread was over.

"Done for the day?" Doris asked as she put the brushes back in her makeup case.

"Almost," said Eliza. "I have some phone calls to return. Then I can pack it in."

On her way back to her office, Eliza met Range Bullock in the hall.

"How's life in the front row?" Eliza greeted him.

Range rolled his eyes. "It's different, that's for sure."

"Are you missing the day-to-day deadlines?" asked Eliza.

"To tell you the truth, not as much as I thought I would," said Range. "When I was producing the *Evening Headlines,* I should have bought stock in Tums. My ulcer has really quieted down since I left."

Eliza looked at Range. His hair was almost totally white now. His skin was pale and there were deep lines at the side of his mouth.

"Come on, Range. You can't tell me that being the president of KEY News is easier than being the executive producer of the evening show."

"It's different," Range answered, smiling. "Now I can be the one who gets to make the new executive producer's life a living hell."

Eliza smiled back. "Well, you certainly look like you could use a little sun," she said. "Why don't you and Louise come over Sunday afternoon? We can lie by the pool and throw something on the barbecue. Murphy and her family are coming over, too."

"Sounds good," said Range. "Let me talk to Louise and get back to you, all right?"

"Fine."

Eliza continued on her way to her office. Paige Tintle, her assistant, was waiting in the reception area.

"For your reading pleasure," Paige said, handing Eliza a legal-size folder.

Eliza opened the folder and perused the first few documents. "How bad is it this month?" she asked.

"Not bad at all," said Paige. "In fact, it's pretty much a lovefest."

Eliza carried the folder to her desk and sat down. She spent more than half an hour reading through the various articles that the clipping service had provided. There was an article from *Good Housekeeping* that included pictures of Eliza and Janie making cookies in the kitchen in Ho-Ho-Kus; and there was an article in *Woman's Day* that chronicled a day in her life, starting with hosting *KTA* in the morning, following her around the Broadcast Center afterward, and accompanying her home to meet Janie. A story in *People Español* highlighted the fact that she had a Guatemalan housekeeper and had taken pictures of Mrs. Garcia at work and with her family, who lived in a nearby town. But it was the piece in *Vanity Fair* that went into extraordinary detail about Eliza's background, her youth in Rhode Island, where her parents still lived; her rise through a succession of local stations on her way to the network; her marriage to John Blake, his tragic death, and the nervous collapse she had suffered after giving birth to their child.

Eliza closed the folder. She wasn't ashamed of that painful period in her life, but she certainly didn't want to be reminded of it.

CHAPTER 7

Mrs. Garcia crossed the camp parking lot and walked around the front of the station wagon. Janie ran ahead.

"Get in the front seat, Janie," called Mrs. Garcia.

Janie turned and looked at her quizzically. "The front? I'm supposed to sit in the back."

"It's all right this time, Janie," said Mrs. Garcia. "Do as I say and sit in the front seat with me."

Janie shrugged but got into the front seat of the car and instinctively reached for the shoulder harness, securing it around her waist. As soon as Mrs. Garcia turned the ignition key, Jane began peppering her with questions.

"What are we going to do? Where are we going? Is Mommy meeting us there?"

"*Oye, hija,* please be quiet. I have to pay attention," said Mrs. Garcia as she eased the car through the camp gates.

"Pay attention to what?"

"Pay attention to my driving," answered Mrs. Garcia.

There was a puzzled expression on Janie's face. Usually, Mrs. Garcia was happy when they rode in the car together. Sometimes they sang Spanish songs and sometimes they played games. Mrs. Garcia would point out something along the road and teach Janie the word for it in Spanish. But today, Mrs. Garcia looked very worried or very mad. Janie couldn't decide which one.

"Look, Mrs. Garcia," said Janie, trying to get the woman's attention and approval. "Look at the necklace I made this morning."

Mrs. Garcia glanced over at the beads that encircled Janie's neck.

"Very nice," she said.

"See? The beads have letters on them.

It spells my name. J-A-N-I-E." The child patted the beads with satisfaction and waited for her caretaker's reaction.

But Mrs. Garcia didn't respond.

"What's that?" asked Janie, pointing to a squirrel running across the winding country road.

"*Una ardilla,*" answered Mrs. Garcia.

"And that?" Janie gestured toward a crumbling stone wall at the side of the road.

"*Un muro de piedra.*"

Janie looked out at the unfamiliar stretch of road. "Hey," she protested. "This isn't the way home."

"We're not going home, *mi hija.*"

"Then where *are* we going?" asked Janie. As she leaned forward in her seat and turned her head, trying to get a full look at Mrs. Garcia's face, Janie caught a glimpse of movement in her peripheral vision. Restrained by her seat belt, she twisted around as far as she could and saw the distorted face of the man in the backseat.

CHAPTER 8

P.J. Clarke's at Lincoln Center was crowded at lunchtime, but two women were shown to a table the minute they came in the door. Heads turned as the KEY News anchorwoman and psychological expert walked through the restaurant.

"So how's everything going?" Dr. Margo Gonzalez asked once they were seated.

Eliza spread her napkin across her lap. "My life is an embarrassment of riches, Margo. Janie is healthy and seemingly happy. KEY let me go back to the mornings. Mack and I are back together again, or as together as you can be when one lives here and the other lives in England. I keep waiting for the other shoe to drop."

A tall, thin young woman dressed in white shirt, black pants, and black tie came up to the table and took their drink orders.

"What are you going to have?" asked Eliza as they scanned the menu.

"I love their crab cakes," said Margo.

"I'm going for the hamburger," said Eliza, putting the menu down. "I can't resist them here."

"Think it could change anytime soon?" asked Margo after the waitress took their orders.

"Could what change?" asked Eliza.

"Do you think Mack might get transferred back to the States?"

"He's got his agent lobbying for that, but we'll see." Eliza bit her lower lip and looked down at the tablecloth.

"What's wrong?" asked Margo.

"Nothing. Everything's fine."

"All right," said Margo, "but that face doesn't look like 'nothing.'"

Eliza looked up. "I don't know. I know

I don't have anything to complain about. There are so many people in the world with real problems, but, honestly, I've been feeling sort of anxious lately."

"I can understand that," said Margo. "You have lots of wonderful things in your life, but you have a lot of pressure as well. You're a single mother, you have one of the world's most visible and demanding jobs, and you're trying to juggle a long-distance romantic relationship that requires a great deal of trust."

Eliza smiled. "I didn't invite you to lunch for a free therapy session, Margo."

"I know you didn't," said Margo. "You're my friend now, Eliza, and I don't treat friends. But anytime you want to talk, woman-to-woman, I hope you'll call on me."

CHAPTER 9

The black van was hidden from view, parked behind an abandoned dry-cleaning facility in a town fifteen miles north of Camp Musquapsink. The driver waited for the Volvo station wagon to come into view.

Where are they? If everything had gone according to plan, they should have been here by now.

Through the open window, she thought she heard a car approaching. She strained to see the vehicle that should be coming around the corner of the building, and started to pull on her mask. But instead of the white station

wagon she was expecting, a red convertible swung into view.

The top was down and she could see
four young people in the car, two boys and
two girls. *High school kids,* she thought.
Maybe they were sneaking back here for
a little make-out session. If that was the
case, they'd be almost as distressed to
see her as she was to see them.

As the convertible approached, she
decided she had no choice other than to
play it cool. Quickly pulling off the mask
and dropping it in her lap, she looked directly at the convertible's passengers as
the car passed alongside the van. The
convertible circled the parked vehicle
and then drove back in the direction from
which it had come.

Steady, she thought. *Steady.* It was
just kids. They weren't going to be paying any attention to news reports over
the days to come. And even if they did
hear about everything, they weren't going to make any connection between the
woman in the black van behind the old
dry-cleaning plant and the kidnapping of
Eliza Blake's daughter.

Tears were running down Janie's cheeks.

Mrs. Garcia glanced over from the driver's seat. "Don't cry, *hija,*" she said in a soothing voice. "Everything going to be okay."

"I want Mommy," Janie sobbed. She raised her hands to wipe at her tears, smearing the green face paint.

"And your mommy wants you, too, kiddo. You can count on that," said Popeye in the backseat of the station wagon.

Janie felt the hot breath, seeping through the mouth opening of his mask, against the nape of her neck. She reached backward to wipe the feeling away. The man grabbed her hand.

"What do you think you're doing?" he said.

"Nothing." Janie sniffled.

"It better be nothing. I've heard you're a smart little girl. So don't do anything stupid. And stop that damned crying," he demanded. "Or I'll give you something to really cry about."

Janie tried to control her sobs, but realizing with every minute she was getting farther and farther from her mother, her crying continued. Soon she was hiccupping as well.

"For God's sake, get her to stop, will you?" demanded Popeye, pressing the tip of his gun against the back of Mrs. Garcia's head.

"She can't help it," said Mrs. Garcia. "She scared."

"What the hell good are you if you can't control the kid?" the man asked angrily.

The tone of his voice made Janie sit up straighter. What if the man hurt Mrs. Garcia? What if he took her away? Then she would have no one to take care of her and she would be alone with the horrible, smelly man. Janie willed herself to stop crying, but the hiccupping continued.

"Turn in up there," Popeye instructed.

The station wagon slowed and pulled into a deserted parking lot where weeds were growing up through the cracks in the macadam.

"Now drive around to the back of the building."

Janie looked up over the dashboard, trying to see what was ahead.

"Pull up next to the van and park," the sailor commanded.

Mrs. Garcia did as she was told. As the Volvo came to a stop, the woman in the front seat of the black van finished sliding the mask over her head.

"Now, both of you, get out."

Mrs. Garcia and Janie obeyed while the man kept his gun aimed at them. A toothy-grinned Olive Oyl got out of the van and, walking around to the back, opened its double doors.

"Go ahead," said Popeye. "Get on back there."

Mrs. Garcia took Janie's hand and started walking slowly, wondering if there was any chance at all that they could break away and run. But the gun aimed in their direction made the odds of getting away next to nil. Even if she were willing to try anything herself, she couldn't risk Janie's life.

The sailor got out of the backseat of the station wagon and followed them. As they got close to the van's rear doors, Olive Oyl held out two cords made of rope. She swapped the rope for the man's gun and kept it pointed in the direction of Mrs. Garcia and Janie while Popeye expertly tied their wrists behind their backs.

"Okay, climb in," the man growled.

Mrs. Garcia struggled to lift her leg high enough to get a foothold on the van floor.

"You should get yourself on a diet, lady," Popeye grunted as he got behind Mrs. Garcia and tried to lift her. With his pushing her, Mrs. Garcia rolled awkwardly into the back of the van.

"Now, little princess, it's your turn."

As the man reached down to lift Janie, the little girl leaned forward and bit him as hard as she could.

"Jesus Christ," the man yelled, pulling his wounded hand from Janie's mouth while smacking the child's face with the other. He ripped the feathered construction-paper band from Janie's head and threw it to the ground.

"Calm down, sailor," said the woman. "Get hold of yourself. That temper of yours could ruin everything."

CHAPTER 10

A blue Lincoln Town Car turned into the driveway on Saddle Ridge Road. The driver got out and opened the rear passenger door.

"Thanks," said Eliza as she emerged. "See you in the morning."

"Yes, ma'am, see you then."

As the car pulled out of the driveway, Eliza walked around to the backyard. She could hear Daisy's loud barking. Eliza strode out over the expansive lawn to the doghouse.

"Hey, Daisy," she said as she bent down and smoothed the dog's golden coat. "How are you, girl?"

Usually a loving pat and a few gentle words were all it took for Daisy to settle right down. But this afternoon, the dog continued to bark, rapidly wagging her tail.

"What's the matter, girl?" asked Eliza. "Have you been out here too long?"

Eliza unclipped the dog from the leash. Daisy bounded for the house as Eliza followed.

Right away, she noticed that the French doors that led from the patio to the interior of the house were open. Eliza knew that Mrs. Garcia liked to let fresh air in the house. Having grown up in Guatemala, central air-conditioning was foreign to Mrs. Garcia and she found it too cold and too stuffy. The housekeeper thought the air inside the house needed to circulate more. Leaving the doors open whenever she could was her solution.

But Eliza noticed that the sliding screens had been left wide open as well. Maybe Mrs. Garcia had entered with her arms full of groceries and forgotten to come back and close the screen doors.

Eliza walked through the open doorway. "Mrs. Garcia," she called, "I'm home."

The house was quiet.

Eliza put down her bag on the kitchen counter and took a bottle of water from the refrigerator before heading upstairs.

"Mrs. Garcia?" she called when she reached the top of the staircase.

No response. Eliza went from room to room, the thought crossing her mind that Mrs. Garcia could have had a heart attack or something and could be lying somewhere, unable to answer. It was a relief to find each room in order, with no sign of Mrs. Garcia.

Glancing at her watch, Eliza calculated that it would be another hour and a half before Janie arrived home from camp. Maybe Mrs. Garcia had gone out to do some errands before Janie got back. A check of the garage revealed that the station wagon wasn't there.

Yes, thought Eliza. That's what must have happened. Mrs. Garcia had gone out to the store or the post office. Eliza knew that Mrs. Garcia made quick visits, if there was time after she got her work done, to her daughter and grandbaby in Westwood. Maybe she was over there. But wherever Mrs. Garcia had gone, Eliza

had absolutely no doubt that she would
be back in time to meet Janie's bus.

Eliza changed into shorts, a sleeveless
top, and a pair of sandals. Then she went
downstairs again to check the mail. In
the den there was nothing on her desk,
where Mrs. Garcia always left any envelopes and packages.

She walked outside, down the driveway, and opened the mailbox. Diago-
nally across the road, she spotted her
neighbor doing the same thing.

"Hi, Susan," Eliza called out and
waved.

Susan Feeney waved back. "How are
you?" she called.

"Fine thanks," said Eliza. "You?"

"Thrilled to finally have all the workmen out of the house," said Susan, walking closer so she wouldn't have to yell. "I
can't tell you how glad I am to have that
addition finished and have the house to
myself again."

"Well, it looks wonderful," said Eliza.
"They really did a nice job."

"Thanks," Susan said. "The joys of

home ownership never end, do they? There's always something that needs doing. What are you having done now?"

"What do you mean?" asked Eliza.

"I saw the work van in your driveway this morning."

Eliza shrugged. "I didn't know we were having anything done. Mrs. Garcia must have scheduled something."

Eliza stretched out on a lounge chair under the striped awning that shaded most of the patio and began flipping through the mail. After opening a few envelopes and scanning the contents, she put the pile down, lay back, and closed her eyes. *I'm still not adjusted to these early hours,* she thought. *I'm just going to rest for a few minutes.*

When she opened her eyes again, the shadows in the yard were different and Eliza could tell the sun had shifted position. She looked at her watch. It was almost five o'clock. Janie would have gotten home from camp a half hour ago. *That's sweet,* Eliza thought. Mrs. Garcia had kept Janie from waking her mother when she got home from camp.

She rose from the lounge chair, picked up the mail, and went inside the house.

"Janie?" she called. "Mrs. Garcia?"

Eliza listened for a response but heard nothing. She went to the garage again. The station wagon was still gone. She checked the kitchen table and counters looking for a note. Finding none, she looked on the hall table and her desk. Nothing. Nor were there any signs that Janie had even come home. Usually, there would be some arts-and-crafts project deposited on a table, or her camp bag, with its contents of wet bathing suits and damp towels, left sitting on a chair.

Eliza felt her body tense. It wasn't like Mrs. Garcia to take Janie somewhere without leaving a note. She called Mrs. Garcia's cell phone.

"This is Carmen Garcia. Please leave your message and I will get back to you."

"Hi, Mrs. Garcia. It's just after five o'clock and I'm wondering where you and Janie are. Will you call me as soon as you get this message? I'm starting to worry."

Next, she found the phone number for Mrs. Garcia's daughter and tapped in the numbers, identifying herself when Maria Rochas answered. Eliza could hear a baby crying.

"I was wondering if your mother was there with Janie?" Eliza asked as she paced to the living room window. Her eyes searched the road.

"No, Mrs. Blake. My mother didn't stop over today," said Maria. "In fact, I haven't talked to her all day. Is something wrong?"

"Everything's probably fine, but if you hear from her, will you ask her to call me?"

"Of course I will," said Maria. "And when my mother does get there, will you have her call me and let me know everything is all right?"

"Absolutely, Maria," said Eliza. "Thank you."

Clicking off the phone, Eliza told herself to stay calm. Most likely, there was a perfectly good explanation. Maybe Janie had gone to play at a friend's house after camp and Mrs. Garcia was picking her up now. Maybe Mrs. Garcia had realized she needed something from the grocery store and she had taken Janie with her.

Eliza sat on the sofa in front of the picture window, willing the station wagon to pull into view.

CHAPTER 11

Beneath the tear-streaked vestiges of face paint, the redness of the handprint was fading, but the violence of the man's strike had affected her. Janie kept her head down. The blindfold that had been tied tightly when they got into the back of the van made it certain she wouldn't be able to see the people who were separating her from her mother.

She couldn't tell how long they had driven and she had no idea of the route that had gotten them there. But now, she and Mrs. Garcia were sitting side by side on a soft mattress. Janie inched herself closer to her caretaker, desperate to find comfort.

"Mrs. Garcia," she whispered. "I'm scared."

"I am, too, *chiquita.* But don't worry. Your *mamá* and her friends will come and get us."

Janie hiccupped. "You promise?"

"I promise," answered Mrs. Garcia, knowing she had no right to make such a pledge. "Your mommy is very strong. She is very powerful and she will make sure nothing bad happens to us."

Janie was silent as she considered the woman's answer. She wanted to believe Mrs. Garcia, wanted to believe that everything would be all right. But if her mother hadn't been able to protect her from these bad people, maybe she wasn't as strong and powerful as Mrs. Garcia said she was.

CHAPTER 12

One dead end after another.

There was no answer at Camp Musquapsink, which had closed for the night after the last campers left for the day. Calls to Susan Feeney and some other neighbors provided no comforting information. Marcia Demarest, the owner of Demarest Farms, said she hadn't seen Mrs. Garcia but asked Eliza to hold on a minute while she checked with the other workers who manned the big red barn that provided luscious fruit and vegetables, a bakery, a deli, and fresh flowers for its eager customers.

"I'm sorry, Eliza," said Marcia when she came back to the phone. "But nobody has seen Mrs. Garcia or Janie here today."

Eliza bit her lower lip as she considered what she knew.

Daisy had been barking wildly when she arrived home.

The screen doors leading to the house had been left open.

The car was gone and there was no note.

Susan Feeney had seen a work van parked in the driveway this morning, but Eliza hadn't scheduled any work to be done.

It was the last fact that bothered Eliza the most. Mrs. Garcia would have mentioned it if something needed to be repaired. What was that van doing in her driveway this morning?

With a feeling of panic washing over her, Eliza decided it was time to call the police.

CHAPTER 13

"I'm Eliza Blake," she said, trying to keep her voice steady but hearing it cracking. "I'm worried that something has happened to my seven-year-old daughter and our housekeeper."

The Ho-Ho-Kus police dispatcher instantly recognized the caller's name and decided he should contact the chief of police at home. Only fifteen minutes later the chief and two uniformed officers arrived on Eliza's doorstep. Two detectives were close behind.

They gathered in the kitchen and Eliza recounted everything she knew, trying to keep herself composed and her mind focused.

"I know Janie got off to camp safely this morning. I spoke with Mrs. Garcia right after I got off the air."

"That's at nine o'clock, right?"

"Yes," said Eliza.

"Which camp does Janie attend?"

"Camp Musquapsink."

"That's over the state line, in New York, isn't it?" asked the detective.

Eliza nodded. "Yes, in Sloatsburg."

"And you don't know if your daughter came home from camp or not?"

"I could kick myself now, but I fell asleep in the backyard. I didn't really think anything was wrong at that point. I didn't wake up until after the time the bus usually drops Janie off. I've called the camp, but there's no answer."

The detective looked at one of the uniformed officers. "Give the Rockland County Sheriff's Office a call and have them check out the camp," he instructed.

Eliza shook her head. "I don't understand it. Mrs. Garcia didn't mention anything special she had planned to do with

Janie. It just isn't like her to go somewhere with Janie without telling me or
leaving a note."

"How long has the housekeeper
worked for you?" asked one of the detectives.

"About two years now," said Eliza.

"How did you find her?"

"Through an agency," Eliza answered.

"We'll need the name of the agency,"
said the detective.

Eliza looked at him. "Hold it right there,"
she said. "You don't have to go investigating Carmen Garcia. I'd trust her with
my life. In fact, more than that, I trust her
with my child."

Holly Taylor was lifting the London broil
off the backyard grill when the phone
rang. She took a sip of red wine before
she picked up the portable phone from
the table on the patio.

"Hello?"

"This is Officer Kyle Downey of the
Rockland County Sheriff's Office. We're
looking for Holly Taylor."

Holly's face, already flushed from the

heat of the barbecue grill, grew hotter still.

"This is Holly Taylor."

"You are the director of Camp Musquapsink?"

"I am."

"Ms. Taylor, we have a report that a child who goes to your camp is missing."

Holly sat down on one of the cushioned outdoor chairs. She could feel her pulse racing in her ears. *Don't panic,* she told herself. *You must not panic.*

"Oh, no," she said, showing concern but trying to keep her voice as even as possible. "Which child is it?"

"Janie Blake."

Though over two hundred campers registered each summer, Holly prided herself on knowing all of them by name. Some of them, like Janie Blake, had the added distinction of having famous last names, being children of professional sports players, media moguls, and Wall Street barons living in Manhattan or the New York City area. Janie's mother was arguably the most well-known parent the camp had ever had.

The thought that something could have happened to Janie, or any of the campers entrusted to her care, made Holly physically ill. And if the camp was involved in any way, had been remiss in any of its safety procedures, the adverse publicity could be ruinous. Still, Holly knew she should tell the truth.

"Janie was at camp this morning," she said. "But her caretaker came and picked her up."

"What time was that?" asked Officer Downey.

"I'm not quite sure," said Holly. "I think it was right before lunch. But I can check the log we keep in the office. I'll drive over to camp right away."

"How long will that take you, Ms. Taylor?"

"I should be there within half an hour."

"Someone from the sheriff's office will meet you."

Holly hoped to reach the camp and check the log before the police arrived, but when her car pulled into the parking lot, a Rockland County sheriff's vehicle was already there. Two tall, tanned officers in light blue uniforms stood at the entrance to the office waiting for her.

She unlocked the door and the officers escorted her inside. Holly went directly to the reception desk and pulled the leather-bound book from the drawer. She opened the log to the day's notations, quickly seeing that there were only three entries, all of them made before lunchtime. Two children had been taken out of camp by their mothers to go to morning dental appointments. Then, at 11:23 A.M., Carmen Garcia had signed out Janie Blake.

Damn it. Nobody had looked at the log afterward. Nobody had read the words written a full eight hours ago now.

Holly forced herself to hold up the book so the police officers could read the shaky script—an instruction that had been totally ignored.

"Call police."

CHAPTER 14

It was time to catch up. The scrapbook was nowhere near up-to-date.

Nell positioned herself next to the magazine racks at the CVS and waited while a teenager took out last month's issues and replaced them with the current ones.

"Mind if I go through those?" asked Nell, pointing to the pile of outdated magazines.

The high school kid shrugged. "Knock yourself out."

Nell bent over and began to weed through the stack. A few were no-brainers. Eliza Blake smiled from their covers. Others required further scrutiny. Nell read the teasing announcements on each one about what could be found on the pages inside. She located four more magazines that contained what she wanted. After she was satisfied she wasn't missing anything, Nell went to the checkout counter.

"Evening, Nell. Haven't seen you in a while," observed the elderly man at the cash register.

"I'm busy, Charlie."

"I know what you mean," said the man as he began holding the periodicals' bar codes under his scanning gun. "I don't know where the days go sometimes." He scrutinized the dates on the magazine covers. "Hey, Nell, these are old issues. You shouldn't be charged for these."

It was a little game they played: Nell bringing the magazines that were too old to sell up to the register, Charlie letting her have them for free.

"How's your uncle doing?" he asked.

"He's fine, Charlie."

"Tell him I was asking for him, will you?"

"I will," said Nell as she reached for

the long braid that hung down her back and pulled it to the side so it rested on the front of her shirt.

As he slid the magazines into a plastic bag, Charlie looked at the covers.

"I see you're still keeping that scrapbook of yours, huh?"

Nell nodded. "Yes, I am."

"It must be pretty big by now."

"The first and second ones are finished," she said proudly, "and I'm starting on a third."

"You really are crazy about that Eliza Blake, aren't you?" he asked.

Nell smiled sweetly. "I love her. I just love her."

Turning to the neatly stacked magazines on the Formica-topped table, Nell took one from the top of the pile and began flipping through the pages. When she came to the article she was searching for, she picked up the scissors. She cut jaggedly around the edges of the first picture: a smiling mother and a happy child riding bicycles together on a sunny day.

Nell studied the photograph. The light was shining on Eliza's face and the way she was looking at Janie made Nell's chest tighten. She wished her mother had looked at her that way when she was younger. They had never ridden bicycles together, and Nell knew that her mother had never loved her in the same way Eliza loved Janie. Her mother hadn't been good at showing love.

Nell worried sometimes that she had contributed to her mother's death. When her mother got sick, she didn't have the strength she needed to fight. Nell suspected she had used up all her energy on her. Nell's father had taken off when she was a baby, and her mother had raised Nell by herself, along with working as a waitress to earn the money that barely paid the bills.

There were always so many bills. Nell could remember her mother complaining as she hunched over the kitchen table in their tiny rented bungalow, trying to parcel out the money every month, paying the minimum due on the credit card statement and just enough on the utility bills so the heat and the electricity wouldn't be turned off. Still, it seemed the collection agencies were always calling, and there had been many nights when they had used candles to get through the evenings and had huddled together under their quilts to stay warm.

Her mother was forever bringing leftovers home from the restaurant, muttering about how she had to keep her lousy job so they wouldn't starve. She was forced to find activities that didn't cost much. When they splurged, once a year, on Nell's birthday and went to the movies, they timed it to go to the early-bird matinee. They never bought overpriced candy at the concession stand, stopping beforehand to get it at a grocery store. Her mother didn't have time to read to her, so some of Nell's earliest memories were of the story hours she'd attended at the public library. The sessions Nell had there were her happiest, and soon reading and scrapbooking became Nell's favorite activities.

She positioned the photo of Eliza and Janie Blake exactly in the middle of the scrapbook page. Then she artfully arranged star and heart stickers around the picture, creating a display that pleased her. Slowly and deliberately, Nell made her way through all the magazines, cutting and pasting and filling page after page in the scrapbook.

When she was finished with her work, Nell closed the book with satisfaction and a sense of anticipation, knowing there would be more pictures of Eliza to come.

CHAPTER 15

An Amber Alert was issued on surrounding highways while color photographs of Janie Blake, supplied by Eliza, were transmitted to police stations around the country. The local police went from house to house, asking the neighbors if they had seen Mrs. Garcia or Janie that day, or if they had noticed anyone or anything suspicious. So far, Susan Feeney was the only one who had anything to report. She told the police everything she could remember about the black van she had seen in Eliza's driveway that morning. It wasn't much. She thought there had been a dent in one of the van's back doors. From her vantage point across the street, she hadn't noticed any identification on the side of the van, nor had she noted the license plates. She couldn't even say for certain if they had been New Jersey tags. But law enforcement started checking to see if there were any reports of a stolen vehicle matching that description.

Before the long summer evening had slipped into full darkness, Eliza's home was swarming with law enforcement personnel. As the minutes dragged into hours, Federal Bureau of Investigation special agents searched the premises, dusted for fingerprints, and set up their on-site command center in Eliza's garage. Dozens of agents from New York and the Newark field office were out searching and FBI computers in Quantico, Virginia, were spitting out records on sex offenders as well as child abuse and extortion perpetrators. Though no ransom demands had been made, the notation in the camp ledger signaled that something was terribly wrong.

"'Call police,'" said Special Agent Barbara Gebhardt as she looked at her notes. "The housekeeper could have written that just to throw us off."

"It wouldn't be the first time a domestic was in on a kidnapping plot," said Agent Trevor Laggie. "It makes it a lot easier to kidnap somebody when you have access to their home and know their schedule."

Eliza sat on the sofa, face tear streaked, hair disheveled, and arms wrapped around her body, listening to the conversation between the agents. She was using every bit of energy willing herself not to fall apart. She couldn't panic, she had to pay attention. She *knew* Janie and Mrs. Garcia, while none of these people invading her home did. While Mrs. Garcia had been with them only since they'd moved to Ho-Ho-Kus from Manhattan two years before, time and time again, Eliza had witnessed the woman's honesty, dependability, and utter devotion to Janie. The woman who made sure to return any spare change she found between the cushions of the sofa when she cleaned, and whose eyes filled with tears whenever Janie fell off her bike, would never steal Janie away.

If she had knowledge that could somehow help to find her little girl, she had to be in a condition to offer it. Eliza wanted to retreat, wanted to be able to go upstairs, pull the covers over her head, and fall into a deep, deep sleep, only to find, when she woke up, that it was all just the worst possible dream. But that wouldn't help find Janie or Mrs. Garcia. She had to stay focused.

"I'm telling you," Eliza spoke up. "Mrs. Garcia doesn't have anything to do with this. She loves Janie. She would never take her away, not willingly anyway."

Eliza leaned back, closed her eyes, and tried to imagine the scene in the camp office that morning. Mrs. Garcia had been trying to alert whoever was at the reception desk that something was wrong. But why hadn't Mrs. Garcia just spoken out?

"What about the girl who was there when Mrs. Garcia picked up Janie?" asked Eliza. "Maybe she saw something or remembers something that can help us."

"Lisa Nichols," said Laggie. "The camp director provided her address and phone numbers but, so far, we haven't been able to contact her. We have agents going over to her house."

"What about her cell phone?" asked Eliza.

"We've left repeated messages," said Agent Laggie. "She has it switched off."

Eliza felt her chest tighten. The minutes were passing, each one of them taking Janie farther away. She knew the statistics. Every hour that passed made it harder to find a missing child.

Eliza called Range Bullock to tell him what had happened and to alert him to the fact that she would most definitely not be coming in to anchor *KEY to America* in the morning. The president of the news division, in turn, called the executive producer of the morning program. Telling Linus Nazareth ensured that word would spread quickly after that.

Every time the phone rang, the atmosphere on the first floor of the Blake residence grew more electric. Each time Eliza picked up the receiver, she braced herself to hear the voice of the person who knew where Janie was. But each time, the voice at the other end was a friend or colleague who had heard the news.

"The assignment desk just called me. I'll be out there within the hour."

Eliza felt a slight bit of relief when she heard B.J. D'Elia's familiar voice.

"Are you coming out as my friend or as a KEY News cameraman?" asked Eliza.

"Both," said B.J., "and Annabelle is coming with me. She's producing the lead piece in the morning."

Eliza almost had to laugh. Her world was falling down around her and *KEY to America* was gearing up to cover it. How many times had she reported on the various calamities that befell human beings? Hurricanes and floods and fires and murders and business collapses and political scandals and terrorist attacks. Too many times to count, Eliza had reported the stories of people who were disillusioned and dazed and broken and fighting for their lives. Now it was her turn. Now she was the victim every reporter would want to interview, every cameraperson would want to capture.

She hung up the phone, walked over

to the window, parted the curtains, and looked outside. Satellite trucks and news cars were parking on the street in front of the house. The media circus was beginning.

At the same time as she dreaded it, she also welcomed it. Let them all come and do their jobs. Let them write their stories for the front pages of their newspapers or air their videos at the top of every single news broadcast. Let them flood the Internet with articles and the airwaves with reports. The more people who knew that Janie was missing, the more people who would be looking out for her.

Knowing that Maria must be sick with worry, Eliza picked up the phone and called Mrs. Garcia's daughter.

"Hello, Maria. It's Eliza Blake again."

"Yes?" Maria answered, her voice hopeful but tense.

"You haven't heard from your mother yet, have you?"

"No," said Maria. "I was praying just

now when the phone rang that it would be her."

"I wish it was her, too, Maria," said Eliza. "I *so* wish it was her. But I just wanted to keep you posted on what's happening. I've called the police and they are going to be looking for your mother and Janie."

"Jesús mio," Maria said softly.

"Try not to worry, Maria. The police will find them and everything will be fine."

Eliza did her best to sound positive, but she suspected that Maria Rochas knew full well how anxious she was, and how scared.

CHAPTER 16

The carnival workers had turned night into day. Giant spotlights bathed the school parking lot. Strategically spread around the property, a Ferris wheel, a merry-go-round, a fun house, a small roller coaster, and other rides were designed to give the kids gentle pleasure, thrill them, scare them, or make them dizzy. Neon signs, the pinging of bells, and hawking attendants summoned the fairgoers to the booths that offered game winners stuffed bears and goldfish to take home in water-filled plastic bags. The air was thick with the aroma of sausage and peppers, popcorn, and cotton candy.

Hugh Pollock stood at the fence that cordoned off the giant slide and ate his zeppola. Oblivious to the powdered sugar that ringed his mouth, looking upward, he chewed the warm, fried dough. He was transfixed by the blond girl, in the loose T-shirt and denim shorts, climbing the steps to the platform at the top. He watched as she spread the hemp mat on the slide, sat down on it, and then let go of the safety railing. Hugh held his breath.

The girl's yellow hair fanned out behind her as the breeze blew against her. She made her long descent down the slide, her shirt pressing against her chest, indicating the beginnings of adolescent development beneath the cotton. Disappointed, Hugh turned and walked away.

Though the evening was warm, Hugh wore a baggy black nylon jogging suit. He could feel the perspiration on the back of his neck but couldn't tell if it was the heat or the anticipation that made beads of sweat drip down his sides.

He cruised around the fairgrounds, aware that it was getting late. Many of the younger ones had already gone home. Hugh did spot one—a perfect little girl— and followed her for a while. He admired her ponytail swaying from side to side as she walked on thin, hairless legs. But the treasure was being guarded by the man and woman who flanked her, firmly holding her hands. Hugh let them walk away.

"Three tries for a dollar. Come on now, try your skill. Three shots for a dollar."

Hugh looked in the direction of the shouting voice. A group of children were gathered around a game stand, looking longingly at the prizes that hung from the ceiling of the booth. As Hugh got closer, he saw the miniature rifles, attached to a long, low table, pointing in the general direction of the orange rabbit targets that sped across the horizon only ten feet away.

"Want to give it a try, pal?" asked the attendant. "Lots of great prizes here."

Hugh looked with skepticism at the dangling collection of cheap dolls, plastic trucks, and blow-up toys. Then the girl with the bangs and freckles caught his attention. Her eyes glistened with excitement as she stared up at the prizes. She was standing next to a boy who resembled her and Hugh surmised he was her older brother. But he couldn't have been more than eight or nine years old and the little girl looked to be about six or seven. There were no adults around but the booth attendant.

Perfect.

"Which one do you want?" Hugh asked the girl.

She looked at him uncertainly.

"It's all right," said Hugh. "I want to try the game, but there are no prizes that I like. Why don't I try to win one for you instead?"

The girl looked at her brother. He only shrugged.

"Okay," said Hugh as he pulled a dollar bill out of his pocket. "What will it be?"

The girl pointed up at a plastic baby doll with curly white hair.

Hugh bent down, took aim, and fired, each time hitting the target. He stood upright and pointed at the doll.

"For three hits, you only get to pick

from the bottom row of prizes," said the attendant. "You need nine to get the prizes on top."

Hugh dug into his pocket and threw two more bills on the counter. He took his shots but, this time, he missed a few.

"Damn it," he hissed as he took out more money. "I could go to the store and buy the darned thing for less than I'm spending here."

He could feel the little girl watching him. That made his breathing come faster as he took aim again. Finally, he accumulated the necessary points to get the doll.

The child beamed as he handed her the prize.

"What are you going to name her?" he asked.

"I don't know yet," said the child.

"Maybe you could name her after yourself," Hugh suggested. "What's your name?"

"Madison."

"That's a pretty name," said Hugh. He engaged the girl and her brother in conversation as they slowly walked away from the game booth toward the food stands.

"Anyone want a slice of pizza or an ice cream?" asked Hugh.

The children looked at each other again.

"Don't worry," said Hugh. "It's all right." He handed some money to the boy. "Go ahead over there and get yourself and your sister ice cream cones. Madison and I will go over to the picnic tables and find seats."

"It should be all right, Madison. I'll be right back." The boy grabbed the ten-dollar bill and ran.

Hugh took the girl's hand and began to walk toward the picnic area, but instead of finding a place to sit, Hugh continued past the wooden tables.

"Where are we going?" asked the child.

"Back here," said Hugh. "It's nicer back here."

He could feel the child try to pull her hand from his.

"I don't want to go back here," said the little girl. "I want my brother."

Hugh leaned down and swept the child into his arms. He felt her young skin. He buried his nose in her soft hair. Just as he lifted his hand to caress her bare leg, he felt a vibration in his pants.

Crap. He knew who was calling him.

Hugh didn't want to answer, but he had to. He had promised to keep his cell phone on at all times. There would be hell to pay later if he didn't respond now.

He put the child back on the ground, but kept his arm locked around her as he got the phone out of his pocket with his free hand.

"Where are you, Hughie?"

"Nowhere special."

"Don't lie to me, Hughie. Where are you?"

There was no use in trying to hide it. She would be able to hear the roar of the rides and the kids screaming in the background.

"At the carnival."

"What's the matter with you, Hughie?" she shrieked. "You know it's dangerous for you there."

"Quit worrying, will you, Isabelle?"

"Quit worrying? Are you crazy? Of course I'm going to worry. How can you jeopardize everything like this? You know we can't take any chances. You better get back here right now."

At that moment the little girl kicked Hugh's shin, causing him to yelp. Instinctively, he pulled back and the child wriggled free. Hugh didn't try to chase her as she ran to find her brother.

CHAPTER 17

"Can you help us with something?" asked Agent Laggie.

Eliza roused herself from staring at the framed photographs resting on top of the piano. Janie as a baby, wrapped in the pale yellow blanket knit by her maternal grandmother. Janie as a toddler, taking her first steps. Janie on her first day of kindergarten. Janie missing her two front teeth. Janie hugging Daisy.

Janie.

Janie.

Janie.

"Yes, of course. What is it?" she asked as she turned away from the pictures.

She noticed that Laggie was holding a box in his hands.

"Would you come upstairs with me and help collect any articles . . . that would have Janie's scent on them?"

Eliza looked at him, uncomprehending for a moment.

"It might help us later if we have to use search dogs," said Laggie.

"Oh my God, this can't be happening," Eliza whispered as she got up off the piano bench and led the way to Janie's bedroom. The room was tidy, the twin beds made, the toys picked up and stored in the play box and on the shelves that lined two walls of the room.

Agent Laggie took plastic bags from the box he was holding and handed them to Eliza.

"Dirty socks, underwear, pajamas, and anything else you think would help," he said. "Just stow them in the bags."

Eliza opened the walk-in closet. A large canvas hamper stood at the rear. It was empty. "Mrs. Garcia is so efficient," she said. "She must have done Janie's dirty laundry early this morning."

Agent Laggie looked at her in a way

that Eliza thought communicated his skepticism.

"How about the bathroom?" he suggested. "Janie's toothbrush, her hairbrush or comb?"

Those items were all on the shelf over the bathroom sink. Eliza carefully placed each one in a plastic bag, stopping to catch her breath at the sight of strands of Janie's fine brown hair caught between the bristles on the hairbrush.

"We need Janie's fingerprints, too," said Laggie.

Eliza didn't have to ask him why.

CHAPTER 18

"Mommy," Janie called between sobs. "I want my mommy."

Mrs. Garcia ached to take the child in her arms, but the tightly tied ropes that bound her wrists made that impossible.

"Shh, *tesoro.* You will be with Mommy soon," she whispered. "Just try to rest. If you fall asleep, you can forget that you are missing your mommy."

"I can't sleep," Janie whined. "I want Daisy and I need my Zippy. I can't sleep without Zippy."

A loud banging from the other side of the wall made Mrs. Garcia jump.

"Shut up in there," the man's voice

ordered. "I don't want to hear another word about your mother, your dog, or that freakin' Zippy."

"Please, Janie," Mrs. Garcia whispered. "Try to be quiet and go to sleep, *mi hija*. We don't want the man to come in here again."

"I hate him," said Janie with certainty in her voice.

At any other time, Mrs. Garcia would have corrected the little girl, explaining that it wasn't right to hate anyone. But how could she judge Janie when Carmen herself felt exactly the same way?

TUESDAY
JULY 22

CHAPTER 19

As dawn broke, the reporters, producers, and camera crews camped out in front of the large brick colonial pounced on anything that moved. They called out questions and shot video of police cars and government sedans coming and going, as well as video of a black Lexus with New York tags pulling into the driveway. Its occupants were a somber-faced elderly couple.

"Are those her parents?" asked the CBS reporter.

"I don't think so," answered his producer. "Her parents live in Rhode Island, but I think her in-laws live around here."

"The parents of her dead husband, right?" asked the reporter.

"Yep," said the producer. "You got to feel sorry for them. They've already lost their son. They have to be frantic at the thought of losing their grandchild."

Katharine and Paul Blake came in the house and headed directly to their daughter-in-law's side. They found Eliza huddled on the sofa, a handmade afghan draped around her shoulders. She looked pale and her face was devoid of expression. She rose when she saw them and took their hands in hers.

"You're cold as ice, honey," said Katharine, wrapping her arms around Eliza.

"Oh, Katharine, I'm just so scared," Eliza whispered.

"I know you are, dear. We all are."

"If something happened to Janie, I couldn't bear it."

"None of us could, sweetheart," Katharine agreed. "But I've got to make myself believe that Janie is going to be fine. All of us have to believe that or we aren't going to be able to get through this."

"We're here now, Eliza," said Paul. "Why don't you go upstairs and try to get a little sleep?"

Eliza shook her head. "There's no way I'd be able to sleep."

"Well, rest then. Just go up and lie down for a while."

"Thanks, Paul, but I want to stay down here so I know what's going on."

"I'm going to make some tea," said Katharine. "A cup of tea will make us all feel better."

As she watched the thin figure walk toward the kitchen, Eliza felt a lump in her throat, remembering the way Katharine had acted when John was dying. Positive, capable, and determined while in no way denying the gravity of the situation. Eliza had always admired Katharine for the way she had conducted herself over those excruciatingly painful months. Katharine knew that her son was going to die, yet every single time she had come into that hospital room at Sloan-Kettering, there had been a warm smile on her face. Eliza had always marveled at how Katharine had been able to do that, but never more than right now when she herself felt abject terror at the prospect of losing her own child.

Eliza knew she had to hold herself together, but she could feel herself slipping away. She wanted to retreat, to withdraw and protect herself, insulate herself from the horror around her. But she knew she had to fight the urge to shut down. She had to keep her mind clear, stay involved, because there might be something only she could contribute that would find Janie. Eliza was fighting for some sense of control in the face of this nightmarish situation that was completely beyond her ability to manage.

"I think we should send some coffee to the guys out there on the street," said Eliza, shaking herself into action. She followed her mother-in-law to the kitchen.

A police officer guarded the front door. Annabelle Murphy and B.J. approached and flashed their KEY News ID badges.

"We're friends and colleagues of Ms.

Blake's," said Annabelle. "Would you please let her know we're here?"

They waited on the front stoop as the policeman opened the door and spoke to another officer inside. Two minutes later, Annabelle and B.J. were allowed entry. Eliza came hurrying toward them and hugged them tightly.

"Oh God, Eliza. I'm just so sorry," said B.J.

"I know you are. I know you are, Beej."

Annabelle pulled back and looked at her friend. "How are you holding up?"

Eliza stared straight into Annabelle's eyes but said nothing.

"Yeah, I get it," said Annabelle. "This is the worst."

Eliza shook her head. "No, I can think of one thing worse," she said.

"Don't, Eliza. You'll go out of your mind if you think about *that*."

Eliza managed a weak smile. "I already have been," she said.

Annabelle, uncharacteristically, was at a loss for words. She was a mother herself. Sometimes when she lay in bed at night and sleep wouldn't come, she'd imagine what she would do if anything bad happened to one of her children. When she really wanted to torture herself, she let herself think about actually losing one of the twins. But that scenario always led to the realization that, even if one of her children died, she would still have to go on for the other one. She wouldn't be able to let herself die as well, as much as she might want to.

Janie was Eliza's only child. There was no other to force Eliza to keep going if she lost Janie. But right now, the memory of the nervous breakdown Eliza had suffered after Janie's birth made Annabelle fear that just the pressure and worry of the immediate situation might be overwhelming.

"Have you taken anything?" Annabelle asked quietly. "Just something to take the edge off?"

"No," answered Eliza. "I want to be clearheaded."

"Listen, Eliza. I'm talking to you as a friend. Margo will give you something that won't dull your mind, but it will lift the mental pain a little bit. You really have to, if not for yourself, then for Janie. What good will you be to her if you collapse?"

Eliza's mouth was set in a tight line as she listened.

"I'm going to call Margo and see what she thinks," said Annabelle as she pulled out her cell phone.

"Don't do that," said Eliza. "You'll wake her."

"Are you kidding me?" said Annabelle as she tapped the keypad. "Margo would be furious if we didn't call her."

"Yeah, good idea," said B.J. "Let's get her out here, too. We'll do some brainstorming and figure all of this out."

Annabelle nodded. "B.J.'s right," she said, taking Eliza's hand. "We'll all help as much as we can, Eliza. You aren't alone."

CHAPTER 20

On the bottom floor of the KEY News Broadcast Center, Joe Connelly sat in his office adjoining the main security center. He was focused on the information on his computer screen. Joe clicked from entry to entry, sipping a cup of black coffee and looking for anything that could help in the search for Janie Blake.

The ABERRANT BEHAVIOR computer file currently had over eighty cases culled from mail and telephone threats coming into KEY News headquarters and KEY affiliates around the United States. Some of the cases were simple; others were not.

Over the years, Eliza Blake had received lots of bizarre correspondence, but not all that many threats, surely not as many as her predecessor in the *Evening Headlines* anchor chair, Bill Kendall, had gotten. But the number of truly disturbing letters had risen in the last few months. Joe was certain that was because of all the publicity that had heralded Eliza's return to the morning program. The woman's face had been everywhere, on billboards, buses, and magazine covers. Published stories about her professional and personal life had been too many to count. Joe knew the people in the publicity department had their jobs to do, whipping up viewer interest, but that didn't make his job any easier. The more that was out there in the press about Eliza, the more the crazies wrote their letters.

Most of the letters that came addressed to Eliza were nuisances, and not anything truly alarming. After years of experience, Joe had learned what to dismiss and to what he should pay attention.

Joe knew the FBI was going to call him and he wanted to be ready. He separated any letter in the file that made reference to Eliza's daughter. Then he read them again. Most of them seemed benign.

Happy Birthday, Eliza. I'm your biggest fan. I hope you have a wonderful day with your little girl.

Read the article about you in Redbook, Eliza. That picture of you and Janie was the cutest.

Watched you on your first morning back on KEY to America. You looked wonderful. Why don't you bring Janie to the set sometime? I would love to see her.

Joe continued to read, stopping to study one letter again and again.

Dear Eliza,

I watch you on television and read all about your career at KEY News. I think not only are you a wonderful newswoman, but you are the world's best mom. You seem to love Janie so much. I wonder if she knows how lucky she is. Janie is such a beautiful child, wouldn't it be terrible if something happened to her? Can you imagine what your life would be like without her? Janie better appreciate how lucky she is to have you, because it only takes a moment for life to change forever.

Evaluating a letter was always a judgment call based on experience and intuition. Joe Connelly's gut told him he had something here the FBI would want to see.

CHAPTER 21

Mrs. Garcia listened to the occasional hiccup coming from Janie who, after crying for her mother; her dog, Daisy; and Zippy, her beloved nighttime companion, for hours, had finally fallen asleep. From outside, she could hear the sound of birds calling to one another. Mrs. Garcia hadn't slept at all, but the chirping birds told her that morning had finally come. Yet it wasn't a normal morning, heralded by familiar and reassuring birdsong. Today was much different from yesterday when she had gotten up, washed and dressed, and then seen to it that Janie was fed and safely off to camp.

Safely off to camp.

Nothing was safe now. These people who had invaded her world were heartless and ruthless. Mrs. Garcia couldn't be certain what the day ahead would bring, but she trembled at the prospect.

The blindfold was still tied tightly around her skull. That, and the anguished worrying she had done all night, had given her a pounding headache. She felt helpless and terrified but she tried not to cry. How was she going to get herself and Janie away from these horrible people? And if she did try anything, would it only make matters worse? Would they hurt Maria and Vicente and Rosario as they had threatened to do?

The fear she felt at the prospect of harm coming to her family didn't outweigh her determination to save Janie. Mrs. Garcia pulled again at the restraints that bound her hands, wincing as the ropes cut into her flesh. The man had tied her up so tightly that there was almost no give.

Mrs. Garcia strained to hear in the darkness. *Where is he now? What is he doing? And where is the woman who was helping him?*

Mrs. Blake must be beside herself, she thought. But Janie's mother had undoubtedly called the police by now. The American police were very smart. They would surely come and save them from these monsters.

In the meantime, it was her responsibility to keep Janie safe. She inched her body closer to the child's. She could hear the sound of somebody stirring in the next room.

Where are they?

CHAPTER 22

"The network morning programs are all starting in less than half an hour. We should give them something," Eliza said. "I have to go out there and make a statement in time for the shows."

"Let me do it," said Annabelle, reaching over and rubbing Eliza's arm. "The media is our friend here, Eliza. We can reach millions of people. We'll let them know that Janie is missing and get her picture circulating. We can do more to find Janie in a few seconds than if we nailed flyers to trees and telephone poles every day for a year."

Eliza agreed with Annabelle. The

public had to be informed about Janie before they could ever help find her. Eliza knew that it would be important to humanize Janie, emotionally linking the public to the outcome of the search for her child.

But Eliza also knew very well what it would be like if she went outside to face the press. They would pounce on her and she would be the focal point of the story. There would be questions about how she felt, how she was holding up. It might be better to have the facts laid out to the press by someone else so that the focus would be only on Janie and Mrs. Garcia's disappearance.

Eliza looked over at Katharine and Paul, who had been sitting there listening to the conversation. Her in-laws suddenly looked so frail and old and there was no way Eliza was going to ask them to trot outside and answer a barrage of questions. They were under enough pressure as it was.

"Let me do it, Eliza," Annabelle repeated.

"God, that would be great," said Eliza. "But do you really want to?"

"You'd do it for me, wouldn't you?" Annabelle asked.

"What about your *KTA* assignment?"

"Unfortunately, I've done enough of these 'heartbreaking news' things that I can handle both jobs, at least for this morning. Harry Granger is out there, and you know him—he barely needs to be produced at all. It's not his first time at the rodeo. And B.J. is out there, too, now. He doesn't need to be told what pictures to get; he has better instincts about that than I do."

"Still . . . ," Eliza said uncertainly.

"Don't worry," Annabelle insisted. "There are other producers out there, too. We aren't leaving Harry twisting in the wind. After the broadcast, if you want me to continue to be your spokesperson, I can ask Linus for a leave until Janie comes home."

Annabelle went outside to join the news personnel on the street in front of Eliza's house. Immediately, she was surrounded by colleagues from ABC, CBS, CNN, NBC, FOX, and the local television and radio stations, as well as reporters from the *New York Times,* the *Wall Street Journal,* the *New York Post,* the *Daily News,* the *Record,* the *Star Ledger,* and the Associated Press. It surprised no one that the *Enquirer,* the *Star,* and the *Mole* were also represented. This story was tailor-made for the gossip tabloids' front pages. Photographers from tmz.com, ready to stream the latest video to the popular celebrity news Web site, were there, as well as aggressive paparazzi drooling for the sensational shots that would command top dollar.

"I have a statement, everybody," Annabelle announced.

She waited while the photographers, camera crews, and reporters with microphones and notebooks jostled into position.

"I am Annabelle Murphy, A-N-N-A-B-E-L-L-E—that's one word—M-U-R-P-H-Y. I am a producer for *KEY to America* and a colleague and friend of Mrs. Blake. I have a short statement to read and afterward I'll take a few questions."

Annabelle cleared her throat and began to read from the announcement she and Eliza had composed.

"Yesterday, at approximately eleven forty A.M., Janie Blake, age seven, was taken by Carmen Garcia, Mrs. Blake's housekeeper, from Camp Musquapsink, a children's day camp in Sloatsburg, New York. Neither Janie nor Mrs. Garcia has been seen or heard from since. Local and state police in New Jersey and New York as well as the FBI are investigating. The National Center for Missing and Exploited Children has also been contacted."

Annabelle paused and swallowed before continuing. "Mrs. Blake is asking anyone who has any information that might help find Janie to please call their local police department. Later in the day we hope to have set up a designated number to call."

The CBS reporter shouted out the first questions. "Was the housekeeper scheduled to take Janie from camp? Was this something planned, something that Eliza knew about beforehand?"

"No," said Annabelle. "Eliza has no idea why Mrs. Garcia took Janie out of camp yesterday morning."

"Does that mean the police think Mrs. Garcia kidnapped Janie Blake?"

"You'll have to ask the police," answered Annabelle. "But Eliza does not think that Janie was kidnapped by Mrs. Garcia. She also believes that Mrs. Garcia would never take Janie without letting her know where they were going. She thinks Mrs. Garcia was somehow forced to take her child."

"But she does think Janie was definitely kidnapped?"

"Eliza doesn't know exactly what to think," said Annabelle. "As you can imagine, there are many nightmarish scenarios running through her mind right now."

"Was this her first year at camp?" asked a local newspaper reporter.

"I don't know. I'll have to get back to you on that."

"How long has Mrs. Garcia worked for Eliza?" asked the reporter from the *Daily News.*

Annabelle thought back. "I think about two years."

"What is her background?"

"I know she came with impeccable references."

"Is she a United States citizen?"

"I'm not sure about that," said Annabelle. "I'll have to get back to you."

"Has there been any ransom demand made?" asked the *New York Times* reporter.

"No."

"Then perhaps they could have been in an accident," suggested the Associated Press reporter.

Annabelle took a moment before responding. The note that Carmen Garcia left in the camp log indicated that she was signaling for help. Or perhaps more troubling, she may have written the note to shift suspicion away from herself. Either way, a car accident wasn't high on the list of possibilities. Annabelle didn't want people searching ditches instead of focusing their attention on a full-scale hunt for whoever had taken the child.

"We have reason to believe that is not the case," said Annabelle.

"What reason?" called the NBC reporter.

"I'm not at liberty to say," said Annabelle. "You'll have to ask the police or FBI about that."

"When will the police or FBI be coming

out to talk to us?" asked Harry Granger. Eliza's cohost on *KEY to America* was standing out on the street with the rest of the reporters. Annabelle was supposed to be assisting Harry, doing whatever needed to be done to have him ready to report when the morning program began. Instead, she was helping Eliza. And while she didn't want to neglect Harry, she felt strongly that what she was doing right now was more important. There were other KEY News producers scurrying around out here this morning and they could help Harry. Plus, Harry was a pro, not the prima donna some anchors were. Annabelle was confident he was going to be more than fine without her.

"I don't know about that, Harry. When I go back inside, I'll see what I can find out."

Harry asked a follow-up question. "How is Eliza holding up?"

"About how you might expect," said Annabelle. "She is extremely worried and upset." Annabelle looked down at the ground and then up again. "And she's praying that Janie will come back to her, safe and sound."

CHAPTER 23

"Hughie." Isabelle shook her brother's arm. "Hughie, get up. You have to come watch the news."

He kept his eyes shut. He wanted to finish his dream. But his sister had seen to it now that he wasn't going to find out if the little girl with the dark pigtails and pinafore would take the candy he offered her. *What a lousy way to start the day.*

Hugh got out of bed, pulling his nightshirt down as he shuffled out to the living room. "This better be good," he said.

"Shush," Isabelle said with annoyance. "Just watch."

As he digested the television report,

Hugh bit his thumbnail down to the point where it hurt. Then he gnawed at it some more as he contemplated what Janie Blake's kidnapping would mean.

The camp was in Sloatsburg; the kid's home was in Bergen County. Both of those locations were close enough to his modest ranch-style home that Hugh knew the police were going to come knocking on his door. He was sure of it.

It wouldn't be the first time the cops had come calling. And it wouldn't be the last. Whenever a kid went missing, they loved to look his way and throw their weight around. But they had come to this apartment before and found nothing. They wouldn't find anything this time, either.

Still, Hugh found himself trembling. He shook with fear and outrage. *It's just not fair.*

CHAPTER 24

In a reversal of the usual two-way interview, Harry Granger, on location on Saddle Ridge Road in Ho-Ho-Kus, New Jersey, interviewed former FBI special agent and KEY News contributor Cathy Bonica, who was at the *KEY to America* studio in Manhattan.

"In your years with the Bureau, you worked on some pretty high-profile kidnapping cases, Cathy. What does your gut tell you about this one?"

"Well, first of all, Harry, we aren't even sure that this *is* a kidnapping. Janie Blake and her caregiver are missing. No one saw them taken against their wills. There has been no ransom demand."

"But assuming that this *is* a kidnapping, Cathy, what could be going on here?"

"Well, Harry, there are three types of kidnapping." Cathy reeled off the list. "Kidnapping by a relative or family member . . . that sort of kidnapping is the most common. The other two types are kidnapping by an acquaintance and kidnapping by a stranger."

"Which do you think we are looking at here?"

"It's too early to know," said the former FBI agent. "If a ransom demand is sent, that might give investigators a clue. If no ransom demand is made, it's more than likely this is not a kidnapping with profit as a motive. When a seven-year-old girl is abducted, and it isn't for the money, the worry is it could be for sexual perversion or worse." Cathy paused. "But I think we're getting ahead of ourselves, Harry," she said. "For every kidnapping by someone unrelated to the child, there are over seventy abductions by family members. So, I think it's fair to say that investigators are following the statistics right now and concentrating on Janie Blake's known universe."

"Which would be the housekeeper?" asked Harry. "Is it law enforcement's inclination that there has been foul play by the housekeeper?"

"I'm sure that's their first thought, Harry. They are going to look at Carmen Garcia first, and focus on the family as well. After that, they will move outward . . . to friends and acquaintances, peripheral contacts, sex offenders registered in the community, and finally, and this is the most frightening scenario of all, Harry, strangers."

"Let me get back to something you just said, Cathy. You said that investigators would concentrate on Carmen Garcia and the family first. Did you mean Carmen Garcia's family or Janie Blake's family?"

"Both families, Harry. Nobody will be immune from scrutiny."

CHAPTER 25

Rhonda Billings put down her coffee cup and switched off the television. All the talk of kidnapping and the speculation about what could be happening to Janie Blake was upsetting her. Harry Granger and the others didn't know what they were talking about. Rhonda was tempted to call in to KEY to America and let them know that Janie was just fine.

Rhonda walked around the living room of the ground-floor apartment. She fluffed the pillows on the sofa and straightened the pile of magazines on the coffee table. Then she checked the dial on the air-conditioning unit installed in the living room window. It was a giant machine, but it was the only air conditioner they had and it was going to have to pump extra hard. The forecast was for a scorching day.

Rhonda went to the bathroom, brushed her teeth, and pulled a comb through her short dark hair. She noticed that the gray was getting more and more visible. Over the last few years she had really aged, while Dave hadn't changed very much at all.

Her husband was taking a nap after working the ten-to-six shift, grabbing a few hours' sleep before it was time for her to leave for work at the bakery and he would take over on the home front. Rhonda knew he was relieved when it was time for her to go. She had the feeling sometimes that her husband couldn't stand to be around her. But they had made a promise to stick together, and Dave was the type of person who kept his promises even when he didn't want to.

So, while she was at work, it would be just Dave and her precious girl together, for most of the day. Now she was glad Dave worked the overnight shift, because that meant he was available for Janie, to watch over and protect her. She was worried though, because Dave could be so intolerant. He could have such a temper. That wasn't good for a young child. A child needed patience and understanding and gentleness, and Rhonda had those things in abundance. She also had so much love to give. There would be enough love for both Dave and Janie. Dave didn't have to be jealous or think she would forget about him. She could never forget about Dave. They had been through too much together.

Rhonda walked on bare feet into the kitchen and pulled a box of cereal from the cabinet on top of the refrigerator. She shook Cheerios into two plastic bowls and then poured milk on top. She put the bowls and two spoons on a tray and carried breakfast down the hallway. She wanted to make sure Janie had something to eat before she herself left for work.

The bakery had not yet opened for the day, but the baker had already been in for several hours. Rhonda came in through the rear door, inhaling the aroma of freshly baked bread, crumb cake, and Danish.

She put away her purse, went into the tiny lavatory at the back of the kitchen, and changed into her white uniform. While she was washing her hands, Rhonda looked into the mirror over the sink and realized she was smiling.

She was happy. For the first time in years, she was actually happy. Having Janie had done that for her. Yet, at the same time, Rhonda felt sorry for Eliza Blake. She was undoubtedly devastated, just as Rhonda had been when she'd lost her little girl. She also knew all too well that Eliza would never recover completely, never feel the same again. But, if Eliza were lucky enough to have another child someday, that would help her go on with her life. That's what was allowing Rhonda to go on with hers.

Eliza was young enough to have more children. That wasn't possible for

Rhonda. It wasn't fair, but that's the way it was. Janie was the gift that evened things out.

Rhonda came out of the lavatory and went over to the shelf that was stacked with flattened cardboard containers. She took one, expertly folded it into a box, and lined it with tissue paper. Rhonda went from tray to tray, filling the box with cookies. Sugar cookies, chocolate chip cookies, oatmeal-and-raisin cookies, and English toffee cookies—and pieces of the baker's signature marzipan. Then she took a second box and filled it with lemon squares and brownies, swaddling each in plastic wrap so they wouldn't bump into one another. Finally, she took both boxes and packed them in a shipping carton.

She stood for a while, thinking about what she wanted to write. A gift card wouldn't be big enough. She ripped a sheet from the pad of bakery order forms and wrote on the back.

Dear Eliza,
   I'm sorry you are going through such a hard time right now. Hav-

ing lost a daughter myself, I know what it's like. My heart goes out to you.

These treats are not as sweet as Janie, but I hope they fortify you in the difficult days you are facing.

You're probably wondering, as I did when my little girl was lost to me, why this has happened. God works in mysterious ways. It will take time to be able to see why Janie was taken from you, or maybe you'll never be able to understand. Unfortunately, sometimes you have to go through unbearable pain before you realize what's truly important in life. Be comforted in knowing that your pain is helping someone else.

Someday, God willing, you'll have another child. Save your money until then so you'll be able to stay home and take care of your baby as you should.

Rhonda read the note over and folded it without signing it. She put the *letter in the box with the cookies and sealed it closed. During her break she would take it over to the UPS office. Eliza should have the cookies tomorrow.*

CHAPTER 26

The sound of the upstairs tenants moving around above her head, and the familiar smell of strong coffee, had roused Maria from a fitful rest. She had barely slept at all, racking her brain trying to recall if her mother had said anything at all that could be a clue to what had happened to her and Janie Blake. She now made her way to the kitchen to put on her own pot of coffee.

Overwrought, overtired, and so upset by what she had seen on television, Maria dropped the uncapped bottle on the floor, spilling milk all over the worn linoleum. As she wiped up the mess, Maria felt her chest tightening. Her mother was missing and so was the child her mother took care of every day. And that child wasn't just any child. That child was the daughter of one of the most well-known women in America.

Mrs. Blake was a nice lady, and it was good of her to call last night to let them know what was going on with the police search, but nice ladies could turn mean if things didn't go their way. Carmen had seen women in the nail salon, smiling so sweetly when they came in for their manicures and pedicures, but changing into snarling witches if they had to wait too long or got a call they didn't like on their cell phones.

If Mrs. Blake was upset, she might blame all of them. Because her own baby was gone, she could blame her mother, Vicente, even little Rosario. The Anglos could be harsh when they wanted to be. And the Anglo police scared Maria most of all.

Rosario was a United States citizen because she had been born in this country. And Carmen's mother had legal working papers, so she was allowed to be here.

But Vicente and Maria weren't legal. They had sneaked into the country because there had been no work for them in Guatemala and because they wanted their child to be born in America.

So far, things had worked out all right. Vicente had found a job at the car wash and made some extra money doing detailing jobs on expensive cars and SUVs. Maria had gotten a position at the nail salon, first cleaning the floors and foot baths and stocking the hot towels, then gradually learning to do manicures. The two of them worked hard and saved every dollar they could just to make the rent each month for the cramped two-room apartment in the basement of a larger house that was occupied by a dozen other Guatemalans.

Someday, Maria hoped, the lawmakers would pass legislation so that she and Vicente could be out in the open, living here without constantly worrying that they would be caught and sent back to Guatemala. That day didn't look like it was coming anytime soon. In the meantime, they tried not to call attention to themselves. But what was happening now was surely going to attract scrutiny.

Maria felt panicked. Vicente had already gone to the car wash, so she was alone with the baby. If the police came, she didn't know what she was going to say to them. What if they asked her to prove she was allowed to be here? What if they took her and Rosario and put them in jail? Worse, what if they took Rosario away from her?

The apartment felt like a trap now. Wanting to get out as fast as she could, Maria hurried to pack the baby's bottles and diapers in the bag she always took to the babysitter. She washed Rosario's face and fastened the tiny sandals on her pudgy feet. Maria scooped the child in her arms and started up the stairs. Just as the baby spit up all over the front of Maria's shirt, the doorbell rang.

Two police officers stood at the door. One was of medium height and build, the other was tall and quite overweight. Maria wondered how he would ever be able to run to catch a criminal. Both wore neatly pressed blue uniforms, heavy black leather gun holsters around their waists.

"May I help you?" Maria asked.

"Buenos días, ma'am," said the medium-size policeman. "Are you Maria Rochas?"

"Yes."

"And your mother is Carmen Garcia?"

Maria shifted the baby on her hip. *"Sí."*

"We have a few questions to ask you regarding your mother."

Maria waited, not inviting them inside.

"When was the last time you saw your mother?"

"Over the weekend. We went to Mass together on Sunday and then she spent the afternoon here."

"You didn't see her at all on Monday?"

"No," answered Maria.

"Did you talk with her on the phone?"

"No, I didn't."

"Do you usually talk to her every day?"

"Yes."

"Does she usually call you or do you usually call her?"

"We usually talk during my break. I usually call her."

"Did you call her Monday at lunchtime?"

"No, I didn't." Maria knew there was no point in lying. There was a way to check the phone records.

"Why not?"

Maria's heart pounded and her face grew hot. Dear God, they were thinking she had something to do with Janie Blake's disappearance, that she had known her mother wouldn't be at the Blakes' house, so she hadn't bothered to call.

"Why didn't you call your mother on Monday, Mrs. Rochas?" the officer asked again.

"I had to work through my break and I didn't have a chance to call her. That is the truth. You can check with my boss."

The medium-size officer wrote down the name and address of the nail salon and the proprietor's name.

"May we see your papers?" asked the heavier one.

Maria thought quickly. "My husband

takes care of all that," she said. "He's not home."

"And where can we find your husband?"

"He is working."

"Where?"

Maria hesitated. "At the car wash."

The officers looked at each other.

"Look, ma'am," said the fat one. "We know that most of the guys who work at the car wash are illegal. That's not what we're here about. We want to find Janie Blake and your mother."

"Is there anything you can think of that will help us find them?" asked the other cop. "Did your mother say anything, tell you anything at all, that might assist us?"

The baby in Maria's arms started to cry. The combination of the morning heat, the smell of spit-up, and the tension made Maria feel nauseous. She struggled to remain erect.

"I can't think of anything. No."

The policemen didn't look pleased. "All right, Mrs. Rochas. That's all for now. But if it turns out you know something and aren't telling us, there will be serious consequences," said the heavy cop.

"Life-changing consequences," said the other cop.

CHAPTER 27

"What the hell were you thinking, Annabelle?" It was Executive Producer Linus Nazareth calling from the control room at the KEY News Broadcast Center.

"Excuse me?" said Annabelle into her cell phone.

"Why on earth would you make yourself the spokesperson for Eliza and go out there and brief our competition?" Linus was shouting and Annabelle could imagine all the people in the control room listening to the executive producer's tirade.

"Because Eliza and I decided it would be the best way to handle it, Linus," she said evenly. "And I want to do anything I can to help."

"Well, you can help Eliza without screwing *us,* can't you?" Linus demanded. "Anything and everything pertaining to this case should air on KEY News first. We should be exclusive on every bit of new information. And there you are, giving it up to the other networks. I saw clips of you on *Today, Good Morning America,* and the CBS *Early Show.* What's the matter with you?"

Annabelle was ready to scream right back at him, but thought better of it. Having a showdown with Linus right now wasn't a prudent thing to do. She had quit on him once when they had gotten into a fight, and this time, Annabelle wouldn't put it past Linus to be looking for an excuse to can her just to even the score and save face. Annabelle knew she would be able to help Eliza far more if she continued to work at KEY News than if she didn't. And the fact was, she needed her job.

"Linus, please, listen to me," Annabelle said calmly. "Think about it. I really didn't have much information to give them, but whatever it was, if it helps find Janie Blake, isn't that the most important thing?"

"Look, Annabelle, I'm sorry Eliza's kid is missing. I really am. But I'm going to say what nobody wants to acknowledge: This is a chance to boost our ratings sky high. The viewing audience is going to be all over this thing—like white on rice. We can pull viewers away from their normal habits. If we offer information that other morning shows don't have, viewers are going to change the channel and watch us. And if they like what they see, we might win 'em over for good. This is a unique opportunity, Annabelle, and I'll be damned if we're going to blow it."

CHAPTER 28

Stephanie Quick paused to compose herself before she entered the Ho-Ho-Kus Police Department building. She ran her fingers through her curly red hair and smoothed out the wrinkles that had accumulated on the front of her skirt during the drive from Pennsylvania. She wanted to make a good impression because she knew she was probably going to have a tough sell.

She finished walking up the cement pathway, opened the heavy glass door, and went inside. A middle-aged officer was stationed at the desk.

"May I help you?"

"Yes," said Stephanie. "And I think I can help you, too."

The officer eyed her warily. "Go ahead," he said.

"I have some information about the Janie Blake case."

The officer looked at her sharply, studying the woman who was standing in front of him. She was probably in her early forties, thin, and dressed in a khaki skirt, a white cotton blouse, and a pair of black flats. Small pearl studs decorated her ears, and the only other jewelry she wore was a tank watch with a thick black strap. He decided that Stephanie Quick looked legit.

"Hold on a minute, ma'am," said the officer. "Let me get one of our detectives."

Within two minutes, Stephanie was sitting in an interview room across the table from Detective Mark Kennedy.

"I understand you have some information on the Janie Blake case," he began.

"Yes," said Stephanie.

Detective Kennedy stayed silent and waited for her to begin.

"I saw Janie Blake," said Stephanie.

Kennedy sat up straighter. "When?" he snapped.

"In the middle of the night," she answered.

"Where?"

"I'm not quite sure where she was, but she was tied up."

"I don't understand," said Kennedy. "You saw her, but you don't know where?"

"I know where *I* was, Detective. But I don't know where *Janie* was. You see, I saw her in my dream last night."

Kennedy sat back in his chair and uttered a deep, long sigh.

"I know, I know," said Stephanie. "You're trained to be skeptical of anything you can't prove with your five senses. You're probably skeptical by nature. But I'm telling you, Detective, you'd be making a mistake if you dismissed me as some sort of nut."

"Ms. Quick, I don't know who you are, so I don't know who I'm dealing with and, to be perfectly honest, I don't really believe in psychic abilities." Kennedy shook his head. "Plus, we can't be committing resources to follow up on information that isn't substantive."

"But my information *is* substantive, Detective. I'm telling you. I do have psychic powers and I've helped other police agencies in the past." She opened her purse, took out a piece of paper, and slid it across the desk. "Here's a list of other police departments I've worked with. You can check with them."

Kennedy glanced at the paper, a list of police departments in Pennsylvania. None of the places was familiar to him. He pushed the résumé aside. Grudgingly, he picked up his pen. He had to cover his bases and take this woman's information, though he already knew how much credence he would give it. "All right," he said. "Shoot."

He went through the motions of taking notes as Stephanie described what she had seen in her dream.

"Janie's hands were tied behind her back," said Stephanie.

Predictable, thought Kennedy.

"She was also blindfolded," said Stephanie.

Anyone could come up with that, thought Kennedy.

"And there was paint smeared on her cheeks," Stephanie finished.

Original at least, he thought. "Paint? What kind of paint?" he asked.

"Green," replied Stephanie. "And it was streaked because Janie had been crying."

"All right, Ms. Quick," said Kennedy as he rose from his chair. "Thank you for coming in. If we need anything else, we'll be in touch."

"Fine," said Stephanie. "My phone number and e-mail address are on that sheet I gave you. Please don't ignore me, Detective. I'm telling you, I can help find Janie Blake."

Detective Kennedy escorted her to the door. When he got back to his desk, he shook his head as he stuck Stephanie Quick's paperwork in a folder, not bothering to enter the information into the computer.

CHAPTER 29

Eliza was running on adrenaline as she paced the kitchen floor. She hadn't slept, hadn't eaten, and her brain was in overdrive. She kept going over and over what had happened, trying to make sense of it. At the same time, she was worrying about the future, trying to figure out how to get her daughter back. She already had decided, whatever a kidnapper wanted, she would pay. Getting Janie and Mrs. Garcia home safely was worth any price.

"The phone here is unlisted," Eliza said. "How will whoever has Janie and Mrs. Garcia be able to reach us?"

"We have to consider that whoever has Janie could be someone you know," said Agent Gebhardt. "He or she, or they, could know your phone number. Or, if a stranger has Janie and Mrs. Garcia, he can just ask them for the number, right? Either way, if a kidnapper wants to get in touch with us, he will."

Eliza jumped when the phone rang. She checked the identification bar and felt the first inkling of relief she had experienced since the ordeal had begun. Mack was calling from London.

"It's all right," said Eliza. "It's my . . . uh . . . friend. And he's calling from England, so you can rule him out as a suspect."

"Okay," said Agent Gebhardt. "Answer it, but tell him you can't stay on the line."

Eliza picked up the receiver.

"My God, Eliza. I just heard." Mack sounded so close. She so wished he was.

"Oh, Mack," she said, feeling tears coming to her eyes at the sound of his voice. "I don't know what I'm going to do."

"We'll get through this, honey. I promise we will." His tone was adamant and confident. "Tell me everything."

"I want to tell you," said Eliza, "but we have to keep this line open. Call me back on my cell."

The rooms upstairs were still being gone over for evidence and the first floor offered no privacy at all. Eliza desperately wanted to talk to Mack without anyone hearing. She took her cell phone and walked out to the backyard.

She was halfway across the lawn when the phone sounded. She sat on one of the seats of Janie's swing set and opened the phone.

"Hi," she said.

"Hi," he answered.

For a moment, there was silence, no sound traveling either way over the Atlantic Ocean, as if neither side had the words to convey the enormity of what was happening.

"I'm coming home," said Mack. "I'm getting the next plane."

"Oh, thank you," she uttered gratefully. "I need you, Mack. I don't know if I can get through this. If something happens to Janie . . ." Her voice cracked and she started to sob, deep, gasping sobs that came from her core—sobs she had been fighting since she realized Janie and Mrs. Garcia were missing.

It flashed through her mind, the ways Mack had been there for her over the last two years—and the ways he'd come up short. They'd begun as colleagues, grew to be friends, and, eventually, lovers. Mack had been patient with her reticence, understanding that she had been shattered by John's death and was afraid to offer her heart again.

Not long after Eliza had surrendered to her feelings for him, KEY News in its infinite wisdom had transferred Mack to London where, in a drunken night of loneliness, Mack had slept with another woman. When Eliza learned of it, courtesy of the KEY gossip mill, she had been inwardly crushed and disillusioned. Outwardly, though, she carried on, terminating their relationship and focusing on Janie and her career.

Mack had been exceedingly penitent and persistent in letting Eliza know it. Over time, Eliza had come to realize that he really did love her, that the one-night stand was something he profoundly regretted, a terrible mistake. Finally, she had forgiven him, though she had not been sure she would ever be able to forget.

Yet, as Eliza sat on Janie's swing, Mack's sexual indiscretion seemed like nothing in comparison to what she was facing now. Her daughter's and Mrs. Garcia's *lives* were at stake.

She heard Mack's voice.

"Sweetheart, listen to me, honey. Please, listen to me. Janie's going to be all right. Thinking otherwise will do you absolutely no good and it won't do Janie any good, either."

"I know," she wailed. "I know."

"Eliza, cry now, and get it out. It's probably good to do that. But you have to have faith, sweetheart. You have to try to stay positive."

She couldn't answer him. Eliza rocked

back and forth on the swing, tears running down her cheeks, her body shaking. She couldn't catch her breath and
she couldn't get herself to stop crying;
nor could she see the photographer who
was on the other side of the hedges, the
telephoto lens of his camera pointed
right at her.

CHAPTER 30

"Can't you get that kid to stop hiccupping?"

"She's afraid," said Mrs. Garcia as she turned her head in the direction of the man's voice. She had her arm around Janie's shoulders as they sat huddled together on the mattress. Mrs. Garcia had lain awake all night and listened as Janie hiccupped softly and sporadically as she drifted in and out of sleep. Once Janie awoke, the hiccupping had increased again.

"Well, she's driving me crazy." The man bent down and brought his face close to Janie's. "Cut it out, little girl. If you know what's good for you, you'll cut it out right now."

From behind her blindfold, Janie felt the meanness and anger in the man's voice. She hiccupped again, more deeply this time.

"Damn it, kid. What did I just say?"

Janie pulled back, afraid that she was going to get another slap across the face.

"Please, *señor,* leave her alone," pleaded Mrs. Garcia. "She can't help it. She is very scared of you. That makes her do this. If you make her more scared, she'll only do it more."

They listened to the sound of the man's footsteps as he paced the room, muttering to himself.

"I have to go to the bathroom," Janie said softly.

"Again?" asked the man. "You just went."

"I have to go again."

"Where are your manners, little girl? You have to ask me nicely. 'May I go to the bathroom, *Daddy.*'"

"You're not my daddy," Janie said firmly.

The man bent down to her again and she could feel the heat of his breath as he spoke. "You'd better get used to it, little girl. Until further notice, I *am* your daddy."

The kidnapper covered his head with the mask before taking off Mrs. Garcia's and Janie's blindfolds and untying their hands. Unaccustomed to the light, both of them rubbed their eyes.

"Now remember," he said as he led them to the bathroom, "I can hear everything you say or do in there so don't try anything funny." He patted the microphone still attached to Mrs. Garcia's blouse. "Do what you have to do and get back out here."

While Janie sat, Mrs. Garcia checked out the room in the light of day. The space was clean but small, with barely enough room for a toilet, a tiny sink, and a shower stall. The floor was linoleum and the bat-and-board walls were painted white. Above the toilet was a window. Mrs. Garcia realized the room was at ground level as she leaned over to look out.

"*Ay, Dios mio*," she said softly. "Where are we?"

"Never mind where you are," said the gruff voice coming from the other side of the door. "Finish up and get back out here."

CHAPTER 31

Lisa Nichols sang along to her new Bon Jovi CD as she rode to camp. That she was late for work didn't bother her. The night she'd just had was well worth a disapproving look from the camp director, a dock in pay, or even dismissal for her tardiness.

She was completely unaware that, when she didn't answer her cell phone, deputies from the sheriff's office had gone to her parents' house, the address listed on her Camp Musquapsink personnel form. The parents were under the impression that Lisa was sleeping over at her girlfriend's house, but a phone call to the friend determined that Lisa wasn't there. After some pressuring, the friend admitted to promising Lisa that she would serve as an alibi while Lisa slept over at her boyfriend's apartment. Neither the girlfriend nor Lisa's angry parents knew the young man's address or cell phone number.

As her car neared the entrance of the camp, Lisa saw the news vans and police vehicles gathered on the road. Her first thought was that something could have happened to one of the kids; her second thought was relief that she couldn't have had anything to do with it since she hadn't even been there yet this morning. She slowed and came to a stop when she reached the gate.

"ID please, miss," ordered the officer standing guard.

Lisa rifled through her purse, found her wallet, and pulled out her college identification card. She handed it to the officer, who perused it and handed it back to her.

"The witness just arrived," the officer said into the radio attached to his shirt.

Looking up at him from her open window, Lisa's face expressed her puzzlement. "Witness? Witness to what?" she asked.

"Go directly to the reception office, miss." The officer waved Lisa on.

Outside the main building, a few uniformed officers awaited her arrival. As Lisa got out of the car and walked toward them, one of the officers broke off from the group and escorted her inside the building. Holly Taylor was standing at the front desk, a grave expression on her pale face. Even scarier was the fact that Lisa's parents were standing beside her boss. Her father was glowering; her mother looked like she had been crying.

"Lisa, these people have some questions to ask you," said her father in the controlled voice he used when he was truly angry. "They're with the FBI."

Introductions were made.

"What kind of questions?" Lisa asked worriedly.

"Janie Blake never came home after camp yesterday," said one of the agents. "Do you know anything about that?"

Lisa swallowed. "I know her maid

came and signed her out yesterday, before lunch. Janie was really excited."

One of the other agents was taking notes. "So, give us a description of exactly what Janie Blake looked like the last time you saw her," he said.

Lisa spoke slowly and deliberately. "She was wearing her camp uniform, the Musquapsink T-shirt and the navy shorts, and she had a construction-paper band around her head with a big yellow feather attached to the back . . . and she had stripes of green paint on her cheeks. It was Native American Day."

The first agent resumed his questions. "And what did her caretaker say when she came in to get her?"

Lisa tried to remember. "Nothing, really. I was collating some papers and I think she asked me what I was doing."

"Anything else?"

"I think she said something about Janie's mother meeting them at home with a surprise. That's it. Then she just signed the log and they left."

"Did you check her signature?"

Lisa's face reddened. "No, I guess I didn't," she said softly.

CHAPTER 32

To escape the bustle and tension inside the house, Eliza and Annabelle went out to the patio. Annabelle carried a yellow legal pad that she placed on the white wrought-iron table as they sat down.

"I've been looking around on the Internet, Eliza, and there are some things we should be doing." Annabelle was taking on the functions she knew well as a producer: researching, planning, and organizing. "The FBI and the police are doing their jobs, but we have to do ours. Someone may have seen Janie or will come forward with information that will help us find her. We have to get the word out there."

Eliza took a deep breath, considering what Annabelle was saying. She thought about some of the missing-children cases that had gotten heavy media attention. Tragically, having the coverage didn't necessarily mean there was a happy ending to the story. How many times had she read the copy from the teleprompter and informed the nation that a missing child had been found alive? On the other hand, how many times had she told the audience that a missing child had turned up dead or never turned up at all? She knew she could ask somebody in the KEY News research department to find out the statistics on the resolution of missing-children cases, but she had a feeling that the answers would terrify her even more than she already was.

Annabelle was staring at her. "Eliza?"

"I brought this on myself," Eliza whispered.

"Don't be ridiculous. You did not."

"Yes, I did. Exposing Janie this way, doing all those interviews, letting all those stories be done and pictures be taken, leaving her open to some sick individual who would abduct her for whatever twisted reason. Oh, God. I might as well have given them instructions on how to get at her. Anyone could know where we live, anyone who wanted to could figure out our schedules, where she would be. This is my fault."

Annabelle reached forward and wrapped her arms around her friend. "It's going to be all right, Eliza. It will be. It has to be."

Eliza tried hard to think clearly. If media exposure had put them in this position, media exposure might be able to bring Janie back home. Annabelle was right. Besides, what other choice did she have? This was the fight of her life and she would do everything possible to get her little girl back.

"All right," she said with determination. "What are we going to do?"

Annabelle consulted her notes. "We're going to get a designated hotline number set up where people can call in with information," she said. "And we'll set up a Website: www.findjanie.org, or something like that. The guys at KEYNews.com can help us with that. And, of course, they'll post information on the KEY News Web site as well. I'm sure there will be millions of hits on KEYNews.com because that will probably be the first place on the Internet people will go to find out what's happening."

"Shouldn't we include Mrs. Garcia's name in the Web address?" asked Eliza.

"We need something that people will remember easily. 'Find Janie and Carmen' doesn't cut it," said Annabelle.

Eliza smiled in spite of herself at Annabelle's matter-of-factness. But as she tried to listen intently to Annabelle, Eliza's mind kept wandering to thoughts of Janie. Where was she? What was she thinking? She must be terrified and unable to understand why anyone would take her away from her secure little world.

Please, God, Eliza prayed. *Let her be safe. Please, just let whoever took her call and ask for money. I'll pay whatever they ask if I can just have Janie back, healthy and unharmed.*

Annabelle was continuing to talk as

she checked off the items written on the pad.

"You have a fax machine, right?"

"Yes, in the den," Eliza said, trying to sound positive.

"Good," said Annabelle. "We'll need it to issue press advisories. And I'll need some good pictures of Janie, and Mrs. Garcia, too, if you have any. We have to get missing-child flyers made. We can get volunteers to post them around here . . . and we can offer the flyers on our Web site so that people out of the area can download them."

Eliza nodded. "I already gave the police a picture for TRAK, the Technology to Recover Abducted Kids, and it was sent out to various state law enforcement agencies. Wait a minute," she said as she got up. She went inside the house and came back with a silver frame. "How's this?" she asked as she handed it to Annabelle.

Annabelle looked at the picture. Janie smiled broadly as Mrs. Garcia stood behind her, wrapping the child in a towel.

"Sweet," Annabelle remarked.

"It was taken on the Fourth of July,"

said Eliza. "We swam and had a barbecue that afternoon before we went over
to Ridgewood for the fireworks. Janie
was so excited. She loves fireworks. That
was less than three weeks ago." Eliza's
voice trailed off.

"All right, we'll use this," said Annabelle, trying to pull her friend out of
a reverie that wasn't going to help her.
"Here's the hardest part, Eliza. It's time
to go and talk to the vultures out there.
You have to look into the cameras and
tell Janie that you love her and that you
are coming to get her. You have to beg
whoever has her to give her back, and
you have to ask the public to help you
find her."

Eliza considered Annabelle's words,
thinking of some of the parental pleas
she had seen televised over the years.
The dazed parents, trying to hold themselves together as they begged for the
return of their child. In their most desperate hours, expected to go out there
and face the cameras and the barrage
of questioning. *How were they able to
do that?*

But she knew the answer. They had been able to do it because they felt their child's life depended on it.

"All right," she agreed quietly. "And, Annabelle?"

"Yeah?"

"Thank you."

"You're welcome."

"Annabelle?"

"Yes?"

"Tell me it's going to be all right."

"Yes, honey, it is going to be all right," said Annabelle, giving Eliza the answer she needed to hear. She knew it wouldn't do Eliza any good to tell her what else she had learned in her research. The vast majority of kidnapped children who were murdered—were dead within three hours of their abduction.

"I want to offer a reward."

Eliza stood beside the table where the FBI agents were stationed.

"I was thinking of a quarter of a million dollars," said Eliza. "Do you think that seems like enough?"

Trevor Laggie whistled softly. "That kind of dough sure sweetens the pot. Just be prepared for people coming out of the woodwork with leads that turn out to be nothing."

CHAPTER 33

The men were busy, spraying wind-
shields and scrubbing hubcaps. They
kept working when they saw the police
car pull into the service area, but they
watched quietly and warily, hoping not
to call attention to themselves, ready to
run if they had to.

"Which one of you is Vicente Rochas?"
asked a heavyset cop.

The men put their heads down and
concentrated on their cleaning tasks.

Seeing that no one was going to volunteer any information, the police officers walked into the office.

"We're looking for Vicente Rochas."

"He's out there working, isn't he?" answered the cashier.

"Will you come and point him out to us?"

The cashier locked up her register and followed the policemen outside.

She looked around the lot. "I don't see him, but I know he was here this morning." She turned to one of the workmen. "Hey, Miguel, where's Vicente?"

The workman shrugged.

One of the policemen stepped forward. "Listen up, fellas. If you know what's good for you, you'll tell us where Vicente Rochas is."

No one said a word.

"Don't make us go around checking your working papers, guys. If you want to stay in the good ole U S of A, you'll tell us where Vicente is."

At the side of the building, the door to the men's room opened and a man with a small frame and caramel-colored skin came out slowly.

"I am Vicente Rochas," he said.

They took him to the police car. Vicente sat in the backseat while they peppered him with questions.

No, he had no idea where his mother-in-law was. He hadn't seen her since Sunday when she'd spent the afternoon with him, his wife, and their daughter.

Yes, he knew where the Blakes lived. No, he had never told or shown his friends where the house was.

No, he had no idea where Janie Blake went to day camp.

No, he didn't have working papers.

"Please, don't turn me in," Vicente pleaded. "Don't send me back to Guatemala. There is nothing for me or my family there."

"If you've done nothing wrong, then you have nothing to worry about," said the heavyset policeman. "But we're going to be watching you, Vicente."

CHAPTER 34

A mile a minute. With each minute, Janie could be another mile farther away. She could have been taken over two thousand miles by now.

Eliza stood in the den and spun the globe she kept there, mostly for Janie's benefit. Her fingers traced various routes going up and down the eastern United States or spraying out in varying degrees in a westerly direction. Janie could be in Florida or Canada or Arkansas or Michigan. Janie had last been seen a full twenty-four hours ago. By now, if an airplane had figured into the kidnappers' plans, Janie could be almost anywhere.

Her cell phone rang and Eliza glanced at the tiny identification window. Margo Gonzalez was calling.

"Hi, Margo," she answered, noticing that her free hand was trembling.

"Oh, Eliza, I'm so sorry about all this. I would have called sooner, but I was tied up with a suicidal patient all morning. Are you holding up?"

"Um-hmm."

"I was going to wait till tonight to come out for the meeting with Annabelle and B.J., but I can leave now and be out there in an hour," Margo offered. "I can bring something to help calm you."

"I might take you up on that at some point," said Eliza, "but right now I want to try not to take anything. I want my mind to be clear."

"All right, but just think about it, will you? There's no need for this to be more painful than it already is. Give yourself a break."

"Okay, I'll think about it," said Eliza.

"And make sure you eat and get some rest."

"I will," Eliza promised.

"All right. And I have something else I need to talk to you about, Eliza. Something that, under these circumstances, seems so ridiculous to even bring up. But I wouldn't want to do anything without running it by you first."

"What is it?"

"Well, I got a call from Linus this morning. He asked if I would be willing to fill in for you while you're out."

"As cohost of the show?"

"I know, I know," said Margo. "It's crazy. I'm still so green when it comes to TV in general and I have absolutely no experience in doing what you do. I told Linus all that, but he says he still wants me to take a stab at it. Who knows what is going through that crazy mind of his."

"Crazy like a fox," said Eliza. "There's always some method to his madness. We just don't know what it is yet."

"Well? What do you think?"

"Do you want to do it?" asked Eliza.

"Not particularly," answered Margo. "In fact, the thought of it really frightens me. But something in my gut also tells me that I should do it, as long as it's all right with you."

"Then do it," said Eliza. "I'm absolutely fine with it, Margo. And you don't have to come out here tonight with Annabelle and B.J. You have to get up too early in the morning."

"Are you kidding me?" asked Margo. "There's no way I won't be there!"

CHAPTER 35

When the FBI agents got to the Broadcast Center, Joe Connelly met them in the lobby and escorted them down to the security center. They sat in his windowless office while Joe shared the contents of his aberrant behavior computer file.

"Naturally, I've been going through this file since we got the news that Janie Blake was missing," said Joe. "There's one letter that keeps haunting me. I leave it to you to figure out if it's completely harmless or something else. You'll see a notation about it on the computer there, but I want to show you the actual letter itself."

Joe opened a blue folder containing the letter and the envelope it had come in, and slid it across the desk to the FBI agents. Without touching the letter, one of them read it aloud.

Dear Eliza,

I watch you on television and read all about your career at KEY News. I think not only are you a wonderful newswoman, but you are the world's best mom. You seem to love Janie so much. I wonder if she knows how lucky she is. Janie is such a beautiful child, wouldn't it be terrible if something happened to her? Can you imagine what your life would be like without her? Janie better appreciate how lucky she is to have you, because it only takes a moment for life to change forever.

"No signature," noted the FBI agent.

"Yeah," said the other. "And get a load of those little hearts and flowers and smiley-face stickers plastered all over it."

CHAPTER 36

It was embarrassing, but Uncle Lloyd said she had to do it. Nell had a standing appointment at the public pool on Tuesdays. She took an exercise class in the water with the old women who had tried to mother her since her own mother died. Any time she missed a class, they checked up on her and, while it usually made her feel good that they cared about her, she didn't like to give them a reason to stop by unannounced. Even though all the attention Janie Blake's abduction had gotten on the news this morning had upset her, Nell had been determined that she wouldn't miss the class today.

As they all waited for the instructor to appear, the women talked about the Janie Blake story.

"Dear Lord, what has this world come to?"

"That poor little girl."

"Her poor mother."

"It just goes to show that you can have all the money in the world and you still can't protect yourself from bad things happening."

"I think it happened *because* Eliza Blake must have a lot of money. She's a target for evil people who want to take advantage of her."

Nell took her long braid and tucked it under her mandatory bathing cap. She listened as the old ladies talked among themselves but she said nothing.

The instructor arrived and the women carefully descended into the pool. Nell moved along with the others, twisting and reaching, following the instructor's directions as best she could. To Nell, the forty-five-minute class seemed to drag on forever.

When the instructor signaled they

were done, Nell got out of the pool and wrapped herself in a towel.

"Everything all right with you, Nell?"

Nell looked around and saw Cora Wallace standing behind her.

"Yes, everything's all right, Cora."

"You're looking kind of pale, honey."

"I'm fine, Cora."

"Are you eating all right, Nell? How about I make you some of my chicken soup?"

"I'm eating fine, Cora. And thanks, but it's too hot for chicken soup."

"You sure? It's no problem. I can bring some by this afternoon."

"Don't do that," Nell snapped.

Cora was taken aback by the tone in Nell's voice. Her smile faded.

"I'm sorry," said Nell. "It's really nice of you to offer, Cora. But I really don't want any."

"All right, dear," said Cora, "but I worry about you, Nell. Since your mama passed, we all want to watch out for you. Are you upset about this Eliza Blake situation? I know how much store you set by her with your scrapbooks and everything."

"I really don't want to talk about it, Cora. And anyway, I've got to get home. I don't like leaving my uncle to take care of things by himself." Nell turned and made her way to the locker room to change.

CHAPTER 37

They would be taking a chance but it was worth a try.

She wondered why it hadn't occurred to her earlier and she cursed herself for not thinking of it when she had gone into the camp office to pick up Janie yesterday.

Mrs. Garcia waited until the next time Janie asked to go to the bathroom. The kidnapper, masked as Popeye again, untied their hands and took off their blindfolds.

Once they were in the bathroom, Mrs. Garcia carefully disconnected the skinny wire that ran from the microphone on the shirt collar to the transmitter on her waistband. She leaned close to Janie's face and stared directly at the child. "Listen to me, *chiquita*," she whispered. "This is very important."

Janie stood still, her eyes wide.

"I am going to boost you up and you climb through that window. Then you are going to run as fast as you can. Just run out to the road and follow it."

"I don't know where I'm going," Janie whispered back.

"Just follow the road, *mi hija*. Keep going until you meet up with people. Then you tell them who you are and that your mommy is looking for you. They will help you. Tell them you need to tell the police."

Janie jumped at the loud pounding on the door.

"What's going on in there?" came the voice from the other side.

"In a minute," Mrs. Garcia called out.

"Hurry up," demanded the voice. "I have better things to do with my time than stand here waiting for the both of you."

Mrs. Garcia looked at Janie. "Ready?" she whispered.

"I want you to come with me," Janie whispered back.

"I can't, Janie. I'm too big and there is too little time for me to try to squeeze through. Be a brave girl. You run and get help."

Pacing back and forth across the room, the kidnapper waited, not particularly concerned. The housekeeper may have been on the chubby side, but she would be no match for him physically if she should get the bright idea to come out and attack him. Actually, there wasn't anything for her to attack him with. He'd made sure there was nothing in that bathroom but a towel and some toilet paper.

"Popeye's waiting," he called. "How much longer?"

"Coming," said Mrs. Garcia.

But the door didn't open—and it dawned on him that he was hearing her actual voice, not a voice transmitted through the microphone.

He grabbed for the doorknob and pushed his way through.

Janie ran down the road, breathing hard, her sneakers pounding on the ground. Why wasn't there anyone around to help her?

She looked over her shoulder, afraid of what she might see. But the road behind her was empty. The man wasn't coming after her, she thought with relief. She kept running until she tripped. She fell forward, the beaded necklace she had made in camp coming from her neck and flying to the side of the road. Janie put out her hands to block her fall but she felt the burning pain as her knees scraped along the ground. She pulled herself up and kept running.

Tears were streaming down her cheeks as she felt the strong hands come from behind and grab hold of her shoulders.

CHAPTER 38

Special Agents Gebhardt and Laggie stood in the kitchen doorway and watched as Eliza sipped a cup of tea at the table with her in-laws. Eliza, Katharine, and Paul Blake were pale and quiet. Eliza's hand trembled as she brought the cup to her mouth.

"Let's take a walk outside," Agent Gebhardt said to her partner.

The FBI agents strolled the perimeter of the property, discussing the case.

"Of course, we have to consider the fact that she is in on this."

"Come on, Barbara, really. I know we should look at the nearest and dearest first, but are you going to tell me that Eliza Blake would actually have her own daughter kidnapped?"

"This world is full of sick stuff, Trevor. You know that. I was stationed at the Columbia, South Carolina, field office when Susan Smith got on TV, sobbing and pleading for the return of her two little boys. Then it turned out she'd strapped those babies into their car seats and let her vehicle sink into the lake. I was there the day they dragged their tiny bodies out of the water. I'll never forget it." Despite the hot July air, Agent Gebhardt rubbed her arms to warm herself.

"Still, Barbara, I don't buy it that Eliza Blake would have anything to do with having her own daughter abducted," said Agent Laggie, "or stage a kidnapping to cover up something even worse."

"I'm just saying," said Agent Gebhardt, "all we know for certain is that Mrs. Garcia took Janie from camp yesterday morning. We don't know if she was forced to do it. We have to look at the possibility that Garcia did it on her own or that Eliza told Garcia to take Janie and knows where they are."

"Then why offer a huge reward? Why would she want people trying to find Janie?"

Agent Gebhardt shrugged. "Offering a reward *looks* good."

"Well, what about the *'Call police'* notation in the camp log? That sounds to me like Mrs. Garcia was trying to get help. She wouldn't do that if she and Eliza had planned it."

"Maybe," said Agent Gebhardt. "Or, as I said before, maybe Garcia just wrote it to throw us off, to make it look like she was under duress. We have to look at every possibility, Trevor."

Agent Laggie shook his head, unconvinced that Eliza Blake should be considered a suspect.

They walked back into the house, not realizing that a sound technician hired by the *Mole* stood on the other side of the hedges aiming a very sensitive parabolic microphone to record every word they said.

CHAPTER 39

Popeye the sailor pulled the ropes so tight around Mrs. Garcia's wrists that she cried out in pain.

"Shut up, *mamacita.* You're lucky I don't beat the hell out of you. Try something like that again and I'll make you wish you'd never been born."

Blindfolded again, Mrs. Garcia could hear Janie hiccupping in between sobs. "My legs hurt," the little girl cried.

"Let me help her," Mrs. Garcia begged as she thought of the glimpse of Janie's legs she had caught before the kidnapper covered her eyes. "Let me wash those cuts out and put some bandages on them."

"Uh-uh. It'll teach the kid a lesson. If she tries to run away, she gets hurt."

"But the cuts could get infected," insisted Mrs. Garcia.

"Nice try," he said. "But now I don't trust you. And besides, I skinned my knees plenty of times when I was a kid and they healed up just fine without anybody fussing over them."

Once he was certain there was absolutely no way either Mrs. Garcia or Janie would be able to free themselves, he left the room, walked outside, and got some plywood from the shed. He covered the bedroom and bathroom windows, pounding in the nails. He then lit a cigarette. After he took a few drags to calm himself, he went back inside the house and made a phone call.

"We've got a problem," he said.

"What is it?"

"It's the damn housekeeper. She helped the kid crawl out of the bathroom window. The brat was halfway down the road before I caught up with her."

"Did anyone see her? Did anyone see you?"

"No," he said. "Fortunately, nobody did. But it was a warning. I've boarded up the windows, but we can't trust the woman. We have to get rid of her."

She wasn't really surprised by how easily his instructions came. "You aren't going to kill her, are you?" she asked with trepidation. This wasn't what they had agreed to when he'd come up with the plan.

"God, no. We don't want to face murder charges; kidnapping is bad enough. I know where to take her."

The blindfold was one precaution, but he decided it would be best to take another. He would drive Carmen Garcia around for a while so she could have absolutely no idea where she was when he buried her.

"Come on, ladies," he said. "We're going for a little ride. You first, princess."

Janie recoiled as the man took hold of her arm, pulling her up from the mattress and away from Mrs. Garcia.

"Where are you taking her?" Mrs. Garcia called, her eyes covered, her head tilted toward the sound of the man's voice.

"Don't you worry about where I'm taking her," said the man. "Just do as I tell you."

He steered Janie out of the room and to the front door.

"My legs hurt," Janie cried as her knees bent as she walked.

"Maybe you'll remember that the next time you get a smart idea about trying to run away. Now quit complaining and climb inside."

Janie felt herself lifted and pushed into the back of the van. She waited, listening, as the man walked away. A few minutes later, Mrs. Garcia was in the van with her and the back doors were closed tight.

The van drove for what seemed like a long time before it came to a stop and the doors were opened again.

"You stay right where you are, princess," ordered the man. "And you, *mamacita*, slide yourself over here."

Mrs. Garcia did not move.

"You heard me," the man growled. "Get moving or I'll take it out on the little one here."

"Please, *señor,*" Mrs. Garcia pleaded. "Let me stay with Janie."

"Uh-uh," answered the man. "You two are a dangerous combination. You've got to be split up."

He reached in and pulled at Mrs. Garcia's arms. She kicked outward, hitting him in the chest. He fell backward, stunned for a moment. When he got back on his feet, he was breathing heavily.

"That's it. Get the hell out of that van or I swear to God, I'm going to break the kid's legs and really give her something to cry about."

Feeling she had no choice, Mrs. Garcia maneuvered herself toward the door. "Don't worry, *niña,*" she said softly. "Everything will be all right. Your mommy is coming, Janie. I know she is. Just keep thinking about that. You'll be with your mommy soon."

The child started to sob. "Please, Mrs. Garcia. Don't leave me. Please."

Mrs. Garcia was pulled the rest of the way out of the van. As the doors slammed shut, she could still hear Janie crying from inside.

Popeye untied Mrs. Garcia's wrists. "You're going to need your hands because there won't be anyone to do a thing for you," he said from behind the mask. "You'll be all alone. And don't waste your time trying to figure out how to escape because there *is* no way."

Mrs. Garcia heard the sound of a hinge creaking.

"Go ahead," said the kidnapper, urging her forward and guiding her hands to the wooden struts that lined the walls. "Hold on to the wall and go down a little bit at a time. Once you get to the bottom of the steps, feel around and you'll find some bottled water, some packages of crackers, a box of cereal, and a couple of apples. I'd eat those first, before some insect or little animal starts worming its way into them. And help yourself to anything else you find, though God knows how long it's been down there."

"Please, *señor.* Please," Mrs. Garcia begged. "Don't do this."

"You did it to yourself, lady. You were too smart for your own good. Get going, and be glad this is your punishment." He added, "For now, at least."

With her heart hammering against her chest wall, Mrs. Garcia inched her way down the wooden steps. She counted ten of them. When she reached the bottom, she estimated she was about six feet underground.

The kidnapper's voice came from above. "When I close you up, you can take off the blindfold, but not before."

Mrs. Garcia's head tilted upward as she listened to squeaking noises as hinges moved, then the sound of the lid coming down, and, finally, loud clicks as an iron bolt slid into place and a padlock was fastened.

CHAPTER 40

Members of the press were staked out in front of the Blake house throughout the morning. At lunchtime, a catering truck arrived, providing sandwiches, cookies, soda, and coffee. B.J. D'Elia lined up with the other hungry members of the press. "Who's paying for all this?" asked B.J., fairly certain that it wasn't being charged to the KEY News budget. The news division's budget had gotten tighter and tighter over the years he'd worked there.

"I heard Eliza ordered it," said the FOX reporter who stood in the line in front of B.J.

"That figures," said B.J.

When he got to the counter, he took a chicken salad sandwich, some chips, and a Coke. B.J. found a place to sit in the shade under a tall tree, keeping his eyes on the front door of the house. As he crumpled the plastic wrap that had protected the sandwich in his hand, he saw Annabelle come out of the house. Grudgingly, he started to get up and hoisted the camera to his shoulder, anticipating that Annabelle could be making another statement. The camera crews from the other media outlets did the same thing as a throng of reporters and producers, eager for any new scrap of information, surged forward.

Annabelle put up her hands to stop them. "Hold it, everybody," she called out. "I don't have anything for you. Just relax."

"Come on, Annabelle," yelled the CBS reporter. "What's going on in there? Any news?"

"Honestly, the only thing I have to tell you guys," said Annabelle, "is that the FBI is going to hold a press conference at four o'clock."

"Where?" yelled an NBC producer.

"Right out here in the driveway," said Annabelle.

"What do you expect them to say?" The CBS reporter wasn't giving up.

Annabelle tried not to show her exasperation. "I wouldn't presume to speak for the FBI," she said. "That's it, guys. That's all I've got."

Almost instantaneously, the scores of reporters and producers pulled out their cell phones and called their respective broadcast producers and assignment editors, apprising them of the information about the FBI press conference. Annabelle continued to walk down the driveway toward B.J.

"How's it going in there?" he asked when they both had taken a seat beneath the tree.

Annabelle sighed deeply. "It's horrible, Beej. Just horrible. I feel so sorry for her. And there she is, worrying about me in the middle of it all. She insisted that I go out and work so Linus won't be ticked off."

"How is she holding up?" B.J. asked.

Annabelle shook her head. "I guess

as well as can be expected. She's putting on a brave face, but she hasn't slept, she isn't eating, and she's wound tight. I just hope she doesn't snap."

"Well, I don't like just hanging around and doing nothing," said B.J. with anger and frustration in his voice. "Anybody could be sitting here, staking out the house, waiting for the feds to come out and feed us a few crumbs. We should be out doing something, Annabelle."

"I feel the same way, Beej," said Annabelle. "That's why I called Linus and asked him to send out another camera guy. Once he gets here, you and I are taking a little trip to Camp Musquapsink."

"But I thought we already had a crew there this morning," said B.J.

"We did," said Annabelle. "They got their shots of the camp and the police hubbub outside. But, after they saw the FBI agents leave, they left, too."

"So what are we going to get that they didn't get?"

Annabelle shrugged. "I don't know," she said. "But the camp is the last place Janie was seen. It's as good a place as any to start figuring out what happened to her."

Yellow police tape still draped parts of the entrance and reception areas, but the KEY News crew car was able to drive directly into the parking lot. Annabelle got out first and went directly into the office. She identified herself and asked to see the camp's director.

"Holly is busy right now," said the girl at the desk. "She's taking phone calls from parents."

"That's all right," said Annabelle. "I can wait awhile."

"I don't really know how long she'll be," said the girl. "Can I help you?"

Annabelle thought quickly. For all she knew, once Holly Taylor came on the scene, she might shoo them off the property. It wouldn't hurt to try to pump the girl.

"Obviously, I'm here about Janie Blake's abduction," said Annabelle.

The girl nodded.

"You weren't by any chance staffing

the desk when her caregiver came and took Janie from camp yesterday, were you?"

"No," said the girl, shaking her head. "That was Lisa."

"Can I talk to Lisa, then?" asked Annabelle.

"She's not here," said the girl. "Actually, Holly fired her today."

"I see," said Annabelle. "I guess I probably would have fired her, too. Lisa should have checked that caregiver's signature when she took Janie out of camp."

"I guess so," said the girl, "but I can understand how it happened. Sometimes we have too much to take care of and we can't pay attention to two things at the same time."

"Why? Was Lisa taking care of something else?" asked Annabelle.

"I heard she was collating song sheets," said the girl. "She was only trying to get her work done, just like all the counselors do. I feel really sorry for Lisa."

"Maybe she'd like to talk about what happened, give her side of the story," suggested Annabelle. "Do you think you could give me her phone number and I could call her?"

The girl shook her head. "No, I shouldn't give out Lisa's personal information, but I could call her and tell her you'd like to talk to her. That way she can get in touch with you if she wants."

"That sounds fair," said Annabelle as she took a business card from her wallet and put it on the desk. "My cell number there is the best way to reach me."

Annabelle glanced at her watch. "I have a deadline," she said. "If Ms. Taylor isn't going to be able to talk with me soon, I'll have to get going."

"I don't know what to tell you," said the girl. "But Holly went out and spoke to everybody when all those media people were here this morning. I don't know if she'll want to speak with you even when she does finish with her phone calls."

Annabelle knew that the KEY News crew that had been at the camp in the morning had gotten video of Holly Taylor making her statement. Annabelle had been hoping she might be able to snag an exclusive one-on-one interview. In the process, she had also hoped she might be able to glean some new information. The likelihood of that seemed to be diminishing. Annabelle thanked the girl and turned to leave just as a young man walked in the door.

"I've got today's pictures to load, Kim," he said, holding up a digital camera.

"What are those?" asked Annabelle.

"Pictures of stuff that happened at camp today. I have a Web site," the young man said with pride. "I set it up this year. When they get home every day, the kids can log on and look at themselves. The parents like it, too. They can see what their kids have been doing."

"Neat idea," said Annabelle. "What's your Web site's address?"

When Annabelle got outside, B.J. was leaning against the trunk of the car, his camera gear on the ground.

"Got some b-roll," he said.

"You didn't wait for permission?"

B.J. shrugged. "What can I tell you? I'm a bad boy," he said, smiling. "On the other hand, what's the big deal? Lots of pictures were taken here today. I just got a few more."

Annabelle opened the back door of the sedan and took out the carrying case containing her laptop. She opened it and turned it on.

"Good. They're wireless here," she said.

"What are you doing?" asked B.J.

"I want to check something out," she said, tapping the keys until a picture of the Camp Musquapsink sign over the front gates filled the computer screen. On the side of the screen was a list of dates, the days the camp had been open so far. Annabelle clicked on Monday, July 21.

A few more clicks, and the smiling, painted face of Janie Blake appeared.

CHAPTER 41

She glanced at the digital clock on the dashboard, knowing that Skip was waiting for her. But Stephanie really wasn't in any rush to get home. She pulled into a rest stop on the highway and bought a tuna sandwich and a cup of coffee. She decided to sit at a table and eat instead of gobbling it down in the car.

For the rest of the ride, Stephanie listened to the radio reports about Janie Blake's abduction. When she pulled up to the house, she got out of the car, kicking at the dried leaves and pine needles that covered the ground. Skip had never gotten around to raking them. She looked at the house. It needed a paint job. Skip had never gotten around to doing that, either. But Stephanie didn't feel she could say anything. It was his house, not hers.

She walked inside and found Skip watching television.

"You look nice and relaxed," she said as she bent over and kissed him. "How's everything?"

"Fine. I'm just taking a break," said Skip. "How did it go?"

"They didn't believe me."

Skip sat up. "It's always like this in the beginning," he said.

Stephanie went into the kitchen and poured herself a glass of water. "I'm tired of them brushing me off and thinking I'm crazy," she said when she walked back to him. "It's so discouraging. Why won't they listen to me?"

"Look, they'll come around," said Skip. "You've had other cases, and the cops are always skeptical at first. Then they see that you have special gifts. They'll be sure to see it this time, too."

CHAPTER 42

An announcement went out to all law enforcement personnel with an updated description of Janie Blake as given by the camp worker who had seen her last.

As Detective Mark Kennedy read it, the color rose in his cheeks. *Green paint had been on the child's face.*

In recent years, psychic criminology had been gaining some grudging acceptance in law enforcement circles. Detective Kennedy made it a point of keeping up with criminal justice publications, reading the articles about psychics but never being quite convinced of their legitimacy. He knew that there were some in his line of work who believed that a talented psychic could help pinpoint a geographical area where a missing person might be, narrow the number of leads to concentrate on, emphasize information that had been overlooked or come up with entirely fresh information. Kennedy had never bought it.

He didn't want to be a close-minded guy; he wanted to be open to possibilities, but, until now, his only experience with "remote viewing," as they called it, was through television shows and the articles he'd read. Those hadn't persuaded him to believe in anything to do with the paranormal. But the woman who had come to the station this morning was real, and the dream she described, in which Janie Blake had paint on her face, was entirely fresh information that was proving to be true. Information he had dismissed.

Kennedy pulled out the file in which he had stuck the paperwork on Stephanie Quick. It was worth a shot. Maybe the other guys would laugh at him for suggesting that a psychic was credible, but it would be far worse if it turned out that she could have helped them find the Blake child but was ignored.

He picked up the phone and began calling the police departments listed on Stephanie Quick's résumé. It turned out that one of her dreams had provided information that had helped a search party locate a missing woman in the Poconos. And, in another case, she had sat inside the car owned by a man who had never come home from work one night, and she had been able to describe how he had been robbed and murdered as he came out of his office. Later, she said a dream had revealed that he had been buried near a bridge. The man's body was eventually found on the western bank of the Delaware River, not far from where a train trestle crossed overhead.

Kennedy went to Chief Steil and told him about Stephanie Quick and what his research had uncovered.

"You know what? I don't want to touch this stuff with a ten-foot pole," said the chief. "Let's just pass this on to the FBI."

CHAPTER 43

He had been putting off going down to the gas station for as long as he could, but now he couldn't wait any longer to go and pick up his final paycheck. Hugh wished he could just tell that clown what he could do with his pathetic hourly wage, but he needed the money.

As he drove around the reservoir, Hugh braced himself for the unpleasantness that would surely be coming. It wasn't the first time, and it wouldn't be the last, that he'd been let go as soon as the boss found out about his past. How was a guy supposed to straighten up and fly right when nobody wanted to hire him, when everyone was repulsed by him and wanted absolutely nothing to do with him? The pressure of being ostracized and whispered about made it even harder to stay on the straight and narrow.

Pulling into the parking lot, Hugh could see the owner frowning through the window of the service station. Hugh parked next to the building, but before he could get out, the owner was standing beside the car.

"Here," he said, thrusting an envelope through the open window.

"Thanks," said Hugh as he took it.

Without another word, the owner turned his back and walked away. Hugh started to call after him, but thought better of it. He was tempted to tell the guy off. But the last thing he needed was a scene. He didn't want to call attention to himself. And God forbid, he didn't want the cops to be called.

Everybody made mistakes, some worse than others, thought Hugh. He knew that society viewed his mistakes as among the most heinous. Some people felt sorry for him, most people hated him, but none of them wanted to have anything to do with him.

The only one he could count on was Isabelle. She had always been there for him and he thought she always would. He had loved her since she was a little girl, his baby sister who always stood up for her older brother when it should have been the other way around. Even then, Isabelle had sensed that he was different, and vulnerable. And she had been loyal to him all these years, through all the whispers and accusations and the court hearings and the jail time. Hugh knew that Isabelle had suffered the embarrassment and pain of being shunned, just because she had a brother who was a disgrace.

That's why he was doing his very best to please her. Isabelle deserved his devotion and his utmost effort. But it was hard to be good, so hard. There were so many, many temptations.

Hugh put the car into gear and looked in the rearview mirror. A silver SUV pulled up to the pump behind his car. Hugh could see the blond head of a little girl in the passenger seat.

His eyes stayed trained on the mirror as he felt his pulse quicken. He remained in the car, watching the child, until the owner of the service station came out again and chased Hugh away.

CHAPTER 44

A cluster of microphones was set up on the driveway. Members of the media kept their eyes on the house, waiting for the FBI spokesperson to walk out and face the press.

The media people snapped to attention and surged forward when the front door opened. Three people strode out. A tall blond woman and a sturdily built man, both dressed in civilian clothes, along with a distinguished-looking white-haired man in a police uniform took their positions behind the bank of microphones. The uniformed man spoke first.

"Good afternoon. I am Michael Steil,

chief of the Ho-Ho-Kus police. Along with me are Barbara Gebhardt and Trevor Laggie, both special agents with the Federal Bureau of Investigation. I will give an opening statement and then we will take a few questions."

The chief cleared his throat before continuing. "Last night at about six P.M., the Ho-Ho-Kus police received a phone call from Eliza Blake expressing her concern that she had not seen her daughter, Janie, age seven, along with her housekeeper, Carmen Garcia, age fifty-two, at the usual time Janie would have come home from day camp and Mrs. Garcia would have normally been there to meet the child."

A reporter interrupted, yelling out, "Do you have any leads on who kidnapped Janie?"

Chief Steil held out his hands. "Please, let me continue," he said. "There will be time for questions. Due to the public prominence of Ms. Blake, the Federal Bureau of Investigation was contacted immediately."

"Are there any ransom demands yet?" another reporter called.

Chief Steil clenched his jaw, trying to remain calm in spite of the aggressiveness of the press corps.

"I know you all have your jobs to do, and I have mine," he said. "But I'm asking you again, politely, to let me finish my statement before asking your questions." He paused, then began again. "At this time we are treating this as a potential kidnapping and we are asking for the public's help. A neighbor saw an unexplained black van with a dented back door in the Blakes' driveway yesterday morning. We are trying to find that van and asking that anyone in the area who has seen a vehicle matching that description to contact the hotline number that has been set up. Mrs. Blake is offering a two-hundred-and-fifty-thousand-dollar reward for any information leading to the recovery of her child and Carmen Garcia."

While the video cameras recorded, and the photographers snapped away, reporters scribbled in their notebooks as Chief Steil continued. "Also, we have something to add to the description of how Janie Blake looked the last time she was seen. In addition to wearing a white

Camp Musquapsink T-shirt, navy shorts, white socks, and sneakers, Janie had had her face painted that morning at camp. There were green stripes painted on her cheeks and she was wearing a headdress made of construction paper with a yellow feather attached to it when she left the camp grounds. Of course, the paint could have been wiped off right away, and the headpiece discarded, but if anyone has seen a child matching any part of that description, please call the hotline."

Steil held up the picture of Janie and Mrs. Garcia that Eliza had provided. "At the end of the conference, there will be copies of this picture for all of you. Now, questions?"

A dozen hands went up. Steil pointed to the reporter near the front of the pack. "Has there been a ransom demand?" the reporter asked again.

"No, not at this time." He pointed to another reporter.

"What about the housekeeper? What can you tell us about this Mrs. Garcia?"

"Carmen Garcia has worked for the family for two years. Mrs. Blake has the utmost trust in her."

"So you don't think she had anything to do with Janie's abduction."

"Clearly, she had something to do with it since she took the child from camp. But, we have reason to believe that she did so under duress."

"What kind of reason?"

Steil looked at the FBI agents. They had discussed it before they'd come out to meet the press and had decided that they were not going to reveal the details of the notation in the camp sign-out log. If it was made public that Carmen Garcia had tried to alert the camp by writing *"Call police,"* the abductor or abductors might hear that, too, and punish her for it.

Barbara Gebhardt stepped forward. "Certain details of the investigation will not be made public. At this time, we are not ruling anything or anyone out."

"Does that mean you are looking at Mrs. Garcia as a possible suspect?" yelled the ABC reporter.

"We look at everyone in Janie's life as a possible suspect," said Agent Gebhardt.

A succession of questions followed,

none of them eliciting any new information from the investigators.

"Last question," declared Steil, pointing to the CNN reporter at the side of the group.

"Does Eliza have anyone who would want to get at her through her child? Does she have any enemies?"

Steil turned to the FBI agents. "You want to answer that one?" he asked.

Barbara Gebhardt took center stage again. "Eliza Blake is a very well-known figure and has a great deal of popularity with the public. But, as with all public figures, there are some people who aren't fans. We're looking at possibilities in that regard as well."

Chief Steil stepped back to the microphone. "Let me make one thing clear. Time is of the essence here. Every hour that passes makes it harder to find a missing person. Janie Blake and Carmen Garcia could be almost anywhere by now. So we are appealing to the entire nation for assistance in finding them." He nodded to the group assembled before him. "You can all help by getting the word out."

CHAPTER 45

The minute she got home from the bakery, Rhonda checked on Janie. The child's lack of appetite was alarming.

Standing at the kitchen sink, Rhonda was truly concerned that Janie hadn't touched the morning cereal she had left her and had completely ignored the peanut butter and jelly sandwich Rhonda had left wrapped and ready for lunch before she'd gone to work. Rhonda wanted to keep Janie healthy and that meant she had to get some food inside the child.

Spaghetti, thought Rhonda. Every kid loved spaghetti. She remembered how much Allison had loved pasta. She'd loved it from the first time she tasted it, chopped fine in the plastic bowl resting on her high-chair tray.

That's what she would do. She'd pre- pare a homemade marinara sauce and serve Janie a big bowl of pasta for din- ner.

While her husband took a shower and got dressed for work on the night shift, Rhonda poured some olive oil into a cast- iron skillet. She peeled and chopped a couple of cloves of garlic and a white onion and put them in the pan. While the sautéing progressed, Rhonda selected the ripest of the plum tomatoes she had lined up on the windowsill to catch the rays of the summer sun. As she sliced them, her hand slipped and the knife cut her finger. Blood seeped out of the slit in Rhonda's skin.

Watching the vivid redness spread, Rhonda tensed. She reached for the faucet, turning on the water and sticking her hand beneath it. As the blood pooled onto the white ceramic sink, Rhonda's breath came faster.

The sound of the car's loud horn and the screeching of tires filled Rhonda's head. She closed her eyes, succeeding in blocking out the sight of the blood in the sink but unable to blot out the vision in her mind of Allison lying on the blood-drenched pavement, the mangled bicycle tossed on its side, the sneaker thrown loose and lying at the curb.

Rhonda knew it all had been her fault.

She grasped the edge of the sink, taking deep breaths, trying to calm down. She found herself picking up the knife again and wondering what it would feel like to thrust it into the side of her neck.

She struggled to regain focus. Big breath in, big breath out, *that's what Dr. Karas told her to do when she saw it all over again in her head. The bright lights inside the ambulance, the eerie ride to the hospital, the confusion in the emergency room, the grim-faced nurses and physicians.*

Rhonda knew she could call Dr. Karas right now. He could help her through this, as he had done so many times before. He had never, ever made her feel like she was bothering him. But she didn't want to call him. She wanted to see if she could get through it by herself this time because things were different now.

She had once thought that no child could ever take Allison's place, but she had been wrong. Now, she had Janie. Now, she had a reason to live.

CHAPTER 46

Ratings shot through the roof as more than double the number of viewers tuned in to watch the first KEY News evening broadcast since Janie Blake's and Carmen Garcia's disappearance.

"Good evening. I'm Anthony Reynes and this is the *KEY Evening Headlines.*

"Sadly, over the years, this broadcast has reported on many child abductions and missing-persons cases, but none has hit closer to home here at KEY News than the disappearance of seven-year-old Janie Blake, daughter of our own Eliza Blake, and her housekeeper, Carmen Garcia. Janie was taken from camp yesterday morning by her fifty-two-year-old caretaker, and neither of them has been seen or heard from since. As KEY News correspondent Harry Granger reports, police and the FBI are looking for leads and battling the clock."

The entire screen filled with the picture of Janie Blake smiling, green paint brushed across her cheeks, the picture Annabelle Murphy had found on the Web site of daily Camp Musquapsink photographs. Harry Granger's voice narrated over the shot.

"Janie Blake left her house in Ho-Ho-Kus, New Jersey, yesterday morning, looking forward to a day of activities at Camp Musquapsink, a day camp over the state line in Sloatsburg, New York. This picture shows Janie less than an hour before she was picked up at camp by her babysitter a little before lunchtime."

Now the picture provided to the press corps at large appeared on the screen: Janie being wrapped in a towel by the Guatemalan woman. Granger's voice continued the narration.

"When Janie did not return home from camp at the usual time, in the late af-

ternoon, her mother, Eliza Blake, started making phone calls to friends and neighbors, asking if anyone had seen her daughter or her caretaker, Carmen Garcia. By the time police were alerted, over seven hours had elapsed from the time Janie was taken from the camp grounds. Today police admit that, in cases like these, time is not their friend."

A white-haired man wearing a police uniform spoke. The text at the bottom of the screen identified him as Michael Steil, chief of the Ho-Ho-Kus, New Jersey, police.

"Every hour that passes makes it harder to find a missing person. Janie Blake and Carmen Garcia could be almost anywhere by now. So, we are appealing to the entire nation for assistance in finding them."

Now viewers saw Harry Granger standing on the street in front of Eliza Blake's stately brick colonial as he spoke.

"Carmen Garcia has worked for the Blake family for two years and Eliza Blake is said to thoroughly trust Garcia and believe she would never do anything to hurt her daughter. Special Agent Bar-

bara Gebhardt says the FBI is trying to figure out Garcia's role in this.

"Clearly she had something to do with it since she took the child from camp. But, we have reason to believe that she did so under duress."

Shots of the yellow police tape cordoning off the entrance to Camp Musquapsink appeared.

"Authorities would not say why they think Garcia was acting against her will when she took Janie Blake from camp. Nor would they say she wasn't a suspect."

Barbara Gebhardt appeared on the screen again. "At this time, we are not ruling anything or anyone out." A graphic with the picture of Janie and Mrs. Garcia and a telephone number flashed on the screen. "There has been no ransom demand but police are treating this as a potential kidnapping. A neighbor saw a black van with a dented rear door in the Blake driveway earlier in the morning. Police are trying to find that van and asking anyone who sees a vehicle matching that description to call the hotline number."

Agent Gebhardt had the last sound bite. *"We look at everyone in Janie's life as a possible suspect."*

Harry Granger wrapped up the piece. *"In Janie's life and out . . . law enforcement is scrutinizing family, friends, acquaintances, peripheral contacts, sex offenders registered in the community, and, most dauntingly, complete strangers as they try to determine what has happened to Janie Blake and Carmen Garcia.*

"Harry Granger, KEY News, Ho-Ho-Kus, New Jersey."

CHAPTER 47

Agent Gebhardt slammed her fist on the kitchen table.

"Damn it, we're the FBI! How did KEY News get that picture of Janie Blake— and why didn't *we* have it first?"

"We're already checking on the Web site listed on the courtesy graphic they used on the picture," said Agent Laggie, not really answering Gebhardt's questions. "We'll go over it with a fine-tooth comb. Every picture on it will be studied and analyzed."

"We've gotta stop playing catch-up,"

muttered Gebhardt angrily. "This is pathetic. We damn well need to start doing better than this or Janie Blake doesn't stand a chance."

CHAPTER 48

As the interminably long day drew to a close, Annabelle, B.J., and Margo sat with Eliza around the kitchen table, drinking coffee, taking notes, and offering support. Annabelle chewed on the end of her pen, her intensity reflected in her furrowed brow and keen blue eyes that narrowed in concentration. B.J. rubbed his forehead with his thumb and index finger, as Eliza had seen him do many times before when he was nervous. Margo doodled on the yellow legal pad in front of her.

"Nice going, finding the picture of

Janie on that Web site," said Eliza. "But, I think you ticked off the FBI."

"Tough," said B.J. "It will keep them on their toes, knowing that they are competitive with us."

"Right, Beej." Annabelle chuckled sarcastically. "The FBI really feels competitive with us."

"Well, they should," said B.J. "They shouldn't be complacent for a minute, because we're going to be all over this."

"I don't get the feeling they're letting things slide, B.J.," said Eliza. "Basically, I'm pretty impressed with how professional and on top of things they are."

B.J. shrugged. "Then I guess our finding that picture first should show them there's always room for improvement."

Annabelle looked up from her notes. "Here's what I've been thinking about, Eliza," she said, "and tell me if you agree. With Mack coming home, he can act as liaison with the press, and that will free B.J. and me to keep current on developments in the case, following up on any leads and investigating whatever we can. That's what we should really be focusing our energies on. Margo will be able to help us as things come up."

Eliza nodded. "That makes sense," she said. "Any specifics on what direction you're taking?"

"Nothing worth bringing up at this point," said Annabelle. "I want to get my thoughts and notes organized." Annabelle refrained from announcing that when she went home she was going to spend the rest of the night on the Internet, finding out how many pedophiles lived in the area.

"I wish I could go with you out into the field, but I can't leave the house," said Eliza. "I have to be here when the kidnappers call with a ransom demand."

"Of course," acknowledged Annabelle. "But we'll be keeping you posted on everything we find out."

Eliza was bolstered by the strength and conviction she felt coming from her friends. Having them with her made Eliza feel more secure, more hopeful. They emanated positive energy and capable strength. Though Eliza knew their hearts were aching for her, she appreciated that they weren't clucking around her, making her feel like a victim. Feeling sorry for herself wouldn't do the situation any good. Janie and Mrs. Garcia needed people who were committed to finding them, not people who were cowering in fear and doubt about the possibility of a successful recovery.

Annabelle and B.J. got up and started toward the front door. Margo lingered behind and pressed a piece of light blue paper into Eliza's hand.

"It's a prescription," she said softly. "It will help you relax and sleep. Get it filled and take it if you need it."

As Eliza watched the three of them leave, she was filled with gratitude for having friends of this quality rallying around her. Since they had come together just a few months before to investigate the murder of her predecessor on *KEY to America,* Eliza had marveled at the unique skills each of them had brought to the task.

Annabelle was one of the strongest producers at KEY News, able to assemble coverage of anything, ranging from space shuttle launches to movie premieres. Her research and organizational skills were extraordinary and her gut instincts were inevitably right on target. Not much got past Annabelle. Yet her capabilities extended well beyond her professional life, as she juggled raising young children and maintaining a loving relationship with her husband. Eliza deeply admired her.

B.J. was fearless, unafraid to take a chance if that's what was needed to get the best shot or follow the most promising lead. He had physical strength, was quick to size up situations, and added a valuable male perspective to their team. His cynicism disguised a soft and vulnerable heart. B.J. identified with the underdog, was ferociously loyal, and Eliza knew she could always count on him to watch her back.

Margo's years of training and clinical experience in understanding how the mind worked were powerful credentials. She understood human motivations and had laserlike insights. But beneath her professional exterior, Margo was warm, compassionate, and a good friend, always ready to help.

As they put their heads together again, Eliza prayed they could have the same success. This time, as far as she was concerned, there was far more at stake.

After her friends were gone, Agent Laggie approached Eliza. "I couldn't help but hear parts of your conversation with those three," said Laggie.

"And?" Eliza asked.

"I understand that your friends want to help, but we don't want them getting in the way," said Laggie.

"They won't be in the way," said Eliza. "They are professional journalists. They know what they're doing."

"Just as long as they don't jeopardize our investigation," said Laggie.

"I really don't see them as a hindrance, Agent Laggie. I think they'll be a tremendous help," said Eliza. "You needn't feel threatened by them."

The agent's jaw tensed. "The only way they threaten us is by sticking their noses into things that should be left to law enforcement," he said. "If your friends are too ambitious and get involved in areas that should be left to us, it could endanger your daughter. Just keep that in mind."

CHAPTER 49

The curtains were drawn and the room was dark except for the sliver of light that streamed in from the hallway through the crack left open at the door to the bedroom. Eliza lay on her side, legs curled up toward her chest. A cup of tea and some toast lay untouched on the table next to the bed.

She stared into the darkness. She was supposed to be getting some rest, but she couldn't relax, couldn't let go, couldn't erase the new picture of Janie from her mind. The eager, trusting smile on her little girl's face just before she disappeared made Eliza ache with longing.

She wanted Janie back, right here, right now. She yearned to reach out as she had so many times before when Janie had crawled into bed with her, when she'd come in to wake Eliza too early in the morning or wanted to be comforted after a bad dream woke her in the middle of the night.

Eliza extended her arm out across the coverlet, trying to get herself to imagine that Janie was lying there beside her. But her mind wouldn't allow her even the most fleeting mercy. Janie was gone and, though she knew she shouldn't allow her thoughts to wander in such a defeated direction, Eliza realized there was a chance that Janie wasn't coming back.

Tears dripped down Eliza's cheeks onto the linen pillowcase. She lay there, crying, until she heard the footsteps coming up the stairs.

Oh dear God, let it be good news, or, at least, don't let it be bad news. Please, no bad news.

Eliza sat up and turned toward the door as it opened.

"It's me, sweetheart."

Mack stood in the doorway, his broad

shoulders outlined against the light. She reached out to him as he came right to her and took her in his arms.

"Oh, Mack, thank God you're here."

Eliza buried her face in his chest and held on tightly. Mack stroked her hair and spoke to her softly.

"It's going to be all right, Eliza. We'll find Janie. We'll get her back."

Eliza pulled away and looked into his face. It was lit on one side by the light from the hallway, unreadable on the other. "Will we, Mack?" she asked. "Will we get her back?"

Both of them knew that Mack couldn't be sure about what was going to happen to Janie, but he answered with the words Eliza needed to hear.

"Of course we'll get her back. You have to believe that, sweetheart. Janie is coming home."

They held each other in the semidarkness, Eliza telling Mack all that had been happening, her impressions of the FBI and the police, her anguish at the picture of Janie snapped just before she was taken from camp.

"I don't know what I'll do, Mack, if . . ."

"Hey," he said, crooking his finger under her chin and lifting it. "Let's not think about the future. Let's just concentrate on the present. Right here, right now."

Eliza nodded. "Okay," she said. "What I have to do now is go out there and talk to them. They're camped out, waiting to hear from me. There isn't a single thing that can help find Janie more than publicity. Assistance from the public could be the key to getting her back."

Mack listened, knowing that Eliza was right. "All right," he said. "You can do it in the morning."

"No," said Eliza. "I've got to do it tonight so I'll run on the ten and eleven o'clock local news programs, and we'll get more exposure on all the network shows in the morning. I have to do it now, for Janie's sake."

Eliza was blinded by the powerful spotlights that beamed at her as she came out of the front door of her home. She held her hand up in front of her face to block the glare as she walked down the path to the driveway. Flashbulbs popped and cameras whirred while the crush of reporters and videographers jockeyed for position near the bank of microphones.

The harsh white light drained the color from Eliza's already pale face and highlighted her red-rimmed eyes. At the last moment, she had run a comb through her tousled hair and had applied some lip gloss. The normally immaculately groomed and fashionably dressed anchorwoman stood before the microphones wearing a pink T-shirt and white jeans, looking every bit the vulnerable and anguished mother. Mack stood guard beside her.

"First of all, I want to thank every one of you for all you are doing to help us find Janie and Mrs. Garcia," Eliza said softly. "Your efforts in getting the word out can make the difference because somebody has seen something or will see something that will lead us to the people who have them. What you report will make the public aware of what they should be looking for."

A reporter yelled, "Can you speak up a little, Eliza?"

Eliza nodded and cleared her throat before continuing. "Most important, I want to say this. Janie, I love you, sweetheart, and we are coming to get you. I promise, baby. We're coming."

Eliza felt Mack reassuringly squeeze her arm.

"To whoever has Janie and Mrs. Garcia, I beg you. Please let them go." Eliza paused, feeling herself ready to break down. She took several deep breaths to steady herself. "And to all of you who are watching this: If you have seen anything at all, if you know anything at all that you think could help us find my daughter and Carmen Garcia, please, come forward. Call your local police or your local FBI office or call the Find Janie hotline number. Janie is just a little girl and I know she must be very confused and frightened right now. She needs to be home with the people who love her."

Eliza turned and walked back to the house, unable to answer the barrage of reporters' questions that followed her.

CHAPTER 50

Mike was dozing on the couch in the living room when Annabelle let herself into their Greenwich Village apartment. She put down her bag and keys and went to her husband, finding a place to perch on the edge of the sofa. She leaned over and kissed him as he slept.

He opened his eyes.

Annabelle smiled down at him. "Hey, Sleeping Beauty," she said.

Mike ran his hands through his cropped hair as he sat up. "Any news?" he asked.

Annabelle shook her head. "No word,

no ransom demand. Just a hellish waiting game."

"How's Eliza?" Mike asked.

"Hanging on," said Annabelle. "*How* I don't know. If I were in her shoes, I'd be locked up in a padded room already. Thank God our kids are safe, Mike."

"Who'd want to take them?" Mike asked, breaking the tension.

Annabelle smiled. "How are they?"

"Sleeping now, like little angels."

Annabelle got up from the sofa and went to the twins' bedroom. *We really have to get a bigger place soon,* she thought. *Soon, they'll be too old to be sharing a room, a girl and a boy wanting separate spaces.* Annabelle had no idea how they were going to afford a three-bedroom apartment in Manhattan—and Brooklyn was getting more expensive by the day.

Kissing Tara and Thomas on the forehead as they slept, Annabelle was struck by the way her heart filled with the simple gesture. The feel of their soft skin, the sound of their rhythmic breathing, the smell of their freshly shampooed hair gave her such a deep sense of peace and well-being. She tried to imagine how Eliza was feeling, knowing that her only child wasn't sleeping in her own bed and wasn't with the people who loved her.

What was happening to Janie right now? What could they be doing to her?

"I can't watch anymore," said Mike as he switched off the eleven o'clock news. The show had been almost entirely about Janie Blake's disappearance. Eliza had been featured prominently, pleading for the return of her daughter and Carmen Garcia. "And you should come to bed, Annabelle, and get a good night's sleep."

"In a bit," she said. "I just want to do a little research online."

"Don't be too long, honey. You have to get up early, too." He kissed her on the mouth. "I love you," he said.

As she searched the Internet, going to various Web sites that gave names and addresses for convicted sex offenders, Annabelle was overwhelmed by the number of names listed as living within a fifty-mile radius of Camp Musquapsink, a circle that included parts of New York state, New Jersey, and Pennsylvania. She quickly realized that this was not going to be something that could be easily investigated. She and B.J. couldn't go from house to house, from town to town, checking on pedophiles. A job like that required a coordinated effort by law enforcement. Besides, so far, there was no real evidence pointing to the involvement of a child molester.

Before turning off the computer for the night, she printed out the list of names and addresses anyway.

CHAPTER 51

The concrete floor was cold and hard, but Mrs. Garcia had no other choice but to sit on it. It was either that or stand up, but she was much too tired and much too scared to use the energy necessary to hold herself erect. She wasn't certain how long she had been imprisoned belowground, but she was pretty sure that, mercifully, she had fallen asleep for a little while.

When she considered her situation, when she thought about Janie or about the threat the monster had made against her own family, Mrs. Garcia trembled with fear and hopelessness. And the thought of what he might do to her if he came back terrified her. There was nothing she could do, buried alive, the good Lord and the monster only knew where. So, to save her sanity, she tried to conjure up what it had been like to sleep in her own bed, with the comfort of her clean cotton sheets and soft quilt. She tried to imagine the aroma of fresh-brewed coffee. She wrinkled her nose in distaste at the real smell she inhaled. This place was dank and musty.

She huddled with her back uncomfortably pressed against a set of wooden shelves. She reached out in the darkness and felt a smooth, rounded surface. Her fingers closed around it and she recognized it as a glass jar. There were others beside it on the shelf.

Her body ached, her throat was sore. She cried out anyway.

"Help. Please, is anyone up there? *¡Auxilio, soccoro, ayúdenme, por favor!*"

The walls of the root cellar closed around her voice as if to snuff it out. She prayed and strained to hear a response, but no one answered her.

WEDNESDAY
JULY 23

CHAPTER 52

Eliza blake suspect in daughter's disappearance!

The *Mole*'s blaring front-page headline crowned a color picture of Eliza sobbing as she sat on a child's swing in her backyard. Inside, the accompanying article stated that the FBI considered Eliza a suspect in Janie's abduction.

"Son of a bitch," said B.J. D'Elia when Annabelle showed him the celebrity gossip magazine. He grabbed the publication from Annabelle and marched across the road to where the reporter who had written the article stood drinking a cup of coffee. He thrust the paper in the guy's face.

"Where the hell do you get off writing this kind of trash?" B.J. shouted.

The reporter shrugged.

"You lying bastard," said B.J., his face reddening. "I should rip your head off for writing lies like this."

"Hey, big shot, those aren't lies."

"The hell they're not," said B.J. "And when this thing is over, I'm going to make sure Eliza and KEY News sue your ass for libel."

"Be my guest, but they won't win," said the reporter smugly. "Because we have the tape to prove that every word of that story is true."

B.J. flinched.

"That's right, buddy," said the reporter. "The FBI *is* looking at your precious Eliza. The feds suspect she may not be the mother-of-the-year she has everybody thinking she is."

CHAPTER 53

Rhonda woke up early. As she came out of the bedroom, Dave was just coming in the front door of the apartment.

"How was work?" she asked, giving him a peck on the cheek.

"All right," Dave answered.

Rhonda studied her husband's face. His coloring wasn't good and he looked exhausted. She was afraid she was expecting too much from him. He worked all night, then grabbed only a few hours of sleep before taking over the child-care duties. While she wished she could be home to take care of Janie during the daylight hours, they needed both sala-

ries to make ends meet. So she went to the bakery during the day. She got to spend evenings with Janie but also got to sleep while Janie slept. Dave, on the other hand, was continually sleep deprived.

"Let me make you some breakfast," said Rhonda.

"No thanks," answered Dave. "I just want to crawl into bed."

He went into the bedroom, shutting the door behind him.

Rhonda walked into the living room and turned on the television, keeping the volume low so as not to wake Janie. She went into the adjoining galley kitchen, filled the kettle with water, and put it on the stove to boil. Then she took a carton of eggs from the refrigerator. As she cracked the eggshells on the side of a mixing bowl, she heard the words coming from the TV. Wiping her hands on a dish towel, she went back to the living room and sat down to watch and listen more closely.

Eliza Blake was on the screen. Rhonda almost didn't recognize her. The woman didn't look like herself. She was even paler and more washed out than Dave. Eliza stared into the camera, glassy-eyed, while she spoke.

"She needs to be home with the people who love her."

Troubled, Rhonda switched off the set. What was Eliza Blake talking about? Janie was already home with people who loved her.

CHAPTER 54

Katharine stood in the kitchen doorway. "Linus Nazareth is on the phone, honey."

Eliza took the phone from her mother-in-law and held it to her ear.

"I just wanted to check and see how you're holding up, Eliza."

"Oh, thanks, Linus. All right, I guess."

"I could kill those lousy bastards for writing that trash."

"What trash?" Eliza asked.

There was silence on the line.

"Linus?"

"Forget it."

"What trash, Linus?"

"All right, you're going to hear it sooner or later. It's the *Mole*. That rag is saying the FBI is looking at you as a suspect. But that really isn't a big deal. Everybody knows that the people closest to the victim are always viewed as suspects first. Nobody is going to take what the *Mole* says seriously and think that you could actually be in on Janie's abduction."

"As if this nightmare isn't bad enough, now it's getting worse?" Eliza asked, her voice going higher.

The other people in the kitchen stopped what they were doing and looked at Eliza.

"I don't believe this is happening," groaned Eliza as she sat in a chair.

"You know what I think?" The executive producer of *KEY to America* didn't wait for an answer. "I think you should come on the show and talk about it all. Get your side of the story out there."

"What side of the story, Linus? There aren't two sides. There's only one. My daughter and a woman I care very much about are missing and I want them back."

"You know what I mean, Eliza. Come on. Let Margo Gonzalez interview you and the people at home will see what a loving mother you are and that you could never hurt your kid."

"Now I have to prove to America that I love my child? That's absolutely ludicrous. I won't do it, Linus, no way," she said. "And have somebody fax that *Mole* article to me, will you? I want to see what I'm up against."

When she hung up the phone, Eliza went to find Agent Gebhardt. She paused to control herself before she entered the den where the command center had been set up.

Gebhardt was talking on the telephone, her back to Eliza. "Listen," she said, "these types show up whenever a child is kidnapped. They're all smoke and mirrors."

The FBI agent stood and listened to whoever was talking on the other end of the phone.

"I don't know how to explain that," she answered. "But, officially, the FBI doesn't use psychics. Maybe she's had some coincidences that worked out with other cases she was involved in at those other departments, but that's all they were, I assure you. Coincidences."

Eliza stepped forward and interrupted. "How to explain *what*?"

Gebhardt turned around and saw Eliza standing there. "I'll call you back," she said into the phone. She hung up and gestured to the armchairs next to the fireplace. "Let's sit down," she said.

"How to explain what?" Eliza repeated.

"Some crackpot came into the Ho-Ho-Kus Police Department saying she saw Janie in a dream."

"And?"

"The woman says she's a psychic."

"What else did she say?"

Agent Gebhardt crossed her legs and jiggled her foot. "She said that, in the dream, Janie had green paint on her face."

Eliza leaned back in the chair. "Anyone could know that now. It's been all over the news."

"I've got to tell you the truth," said

Gebhardt. "I don't believe in this psychic mumbo jumbo. I think these people prey on desperate parents who are willing to do anything to recover their children. But, the only thing is, this one came into the station and told her story *before* the public knew about the face paint."

Eliza digested the information. "Where is this woman now?" she asked.

"She lives in Pennsylvania."

"I want to talk to her. Let's have her come here."

"I don't suggest it. We can send a couple of agents up to interview her."

"Why not? Why not have her come here and see where Janie lives, let her be near Janie's things? If she is truly psychic, the proximity to Janie's private world might give her some insights. We don't have anything to lose. And it's a hell of a lot better than spending your time investigating me."

The color rose in the FBI agent's cheeks. "We're just doing our jobs, Eliza. We have to look at everyone, including you. Our job is to find Janie."

"And Mrs. Garcia," said Eliza evenly.

"And my job is to insist that every possibility, every lead, no matter how ridiculous, is followed up on. I don't care if you think she's a phony. I want to talk to this woman."

CHAPTER 55

"You're listening to 1010 WINS. You give us twenty-two minutes and we'll give you the world."

Alec couldn't wait for the time when he could afford to get his own car and wouldn't have to listen to this boring station every time his mother let him borrow hers. As he leaned over, about to adjust the dial, he heard the newscaster's voice.

"The search continues for Janie Blake, the seven-year-old daughter of KEY News anchorwoman Eliza Blake, who disappeared with her babysitter on Monday. Police are looking for a black van with a dented rear door that they think could be related to the case."

Alec thought of the van he had seen behind the old dry-cleaning plant on Monday afternoon when they had sneaked back there to smoke some more weed. The van was black, but he hadn't noticed if the back door had been damaged. He had been too stoned to notice.

But he did remember the woman sitting in the front seat of the van. She had stared right at him, her eyes penetrating and defiant. He felt there was something scary about her, but had chalked it up to his own paranoia. But what if the woman in the van actually had something to do with the little girl's kidnapping?

Alec pulled out his cell phone to call his best friend and explained what he'd heard on the radio.

"Did you notice if the back door was damaged?" Alec asked.

"Yeah, it *was* dented. I remember looking at it and thinking that it would cost a lot to have that fixed."

"Do you think we should tell the police?" Alec asked.

"I don't know, man. We'd have to explain what we were doing out there."

"Yeah, you're right," Alec agreed. "And that wouldn't be cool."

CHAPTER 56

Janie was curled up in the fetal position, cold, afraid, and alone. To divert herself, she tried to think about some of her favorite stories. The one that kept coming into her mind was Hansel and Gretel, where the little boy and girl had left a trail of crumbs as they went deeper and deeper into the dark forest. That had been a good plan, but the birds had eaten the pieces of bread, and Hansel and Gretel were left in big trouble. Just like she was.

She was worrying about what had happened to Mrs. Garcia and wondering if her mother would ever come to find her when she heard the door open.

"You've got to eat something," his voice growled.

Janie shook her head.

"Don't give me a hard time, your highness. Now get up and eat."

Janie felt the man's tight grip on her arm as he pulled her up into a sitting position. She cried out as her knees scraped against the mattress. She felt the man push against the hot skin around the wounds and she whimpered some more.

"Stop crying, goddamnit. You did that to yourself and now I'm stuck listening to you whining about it. Open your mouth," the man commanded.

She hiccupped as she tried to get control of herself.

"Daddy told you to open your mouth." She felt his hand grab her chin and pull it downward. "Now do it."

"Please. You're hurting me. Stop."

"Do what you're told and I won't have to hurt you, kid."

She opened her mouth. She forced herself to eat three mouthfuls of the cereal he spooned into her before throwing up all over herself, the mattress, and him.

He closed the bedroom door, peeling off his shirt as he walked down the hall to the kitchen. Pulling a plastic trash bag from beneath the kitchen sink, he scraped the vomit from his shirt into the bag. As he washed his hands, he swore to himself. When he had come up with this plan, he hadn't fully understood just how much of the dirty work was going to fall on his shoulders.

The phone rang.

"Well, did you take care of the maid?"

"Yeah. *Mamacita*'s not going to be giving us any more grief."

"Good. Now there's something else we've got to do."

"What?" he asked as he ripped off a paper towel from the roll on the counter.

"We've got to hide the van. It's all over the media . . . the cops are looking for a black van with a dented back door. Get rid of it and just use the Jeep from now on."

"Great. Where should *we* put it?"

"What's with the sarcastic tone?"

"Well, it's interesting you always say *we*, when *I'm* doing all the work here."

"Hey, this was all your idea. You knew going in that you would be the one taking care of her most of the time."

"Try *all* of the time," he snarled. "You're not here enough."

"I'm there as much as I can be."

He didn't answer.

"Remember? You said this would make things better for us," she said.

"I know I did. But maybe I'm not cut out to be a daddy."

"Don't say that now, not when we're in the middle of everything. You just have to hang in there."

"Easy for you to say. She didn't just puke all over you."

"She's sick?"

"Who knows? When I tried to get her to eat something, she threw it all up, back at me. Maybe she's getting a bug, maybe she's nervous. How am I supposed to know what's wrong with her? That's a woman's job."

Now that the kid didn't have the old lady anymore, he figured it would be a good idea to give her something to keep her occupied. Not for her sake but for his.

He took the small television with the built-in VCR from the other bedroom and carried it across the hall. Cracking the door, he peeked inside and saw that Janie was sleeping.

Finally. Now if she'd only stay asleep.

He put the TV down on the floor outside the small room, stole out of the house, and quietly opened the driver's-side door of the van. Reaching in, he put the vehicle in neutral. He stood at the side of the open door, steering with one hand and using all his strength to push the van forward and into the large shed. Afterward, closing the wooden doors of the shed, he was satisfied that he had barely made a sound.

CHAPTER 57

She heard noise coming from above her. The sound moved from one side of the ceiling to the other and then it stopped.

Mrs. Garcia got up from the floor of the root cellar. She looked up and called into the darkness.

"Help! I'm down here. Please, help."

She waited. No answer, but she heard another, different sound. A quick, rhythmic noise. Footsteps?

She screamed frantically. *"¡Auxilio, soccoro!* Help! I'm down here!"

The sound grew fainter until it faded

altogether. The only thing Mrs. Garcia could hear then was her own labored breathing and the rush of her pulse pounding in her head.

CHAPTER 58

Daisy lay with her head resting on her paws, guarding the door to Janie's bedroom.

"Good girl," said Eliza as she bent down to stroke the dog's soft coat. "You miss them, don't you, Daisy? You miss our Janie and Mrs. Garcia."

The yellow Lab looked up with sad dark eyes.

"She's about two, right?" asked Stephanie Quick as she stopped to pet the dog.

Eliza cocked her head to the side. "That's right. How could you tell that?"

Stephanie shrugged. "Just a guess."

Eliza glanced at Agent Gebhardt whose face remained expressionless. All three women entered the child's bedroom, while Mack stood in the doorway. Agent Gebhardt positioned herself just inside the room, watching intently as Stephanie walked around. She stopped at the plush toy that sat in the small wicker rocker.

"Janie's favorite?" she asked.

"Yes. Zippy," answered Eliza as she heard her own voice crack. "She loves that monkey. Her grandparents gave it to her on her third birthday. She has taken it to bed with her every night since."

Stephanie nodded and continued walking around the room.

"This one is Janie's?" she asked, pointing to one of the twin beds beneath the window.

Eliza nodded.

"May I?" Stephanie asked as she reached for the pillow.

"Why not?" said Agent Gebhardt. "We've already been over this room with a fine-tooth comb."

Stephanie picked up the pillow and wrapped her arms around it, hugging it to her body. She closed her eyes and was silent. "Do you really want me to tell you everything?" she asked when she opened them.

"Yes."

"I see blood."

Eliza took hold of the bedpost to steady herself.

"She's hurt?"

"Yes. It doesn't seem to be too serious, though," Stephanie said softly. "But, Janie *is* in pain."

"Anything else?" Eliza forced herself to ask.

"Yes," said Stephanie. "I see a bridal veil."

"You mean a Communion veil," suggested Eliza. "Janie will be making her First Communion soon."

"No," said Stephanie. "It's definitely a bridal veil."

As Stephanie was leaving, she put something in Eliza's hand. "Hold on to this and keep concentrating on Janie," she said.

Eliza studied the silver medallion emblazoned with the signs of the zodiac.

"And one more thing that's coming through to me," said Stephanie. "John is glad you are still wearing the perfume he loved."

Eliza looked up sharply. How could Stephanie have known about the perfume? Stephanie's words brought the memories flooding back.

On one of the last nights in the hospital with John, he had been dozing as she entered the room. He was very thin, flushed with fever, his breathing was labored. She bent down to kiss him.

John opened his eyes, his gaunt face cracking into a weak smile as he saw her. She smiled back and leaned down to kiss him again. She felt the heat coming from his emaciated body as he held on to her.

Then, in a wheezing voice, he had whispered, "Oh, you smell so good."

She had promised herself then and there that she wouldn't use another scent. And she hadn't.

"Well, what did you think?" Eliza asked.

"I think she's a phony," said Agent Gebhardt.

"I don't know about that," said Eliza. "She blew me away with that remark about my husband and the perfume. How would she know that was one of the last things he talked about?"

"Stab in the dark," said Agent Gebhardt dismissively.

"But she got a lot of other things right, too. Daisy *is* two years old and Zippy *is* Janie's favorite toy. Plus, she picked out Janie's bed."

"First of all, she had a fifty-fifty chance of choosing the right bed," said Agent Gebhardt. "And when you look carefully at both of them, the quilt on the one by the window looks slightly more laundered, more used than the one on the other bed."

Eliza listened.

"Have you ever mentioned the dog in any interviews you've done?" asked Agent Gebhardt.

"Yes," said Eliza. "Several times."

"Did you mention how long you've had the dog?"

"I think I've mentioned that we got her as a puppy when we moved out here to Ho-Ho-Kus," said Eliza.

"Which is something anybody could look up and discover that that was two years ago," said Agent Gebhardt.

"Come to think of it," said Eliza, "in the pictures that were taken for one magazine spread, Janie was holding Zippy in her arms, and I think the caption even read that the stuffed animal was her favorite."

Agent Gebhardt managed a wry smile. "See what I mean? This woman doesn't have any special gift. Anybody could have told you what she did."

"What about the bridal veil?" asked Eliza.

"What about it? The woman is in la-la land."

Eliza forced herself to ask her next question. "What about the blood she said she saw? What about Janie being hurt and in pain?"

"Stephanie Quick knows you're vulnerable, Eliza. She is preying on that vulnerability and banking on the fact that you'll do anything you can to get your child back. She doesn't know if Janie is hurt or not, but by telling you that your child is in pain, she is manipulating you.

She's counting on your maternal need to rescue your child and she thinks you'll grab at anyone or anything that might lead you to her."

"She's right," said Eliza. "I do want every lead followed, and if it's Stephanie Quick who can get Janie and Mrs. Garcia home, so be it."

CHAPTER 59

The police had him on their radar screen, but they couldn't be watching him every minute of the day. If he was careful, he'd be able to get what he needed with nobody being any the wiser.

Hugh found his car turning in the direction of Camp Musquapsink. He knew the route well. He had driven it before.

Rather than keeping him far away, all the attention in the press about the children's day camp had enticed him to come closer. Hugh knew he was taking a chance by going back, but he couldn't help himself. The gnawing hunger inside him needed to be fed.

He snapped on the radio and listened to the latest reports. There was nothing new since the last time he'd listened. The cops were still looking for the black van. That was good. Let them look for the van instead of the car he was driving.

About a quarter mile from the entrance to the camp, Hugh pulled off the road, steering the car along a dirt driveway, overgrown in places with bushes and weeds. At a wide spot, he maneuvered the vehicle, turning it around so that it was pointed in the direction of the road in case he had to make a hasty escape.

He traveled the rest of the way on foot, his nylon pants swishing as he walked. Hugh stopped short of the stone pillars that marked the entrance, watching as a stream of adults proceeded onto the camp's grounds. *There must be some sort of parents' visiting day going on,* he thought.

Hugh knew several spots around the perimeter of the camp that served as his observation posts. He selected the one that had the greatest probability of giving him exactly what he needed.

Through the separation in the fence,

he could see the little girls. In brightly colored bathing suits that hugged their firm, undeveloped bodies, they lined up at the edge of the pool, listening to their swimming instructor while their parents cheered from the sidelines. They were mesmerized by their precious darlings. As was he.

Hugh felt his breathing grow heavier. Perspiration broke out across his brow and trickled down the sides of his face. Feeling his knees weaken, he leaned against the fence.

Isabelle would kill him if she knew he was taking a chance like this.

CHAPTER 60

When Eliza Blake called again to tell Maria Rochas there was still no news about her mother or Janie, Maria listened attentively but said very little, even when Eliza mentioned that she had established a $250,000 reward. It crossed Maria's mind that Mrs. Blake could be testing her, seeing if Maria had information she had been withholding but would offer up now because of the money.

"I hope somebody comes forward with something that helps, Mrs. Blake," she said. "I'm sorry, but I must go now. I have to get to work."

When she came out of the house, Maria noticed the police car driving by. After she dropped the baby off with her sitter, she saw the vehicle a second time. As she walked to the nail salon, she was sure the car was following her. It drove past repeatedly and then circled around to find her again.

During her lunch break, she crossed over Broadway to the car wash. Vicente was working with the group of Guatemalan men wiping, vacuuming, and polishing the cars and SUVs lined up for service. He broke away from the cleaning team when he saw her.

"What is wrong?" he asked, seeing the expression on her face. "Is there news of your mother?"

"No." Maria's voice cracked. "No news."

"What then?" he asked. "What is it?"

"We have to take Rosario and get away from here." Her eyes welled up with tears.

"What are you talking about, Maria?"

"Look over my shoulder, Vicente."

A police car was parked on the other side of the street, the officer inside looking in their direction.

"I know, Maria. They are watching us. But we haven't done anything wrong."

"I know we haven't, Vicente. But do you think that matters? If they don't find Janie Blake, they are going to blame us. And if they do find Janie Blake, they are going to come back to get us and send us back to Guatemala. Either way, we have to go where they cannot find us."

"But we can't leave, Maria. That will make us look guilty. Besides, don't you want to be here if your mother tries to contact us?"

"Of course I want to be here if my *mamá* calls," Maria cried. "I am worried sick about her. I cannot eat. I cannot sleep. But, Vicente, I don't want to be deported. I want us to stay in America."

CHAPTER 61

Mack came back into the house after walking around talking to the reporters staked outside. He found Eliza in her daughter's room, sitting on the bed, Janie's stuffed monkey in her lap. Mack sat down and put his arm around her.

"How's my girl?" he asked.

Eliza stroked Zippy's head. "Janie sleeps with this thing every single night. I don't know what she's going to do without it."

Mack reached over and wiped the tears from Eliza's face. He pulled her close, kissing her cheeks and whispering reassurances.

"This is such a nightmare, Mack. Every time I think of what she and Mrs. Garcia could be going through, I'm filled with just the most awful dread." She closed her eyes and rested her head on his shoulder. "What if they're hurting her? What if I don't get her back?"

"Try not to think like that, honey. It doesn't do any good."

"I know," said Eliza. "I know it doesn't. But I keep thinking about what the psychic said, that she saw blood."

"For God's sake, Eliza. Please, don't let what that nut said get to you. Don't do that to yourself. Honestly, sweetheart, though I can understand that, as a parent, you'll grasp at whatever you think can help, I truly believe you're wasting time and energy with that Stephanie Quick character."

Eliza pulled back and looked directly into Mack's eyes.

"If you had said that to me a few days ago, I would have been in total agreement, Mack. But the world is turned upside down. You know that saying? Extreme times call for extreme measures. Well, things are about as extreme as they can get right now. Maybe it won't be the traditional law enforcement investigation that will find Janie, maybe it will take something that's really 'out there,' beyond anything we would usually think of or trust."

They sat quietly for a while, holding each other. Eventually, Mack broke the silence. "I think you should reconsider the offer Linus made and do that interview, Eliza."

Eliza stiffened. "Why? So everyone can dissect each word I say, and judge every facial expression I make, to determine whether I'm sincere or not? So they can decide if I had my own child kidnapped?" Eliza shook her head. "No thanks."

"That's precisely why you *should* do it," said Mack with urgency in his voice. "We know better than to underestimate the audience. When they see you and listen to you, they'll get a true sense of you."

"At this point, let them think what they want, Mack. I don't really care. I just want Janie back."

"Exactly. The focus should be entirely

on finding Janie, but I have to tell you something, sweetheart. Everyone in the media outside is fixating on you, and even though nobody really believes you are capable of being a part of this, they want to know how you're taking being considered a suspect."

"I don't know if that's sick or just pathetic, Mack." She broke from his embrace and lay back on the bed. "You know, I've been in this business my entire adult life. People have invited me into their homes to tell them about wars, floods, fires, hurricanes, political and business scandals, presidential elections, and everything in between. I have one of the highest credibility and trust ratings in broadcast journalism, and now, all of a sudden, I'm being pulled into this bizarre media circus. That's just wonderful."

"The media's all over this story," said Mack, "and this is a particularly scintillating aspect of it."

"That's disgusting," said Eliza.

"Be that as it may," he agreed, "but that's the way it is."

Eliza was sickened by what she found on the Web.

Not only had the *Mole* published the picture of Eliza on the swing and sobbing on its front page, the gossip magazine was capitalizing on their exclusive photo and selling it to any other media outlet that was willing to pay. Eliza checked the Web sites of all the major networks. KEY.com was the only one that didn't feature the shot.

Knowing she should protect herself and not look further, she was compelled to check anyway. There it was on mediabistro.com, tmz.com, and perezhilton.com, the Web site that promised "Celebrity juice, not from concentrate."

Eliza logged out, aware that these sites were just the tip of the Internet iceberg. Anyone in the entire world, with access to a computer, could see her at her most vulnerable anytime they wanted, and read about the suspicion cast upon her. She was used to being in the spotlight, used to appearing on television, used to seeing her face on the cover of magazines, but there was something about being exposed on the Internet, with its eternal memory and universal scope, that truly unnerved her.

The media kept trying to make this a story about her instead of about Janie and Mrs. Garcia. Eliza resolved to do all in her power to keep the focus where it belonged.

CHAPTER 62

The knock at the door was loud and persistent. Turning off the cartoons and closing the bedroom door behind her, Nell went to answer it as fast as she could. Cora Wallace was standing on the front stoop.

"I know you said you didn't want any," she said, thrusting a shopping bag toward Nell, "but I made you some chicken soup. It's good for you, honey."

Having no other choice, Nell opened the screen door. "Thank you, Mrs. Wallace," she said.

"There's also some articles in there that I clipped from the papers about the kidnapping. In case you missed them, I thought you might want them for your scrapbook."

Nell doubted that she wouldn't have them. She got the same newspaper Cora got and Nell had been vigilant about cutting out every story and picture that appeared.

"That was nice of you, Cora," she said as she leaned out and took the shopping bag. Cora went to give Nell a kiss on the cheek.

"Is that vomit I smell?" Cora asked with alarm. "Have you been sick, dear? I had the feeling you were coming down with something when you were so pale at the pool yesterday."

"I had a sick stomach this morning," said Nell. "But I'm fine now."

"Why don't I come in and sit with you for a while, Nell? We can have a nice little chat. I'll heat up some of the soup and we can talk the afternoon away. I worry about you being out here with nobody but Lloyd to talk to so much of the time."

"I don't think so, Mrs. Wallace," Nell said, begging off. "I feel better now, but

I'm still a little tired. I was going to take a nap."

"Is Lloyd in there with you?" Cora craned her neck to look over Nell's shoulder and into the house.

"He went out for a while."

Cora shook her head back and forth at what she saw in the house. "I can't believe that man still keeps those rifles in the house like that. At the very least, he should have them under lock and key instead of hanging them like trophies on the living room wall."

CHAPTER 63

Alec parked his mother's car back in the driveway, remembering to readjust the radio setting to the station she liked so that she wouldn't nag him later. She was always complaining that he didn't show her enough respect in the way he treated her things.

As he was getting out of the car, his cell phone rang.

"Hey, Alec. It's me."

"Wassup?"

"Did you hear about the reward?"

"What reward?"

"The two hundred and fifty thousand dollars for anyone who has information that helps finds that Janie Blake kid. We should tell the cops about the black van we saw behind the dry cleaner's."

Alec sat down on the front stoop of the house. "When I talked to you before, you said you didn't want to go to the police because they'd find out we were smoking weed back there."

"I didn't know about the reward then. Now that I've thought about it, we can just tell them we went back there to make out with some girls."

"The girls might not like that," said Alec. "Don't you think we should talk to them and make sure they're onboard before we go to the police?"

"I don't think they'll care, especially if we stand to get that kind of money. But I guess you're right. We should talk to them so that we all have our stories straight before we go to the cops."

CHAPTER 64

Taking off her blindfold hadn't made a bit of difference. In fact, in a way, it made things worse. Mrs. Garcia was in total darkness and feeling sheer terror. She could stand upright, but when she lowered herself onto the ground, Mrs. Garcia could barely stretch out to her full length.

A dank, woodsy smell permeated the stale air, causing Mrs. Garcia to cough as she crouched in the blackness. Sporadically, she felt something brush against her leg or her arm or her face and she forcefully swiped at whatever it was.

Where was she? Where was Janie?

What were they doing to her? How would the child survive, all alone with those evil ones? Mrs. Garcia's thoughts overwhelmed her. Baby Rosario was too young to understand, but Maria and Vicente must be so worried. Would anyone find her buried here? Would she die here all alone? She turned for comfort to the prayer she knew so well. Into the darkness, she prayed out loud in Spanish, interpreting the words in her thoughts.

Dios te salve, María, llena eres de gracia, el Señor es contigo. "Hail Mary, full of grace, the Lord is with you. Please, Holy Mother, God is on your side."

Bendita tú eres entre todas las mujeres. "Blessed are you among women. No one has more influence with him than you do."

Y bendito es el fruto de tu vientre, Jesús. "And blessed is the fruit of your womb. You're his mother, and like all good sons, Jesus will do what his mother asks him."

Santa María, Madre de Dios, ruega por nosotros pecadores. "Holy Mary, Mother of God, pray for us sinners. I know I have not been perfect, but I have tried. I promise, I will try harder."

Ahora y en la hora de nuestra muerte. "Now and at the hour of our death. Don't let this be the end. Please send someone to find us. Yet, I think the hour of death is coming for me, Holy Mother. If that is God's will, then that is God's will. I will miss my Maria and her Vicente and my precious Rosario. I have had a good life. But, please, Holy Mother, save Janie. She is so young and so pure."

Amen.

CHAPTER 65

Susan Feeney arrived at the front door with a casserole dish in hand but she was stopped by the two police officers who stood guard. After she identified herself as a neighbor and a friend and waited while one of the officers went inside to check, Susan was permitted entry. Eliza met her in the hallway.

"Oh, Susan," said Eliza, reaching out and hugging her visitor.

"I brought you something to eat," said Susan. "I wanted to see how you are."

"Thank you," said Eliza, taking the dish from her. "That's very kind of you, Susan."

"So many people have been calling me, Eliza, wanting to know what they can do. I hope it's all right with you that I'm organizing a meal brigade. From now on, you'll have food coming in here three times a day from people in town who want to help."

Eliza shook her head and tears welled up in her eyes. "I still can't believe that it's come to this."

"Have you heard anything at all?" asked Susan.

"Sure, the calls are coming in fast and furious, people saying they saw a black van with a dented rear door. Hundreds of them, but none have led to anything yet. First, it has to be decided if a tip sounds like it's worth pursuing and then it has to be followed up on. It all takes time, too much time."

Eliza sank down on one of the steps of the hallway staircase and buried her face in her arms. Susan sat beside her.

"God, I wish I had paid more attention to that van," said Susan. "If only I had thought to write down the license plate."

"Please, don't beat yourself up about

that, Susan. How could you have known?"

"This is just awful. I don't know what else to say, Eliza."

"There isn't anything to say." Eliza reached out and patted Susan's hand. "Just be my friend."

An hour after Susan left, she returned.

"When I got home, I went online," she explained. "I read about some of the things that volunteers can do to help find a missing child. I called my church and they are willing to let us use their community room to set up a volunteer center."

"What would the volunteers do?" Eliza asked uncertainly. "Honestly, I wouldn't want civilians getting in the way of the professional law enforcement efforts."

"Of course not," Susan agreed. "We'll only do what they want us to do, things we clear with them first, only things that can free them up and support their investigation. Things like distributing flyers and helping your family with anything you need."

Eliza thought for a moment. "There is something that I wish somebody would do."

"Name it," said Susan.

"Mrs. Garcia's family lives in Westwood. If somebody could go over and take them some food and ask what else they need, I would so appreciate it."

"Consider it done," said Susan. "What's their address and phone number?"

Susan wrote down the information. "There's something else, Eliza," she said.

"What?"

"People in town have been saying they want to hold a candlelight vigil for Janie. Would that be all right with you?"

Eliza considered the question. "I guess so," she said. "We need all the positive energy we can get."

CHAPTER 66

In an area buried beneath ground level
at the KEY News Broadcast Center, a
dozen men wore surgical masks and latex gloves as they opened every envelope
and package that arrived. An inspection
team had been organized when anthrax
was found at major media outlets after
September 11. In the months and years
that followed, as things got back to normal, the staff was reduced to just two or
three inspectors on a shift. Now, with the
Blake kidnapping, the staff was up to full
strength again as every bit of correspondence and every delivery and shipment
was thoroughly examined.

"Here's a good one," said one of the staffers after he sliced open a package and inspected the contents.

The man who stood next to him craned his neck to see what was inside the box. "Gosh, those look good," he said, reaching for one of the cookies. "Smell good, too."

"Hold on there, bro," said the inspector, pulling the box away. "How can you be so sure that they aren't tainted?"

"I'll take the chance," said the other, snatching a sugar cookie out of the box.

As his coworker chewed, the inspector read the note written on the back of an order form stuck inside the package. He read it again, showed it to some of the other guys in the room and then reached for the telephone to call the security chief.

"I think there's something here you should take a look at, Joe. Can you come on down?"

Joe Connelly read the shaky handwriting:

Dear Eliza,

I'm sorry you are going through such a hard time right now. Having lost a daughter myself, I know what it's like. My heart goes out to you.

These treats are not as sweet as Janie, but I hope they fortify you in the difficult days you are facing.

You're probably wondering, as I did when my little girl was lost to me, why this has happened. God works in mysterious ways. It will take time to be able to see why Janie was taken from you, or maybe you'll never be able to understand. Unfortunately, sometimes you have to go through unbearable pain before you realize what's truly important in life. Be comforted in knowing that your pain is helping someone else.

Someday, God willing, you'll have another child. Save your money until then so you'll be able to stay home and take care of your baby as you should.

There was no signature, but the box and the order form were stamped with the name and address of a bakery in a town Joe knew was about an hour outside Manhattan.

He read the letter again.

> *Be comforted in knowing your pain is helping someone else.*
> *Stay home and take care of your baby as you should.*

Joe didn't like the feeling he got from this one.

When he got back to his office, Joe called Eliza's assistant.

"Paige, it's Joe Connelly. We've got a package downstairs, a package of baked goods. Were you expecting anything like that for Eliza?"

"Not that I know of, Joe."

He read her the letter.

"Ugh, creepy," said Paige.

Joe gave her the information on the bakery. "Ever gotten cookies before from this place or ever heard of it?" he asked.

"No, it doesn't sound familiar," said

Paige. "But let me write down the name of the bakery again. I'll check in my files and get back to you."

"Marzipan Bakery," said Joe. "M-A-R-Z-I-P-A-N."

CHAPTER 67

After polishing all the glass cases and wiping all the counters, Rhonda methodically went shelf by shelf, removing the stale cookies, cakes, and pies. Next, she made a list of treats that needed to be replaced by the baker who would come in overnight and bake the goodies to be sold the next day. Finally, she closed out the cash register and deposited the contents in the zippered bag that the owner would take to the bank. She stashed the bag in the designated spot where the owner would find it when he came in tonight after the bakery was closed.

Rhonda took off her apron and stopped in the tiny bathroom at the back of the kitchen to wash her hands, reapply her lipstick, and run a comb through her hair. She knew that Dave was waiting for her and would be eager for her to get home and take over. But she wanted to make a stop at Wal-Mart first.

She drove the few miles to the store and found a spot in the crowded parking lot. As she walked in, Rhonda was conscious of the security cameras that were aimed at her and everyone else who walked into the place. But she had nothing to hide. She was just a mother coming in to buy things for her child.

In the children's section, some of the summer clothing was already on sale. Rhonda found a cute pair of baby-doll pajamas, pale blue, which would bring out the blue in Janie's eyes. She also selected a pair of yellow flip-flops. In the toy department, she picked out a few coloring books and a large box of crayons. Rhonda opened the carton and was delighted with all the vibrant shades. Surely, Janie would be pleased, too.

At the end of the long aisle, a dis-

play caught Rhonda's attention. Hanging from a fake palm tree was a variety of stuffed monkeys. There was one that looked just like the monkey that Janie had held in one of the magazine articles, the monkey Janie called Zippy.

Rhonda slipped the toy from the tree and proceeded to the checkout counter, excited that she was bringing home something that would please the child. Having Zippy with her again would surely make Janie happy.

CHAPTER 68

She didn't hear the bell the first two times it rang. The third chime cut through the din. Isabelle turned off the vacuum cleaner and answered the door.

"I was wondering when you'd get here," she said when she saw the policeman standing on the stoop.

"Is your brother around?" he asked, looking over Isabelle's shoulder, trying to see inside the house.

"No, he's out."

"Where did he go?"

"To tell you the truth, I'm not sure."

"When will he be back?"

"Don't know that, either."

"Would it be all right if I came in and took a look around?"

Isabelle put her hands on her hips. "Do you have a search warrant?"

The officer looked uncomfortable. "No."

Isabelle shrugged and held up her palms. "Sorry."

"All right, have it your way," said the cop. "But you know, when you don't cooperate voluntarily, it doesn't look good. It looks like you have something to hide."

"We don't have anything to hide," said Isabelle. "Not a damn thing. But because Eliza Blake's daughter is missing, you guys are automatically looking at every convicted sex offender as a suspect. I know how it works."

"Then you know I'll be back," said the policeman as he turned to leave.

Isabelle called after him, "When are you guys going to stop persecuting him? He did his time, he's paid his debt to society. Give him a break."

"Once a pedophile, always a pedophile," said the policeman. "They don't change."

"Yeah, but they can work hard to control themselves," Isabelle said vehemently. "That's what Hughie is trying to do and it doesn't help when you guys are always harassing him."

"You went *where*?" Isabelle stared incredulously at her brother.

Hughie didn't look up from the project he was working on.

"Have you lost your mind, Hughie? What were you thinking? Going up to Camp Musquapsink was *incredibly* stupid. You know how dangerous it was to go back there. A cop was already here. What do you think would happen if he knew you were peering through the fence at the camp today?"

He put down the scissors and looked with remorse at his sister. "I couldn't help myself," he said. "There are so many of the kind I like there."

"Like booze to an alcoholic," Isabelle muttered as she sat next to her brother at the kitchen table.

"What did you say?" asked Hughie.

"Nothing. But, Hughie, you *can't* go back there again. Understand?"

"Um-hmm."

She took hold of her brother's arm and stared into his eyes. "Promise, Hughie. You've got to promise me you won't go back to the camp again."

"I promise I'll try, Isabelle." He picked up the scissors again and started cutting.

"They're going to come back, Hughie. The cops will come back," said Isabelle. "You know that, don't you?"

"Eventually, maybe," said Hughie. "But unless they have something we don't know about, they aren't going to get a warrant and they won't be able to come inside. There's no probable cause here. I've been careful."

Isabelle watched Hughie while he continued to cut. His tongue stuck out slightly over his lip as he concentrated. "Why do you have to do that, Hughie? Why can't you act your age?"

"Don't you think a little girl would like these?" asked Hughie as he held up the paper dolls he had fashioned.

Resigned, Isabelle got up from the table. "I'm going out for a while," she said. "If you need me, call me on my cell."

She left as her brother gathered up his paper dolls and went into the bed-room.

CHAPTER 69

"We've got something. We've got a lead."

Eliza hovered over the FBI command desk, listening intently to every word passing between Agents Gebhardt and Laggie.

"A customer at the Burger King in Frankfort, Kentucky, saw a child matching Janie's description in the front seat of a black van with a dented back door in the parking lot. The guy took a picture with his cell phone and wrote down the license plate number before the van drove away."

"So what happens now?" asked Eliza, taking Mack's hand and squeezing it.

"We find out who owns that van and track it down. The Kentucky State Police are all over it."

Eliza went to the telephone to share the first hopeful news they'd received with Maria, but there was no answer at the Rochas home.

CHAPTER 70

It was awfully quiet in there.

The man opened the door to see what was going on inside the room. Janie lay on the mattress, the blindfold tied around her eyes, her mouth open as she breathed softly and rhythmically. An occasional hiccup jolted her little body.

He walked over to the bed to get a closer look. Those knees of hers were red and angry-looking. Pus had started to coat the scrapes and cuts. He reached out to touch Janie's face. Her cheeks and forehead were hot to the touch.

He closed the door quietly. Wondering if an infection had set in, he decided he should probably get something at the pharmacy before she really got sick. The last thing they needed was a kid with a raging fever, or worse. Now would be the time to go, while she was asleep.

Since the episode yesterday when the old lady had helped the kid out the window to run away, he'd nailed sheets of plywood over the windows in the bedroom and bathroom. Once he locked the door to the room, there was no way for Janie to escape.

Cursing the kid for putting him in this situation in the first place, he got into the Jeep and drove the fifteen miles on curving country roads into town, finding a parking space in front of the drugstore. Inside, he picked up a shopping basket and filled it with gauze pads, cotton balls, witch hazel, antiseptic ointment, and some children's aspirin. He decided to throw in a thermometer as well.

At the checkout counter, the cashier emptied the items from the basket and rang each one up. "Did you find everything you need?"

"Yeah, I guess so," the man grunted.

"Actually, do you have anything for hic-cups?"

The cashier looked up. "We have some things in aisle three, but I don't know how well any of them work. I hear there's no cure for hiccups."

"Screw it then," said the man. "Why waste the money?"

He threw some bills down on the counter, waited for his change, and left quickly.

While he was driving back, his cell phone sounded.

"How is she?"

"She's sleeping."

"Oh, that's good. She needs that. What are you doing?"

"I'm driving back from the drugstore."

"You left her alone?"

"Don't worry. She's not going any-where. I made sure of that."

"What did you go to the drugstore for?"

"To get stuff for her knees."

"They're worse?"

"Don't worry about it," he said. "Worry

about what *you* have to do. Did you send the ransom demand yet?"

"No. Not yet."

"What are you waiting for?" he asked with exasperation.

"The money isn't the issue here," she pleaded. "It's never been about the money. I think we could be making a big mistake in asking for a ransom."

"We've been over this again and again. If we want to get away with this, we have to ask for a ransom so it looks like that's our motive for taking her. Nobody says we have to pick it up. That oughta really confuse the FBI."

CHAPTER 71

Mack made a call to Range Bullock, alerting him to the FBI lead in Kentucky.

"I don't know if you want to send our own crews or let our affiliates cover it if the cops find Janie," said Mack. "But Eliza and I want to make sure that KEY News has the best coverage. I didn't tell the feds I was going to call you."

"Thanks for the heads-up, Mack," said the president of the news division. "I'll get the wheels rolling."

"I wish I could be there when they catch this lowlife," Mack muttered. "I'd wring his neck and rip him a new one while I was at it."

"That's why it's a good idea for you not to be there," said Range. "Besides, Eliza needs you to be with her. How is she, anyway?"

"Most of the time, she's putting up a brave front, but this is killing her, Range. Eliza is strong, but this is beyond what anyone should have to bear. Let's hope this Kentucky lead is the answer, because I don't know how much more she can take."

CHAPTER 72

Once Mack arrived to support Eliza and act as a "family" spokesman and liaison with the press, Annabelle was able to focus on producing. She'd spent the day making phone calls, researching other kidnappings and law enforcement procedure, and devouring every new wire service story about the Janie Blake case.

Over and over, she read that, most often, a child was abducted by someone who was close to or at least knew the child. In Eliza's case, Annabelle suspected there was a very wide field of suspects because so many people with whom Eliza had never even spoken, had never even met, knew her or felt they did.

Annabelle was aware of the fact that Eliza got mail from viewers, some laudatory, some critical. Letters came in with comments about the clothes she wore and the way her hair was styled. Men wrote in that they'd love to date her, women said Eliza felt like a friend. She got letters asking for donations, and requests for speaking engagements at charity events and college graduations. People wanted to know what her hobbies were, what she liked to eat, and where her favorite place to vacation was.

Undoubtedly, there must be some letters that Eliza got from people wanting to know about Janie, thought Annabelle. She picked up the phone, called Eliza's assistant, and explained what was on her mind.

"Sure, she's gotten letters asking about Janie," said Paige. "Most of them are pretty benign. But any that seem the least bit threatening or creepy, I send down to Joe Connelly in security."

"Joe, this is Annabelle Murphy. I'm a *KTA* producer," she reminded him.

"Sure, Annabelle. What can I do for you?"

"I'm calling about the abduction."

"Yes?" Joe's tone turned wary.

"I was hoping that you'd talk to me about any threatening letters or calls Eliza has received, ones that you might be concerned about, or think could be related to this."

"You should know I can't do that, Annabelle."

"Can you tell me if law enforcement is investigating anything in that regard?"

"They'd be remiss if they weren't, wouldn't they?" asked Joe.

"Yeah, you'd think that would be a no-brainer, wouldn't you? But I just wanted to check," said Annabelle. "We had something that we beat the FBI to the punch on last night, a picture of Janie taken at camp just a little while before she was abducted. I'm not criticizing them, but they certainly aren't infallible, are they?"

There was a momentary pause on the line before the security chief answered. "Off the record?" asked Joe.

"I'd rather not, but if it has to be."

"It has to be," said Joe firmly. "No using this information on the broadcasts unless it comes from the FBI. But, yes, they've been looking at some correspondence that's come in."

"Anything in particular?" Annabelle tried.

"Uh-uh, Annabelle. Nice try, but I'm not going to bite," said Joe. "Even if I did give you some letters, you don't have the wherewithal to track down a postmark or analyze handwriting. Those are jobs for the FBI."

Joe was right. Annabelle didn't have the ability to figure out who had sent anonymous letters to Eliza. Yet Annabelle didn't want to give up. She was desperate for something to do to help her friend.

Forget the phone. She went down to Eliza's office to speak with her assistant in person.

"You've got to help me out, Paige."

"With what?"

"I just spoke with Joe Connelly and he's not giving anything up," said Annabelle as she sat and crossed her legs. "He admitted there's been some questionable correspondence that has come in for Eliza, but that's all he would say. What help is that?"

"What do you need, Annabelle?"

"I need something *specific,* something we can look into," said Annabelle. "A name, a place, something we can investigate in hopes that it leads us to Janie."

"And the elements for a good story," said Paige.

"That, too," Annabelle admitted. "But that's not my first concern."

"I know it's not," said Paige. She glanced down at her notepad. She had jotted down the name of the bakery where the cookies and the creepy letter had come from. "I do have something," she said. "But you can never say you got it from me, Annabelle. I want to keep my job and don't want to lose anybody's trust."

"You've got my word," said Annabelle. "I promise. Nobody will ever know where I got the information."

CHAPTER 73

Eliza and Mack, along with Katharine and Paul Blake, sat around the kitchen table. Conversation was minimal. They were waiting, listening for a phone to ring.

A square of lasagna lay untouched on Eliza's plate. "Try to eat something, dear," urged Katharine. "Susan's lasagna is delicious."

Eliza picked up her fork and then laid it down again. "I'm really not hungry," she said.

"Eat anyway," said Katharine. "You need fuel to keep up your energy. If you get sick or collapse, what good will that do Janie?"

Putting some food in her mouth, Eliza chewed slowly, not tasting it. She was thinking about Janie and calculating how far it was to Kentucky and how long it would take to get to her daughter. Eliza had wanted to get on a plane as soon as she heard the news about the black van and possible "Janie spotting" at the fast-food restaurant, but the FBI agents had persuaded her not to do it. Nobody knew where the vehicle could be traveling and, until it was actually found, it made no sense for Eliza to fly anywhere.

A ringing sound cut the silence and Eliza jumped to her feet. Mack followed her into the den, where Agent Laggie held the phone to his ear. With her hands clasped beneath her chin and feeling that she would burst, Eliza forced herself to remain quiet until the agent ended the call.

"Well? Please, tell me they've found her," Eliza begged. "Please."

"They've traced the tags," said Laggie. "The van belongs to a guy in Versailles, Kentucky. The state police and agents from our Cincinnati field office are on their way to his house now."

CHAPTER 74

A modest but tidy brick ranch house stood on a small plot of land at the end of a long country road. A dusty black van sat in the driveway.

Unmarked cars parked just out of sight. The occupants of the cars got out quietly and made their way with stealth toward the house. Crouching and hidden from view by trees and bushes, they watched as a man came out of the house and deposited a plastic bag into a trash can before pulling the can to the curb. As the man started to walk back up the driveway, the law enforcement officers pounced.

CHAPTER 75

"Laggie." The FBI agent answered the call, his voice curt, his expression strained.

Eliza watched him intently. She could feel her own body grow even tenser. As she listened to his side of the conversation and realized what it meant, Eliza felt a rush of intense disappointment and defeat.

It wasn't Janie in that house in Kentucky. It was another little girl whose daddy had taken her to Burger King that afternoon. It was she who had been sitting at the table coloring when the police barged into her house. It was another little girl who was where she belonged, safe at home with her parents. Another little girl who, although undoubtedly con- fused by the excitement and chaos of the police charging into her world, would be soothed and reassured by her mother. Another little girl who would sleep in her own bed tonight.

It wasn't her Janie.

Her Janie wasn't safe, wasn't at home, and didn't have her mommy to comfort her. Her Janie was confused and scared and, if Stephanie Quick really did have psychic abilities, her Janie was wounded and hurting.

Blood. The psychic had seen blood.

Eliza felt light-headed and the room began to spin before her eyes.

When she awakened, she was lying on the sofa. Mack was bending over her, deeply concerned, his eyes studying her intently.

"It's all right, Eliza," he whispered as he stroked her forehead. "It's all right."

For a few seconds she was disoriented but, too quickly, the horror of what was happening came flooding into her mind. *Who has my baby? Where have they taken her? What are they doing to her?* Eliza felt the hope she had been clinging to slipping away.

"No, Mack," she answered. "It isn't all right. And it might never be all right again." Tears seeped from her eyes and she covered her face.

"We're far from the point where we have to give up," Mack said firmly, pulling her hands away. "You have to keep on fighting, for Janie and Mrs. Garcia."

Eliza looked into his eyes and reached up to touch his face. She knew he was right. She had to keep going, had to keep hoping, had to keep paying attention. But she was overwhelmed and overtired and overwrought. She needed more help and she knew it.

Katharine made some tea and toast and watched until Eliza consumed all of it while she waited for her friends to arrive. Within an hour, Annabelle, Margo, and B.J. were at the house. Eliza filled them in on the disappointing false lead in Kentucky and voiced her fears about what Stephanie Quick had said when they'd stood in Janie's bedroom earlier in the day.

"What do you think?" Eliza asked. "Do you think there could be any possible way this woman is legit? Do you think she can really see that Janie is hurt?"

"Anything's possible, Eliza," said Annabelle. "But do I think it's probable? I'm sorry, but I don't."

"I don't, either," said B.J. "I think the whole psychic thing is a load of crap. But I also have to say that I remember my grandmother talking about feelings she had about things that were going to happen, and wouldn't you know, some of them did!"

"She also said something that no one could know about but me," said Eliza. "She told me that John was glad I still wore the perfume that he loved. The fact that John loved that perfume was never reported, never in a magazine."

The three colleagues exchanged puzzled looks.

Eliza turned to Margo. "What do *you* think?" she asked.

"To tell you the truth, I'm skeptical

about supernatural gifts, extremely skeptical. But there is at least some research that supports paranormal phenomena. I have friends and patients who are convinced that extrasensory perception exists. You might be surprised by the number of successful businesspeople who go for palm and tarot card readings, who make their plans according to what the fortune-teller says. Are they all crazy?" Margo shrugged. "But I do know I've seen coincidences and had lucky guesses myself, picked up the phone to call someone just as that same person rang me. Synchronicity."

"So your answer is what?" asked Eliza.

"My answer is, I wouldn't bet the bank on Stephanie Quick and her psychic abilities, not by a long shot," said Margo. "But, at the same time, as long as you don't go overboard and become obsessed with everything she says, maybe it doesn't hurt to at least listen."

CHAPTER 76

Damn it. He had waited too long to clean the cuts and the children's aspirin hadn't done any good. The kid was running a fever and needed professional help. When this was all over, the plan was to return the child to her mother, but in good health.

The lights were on in the Urgentcare Center, but there were still too many cars in the parking lot to risk going inside. One by one, patients and medical personnel straggled out, got into their vehicles and drove away, eventually leaving just one car on the macadam.

"Now, you remember what I told you?"

said the man to the little girl. "I'm going to take off my mask. *Do not look at my face!* And when we get inside, let me do the talking. If you look at me or open your mouth, we're gonna kill your mother."

Janie nodded.

"Come on, kid. Let's go," he said as he lifted Janie out of his Jeep.

Janie cried out as her legs bent at the knees. He could feel the heat coming from the child's body as he carried her toward the building. When they got inside, there was no one in the waiting area.

"Hello?" he called out.

A young woman in a blue smock came to the reception desk. "I'm sorry," she apologized, gesturing to the clock on the wall. "We close at ten o'clock."

"It's just five after, Carol," he said reading her name tag.

"I know," she said, "but the doctor is gone. I'm just straightening up."

"Can't you take a look at her?" he asked. "She's in a lot of pain."

"I really shouldn't," Carol said. "It's against the rules, plus I'm not insured."

"Please," he begged. "Are you a nurse?"

"In training," she answered.

"Well, this isn't brain surgery. The kid just fell and cut her legs, but I'm afraid they might have gotten infected. Couldn't you just take a look?"

Carol regarded the child's flushed face. "All right," she said. "Bring her into the examining room."

With Janie perched on the edge of the examining table, the woman carefully pulled back the bandages wrapped around the child's knees. Tears ran down Janie's cheeks, but she didn't make a sound except for a few hiccups.

"It's all right, honey," said the nursing student. "It's all right to cry. I know it's painful. You really hurt yourself, didn't you?"

Janie nodded.

"How did you do this?" asked Carol.

The man answered for her. "She was running and she fell."

"What kind of surface was she running on?" she asked.

"Dirt," the man answered.

The nursing student directed herself

to Janie. "Do you know when you had your last tetanus shot, honey?"

Janie didn't answer.

"It's all right," he said. "Go ahead and tell the lady."

"I had some shots before camp started this summer," she volunteered.

"Oh, that's good," said Carol. "I'm sure your camp requires that everybody is up to date with their tetanus shots." She looked at the wounds again and shook her head. "These are really nasty-looking, and it's red and hot where her body is trying to fight the infection. I can clean them up, but I think she really needs to start taking an antibiotic. I can't write a prescription for that."

The man gestured to the cabinets that lined the walls. "Don't you have any on hand?" he asked.

"You know, I think we do have some in the other room," she said. "I'll get it after we finish here."

Carol spoke soothingly to Janie as she cleaned out the cuts. "So you're going to camp this year," she said, trying to distract the child. "I used to love camp when I was younger. What camp are you going to?"

"Camp Musquapsink," Janie answered automatically.

The man squeezed his hand around the child's arm and she didn't say another word. He stared at the nursing student but her head was down as she applied ointment and clean white bandages to the wounds. He couldn't see her face.

"All right," she said when she was finished. She headed straight for the door. "That should do it. Just wait here and I'll go see if I can find those antibiotics for you."

The nursing student went to the front desk and quietly rifled through the trash basket. She pulled the well-read newspaper out, looked at the picture of the little girl on the front page, and quickly scanned the article beneath it.

The child in the examining room resembled the girl in the picture, though she couldn't be completely certain. The picture captured Janie Blake smiling, full of life. The child she had just treated was solemn and withdrawn. Her eyes were glassy from fever.

But the article dispelled any doubt Carol had about picking up the phone and calling the authorities.

Musquapsink.

Janie Blake had gone to Camp Musquapsink.

"I told you to keep that mouth of yours shut," sneered the man. "Didn't I?"

Janie's eyes were wide with fear, her bottom lip trembling, but she stared straight ahead, afraid to look at him.

"Didn't I? Answer me," he demanded.

"Yes." The child could barely get the word out.

"Damn you," he hissed.

He opened a succession of drawers in the examining room until he found the instrument he wanted.

Carol made the call to the number listed in the article. Her heart pounded as the phone rang over and over again. Finally, someone answered.

"Find Janie hotline. May I help you?"

"Yes," Carol whispered. "I think Janie Blake is—"

"I'm sorry. Will you please speak up? I can't hear you. Please, repeat what you said."

The young woman started to clear her throat but, before she could, the ice-cold scalpel sliced across it.

She heard a vehicle approaching the house and looked out the window to see if it was the Jeep. It was. Hurriedly, she pulled on her mask.

The front door opened and the child walked in, head down, her knees wrapped in snowy white gauze.

She led Janie into the bedroom and turned on the television set. "You can watch it until you fall asleep," she said. After she shut the bedroom door behind her, she turned her attention to the man.

"I'm glad you took her to the Urgentcare," she said, taking off her mask. "That was the right thing to do."

"Well, I'm glad you're glad," he said, "because that little trip came with a heavy price tag."

"What's wrong?"

"Something came up at the Urgent-care. A situation."

"What kind of situation?" she asked with trepidation.

"The girl who helped us figured out who Janie was."

"Oh my God," she said, sinking down on the couch. "Are you sure?"

"Of course I'm sure!" he yelled. "She was on the phone saying Janie's name when I killed her."

She stared at him, unable to utter a word.

"Didn't you hear me?" he demanded.

"I heard you. I just can't believe what I heard." She covered her eyes with her hands. "What have you done to us?"

He shrugged. "I haven't done a damn thing to us. It's the girl at the Urgentcare who has the problem."

She looked at him with disbelief and

fear. "No one was supposed to get hurt. There was nothing in the plan about anyone getting killed."

"Yeah," he said flatly. "Well, the plan changed."

CHAPTER 77

Just before midnight, the ransom demand came by fax to the KEY News Broadcast Center in New York City. The number to which it had been sent was the one available on the KEY News Web site.

We have Janie Blake. She is alive and well but wants to come home. To get her back you have to pay two million dollars in unmarked bills. Get the money ready and we will be in touch with further directions.

The FBI was able to determine that the fax had been sent from the FedEx and Kinko's Office and Print on West Seventy-second Street in Manhattan.

THURSDAY
JULY 24

CHAPTER 78

"Wake up, Eliza, wake up." Mack shook her arm.

Eliza bolted upright. "What? What is it?" she asked fearfully.

"There's been a ransom demand, Eliza."

"She's alive then," Eliza whispered, closing her eyes. "Thank you, God. Thank you."

"They say she's fine," said Mack.

"What do they want?"

"Two million dollars," answered Mack. "They want it in unmarked bills. The fax said to get the money together and they'll let us know what to do next."

Eliza looked at the clock on the bed-side table. It was far too early in the morning to reach anyone at the bank. But she had the home number for her personal investment counselor, Kathy Joyal. Eliza knew that Kathy would willingly take her call at any hour, especially in this situation.

Eliza reached for the phone, profoundly grateful that there was finally something she herself could do to get her child back.

Though Mack said he wanted to grab a few hours of rest, Eliza knew there was no way that she'd be able to go back to sleep. She went to the kitchen and put on a pot of fresh coffee. As she offered the black brew to the agents posted in the garage, she could feel a change in the atmosphere. Last night, when the Kentucky lead had turned out to be bogus, the mood had been morose. Now, even though it was the middle of the night, the agents were wide awake and energized. The FBI was expert in dealing with ransom demands and the fax was just what they had been waiting for.

"Do you think they'll fax again?" asked Eliza.

"It's hard to say," considered Agent Gebhardt. "We may not be dealing with a mastermind here. He's already making mistakes."

"What kind?"

"Well, it wasn't too bright to send the fax from Kinko's," Gebhardt answered. "Too easy to trace and lots of people around as witnesses."

The time passed very slowly. At 5:00 A.M., Eliza turned on the television set. The early morning WKEY-TV news broadcast led with the abduction.

"Day four in the Janie Blake story and the seven-year-old daughter of KEY News anchorwoman Eliza Blake is still missing after her disappearance Monday morning from the day camp she was attending."

Video of a one-level brick house appeared on the screen. "Yesterday, law enforcement officials, acting on a tip, stormed the house of a Kentucky family, suspecting that Janie was being held inside."

A clean-shaven man with a slightly receding hairline spoke. "I understand. I truly do and I don't harbor any ill feelings. I have a daughter of my own and, if she was missing, I would want the police to do anything they could to find her."

Eliza wrote down the man's name, intending to ask Paige to send some flowers or a fruit basket to the family. Then, it suddenly occurred to her that since the fax demanding a ransom had been sent to KEY just before midnight, the news organization must know about it by now. Yet, there was no mention of it on the local broadcast. She was relieved about that. She wanted Janie back, safe and sound, and she didn't want media coverage jeopardizing that goal.

To be on the safe side, she called Range Bullock at home. He agreed that KEY News would not report that a ransom demand had been made; in fact, he had already issued that directive. "You can imagine how well that's going over with Linus," said Range. "Anything to drive the story and drive ratings."

"It must be killing him," said Eliza. "I'm going to call him myself to thank him for holding back."

She called the *KEY to America* news-room and asked for the executive pro-ducer.

"Eliza?"

"Yes."

"It's me. Annabelle."

"What are you doing answering the phone?"

"It's mayhem around here. Everybody is pitching in and doing something," said Annabelle. "I heard about the ransom demand. How are you?"

"Actually, I think it's a good thing," said Eliza. "At least now we've heard from these monsters and that gives the FBI something to go on."

"Right," said Annabelle. "The boss is champing at the bit to report it."

"I'll bet he is," said Eliza. "That's why I want to speak with him. I don't want anything screwing this up."

"All right, I'll get him," said Annabelle. Before getting off the phone, she added, "I hope this whole thing is over soon, Eliza. I'll be out there later this morning with B.J. And remember, you can call me anywhere, anytime."

The start of the conversation with Linus Nazareth was short and to the point. Linus made a big deal over the fact that he was holding back on the ransom demand information and Eliza thanked him profusely for doing so.

"Now that we're absolutely clear about that, how's it going there? How do you think Margo is doing with the show?" Eliza asked. "I thought she did well on the little bit I caught yesterday morning."

"Ah, she's all right," said Linus. "But she isn't you. Don't worry. Your job is secure."

"That's the last thing on my mind, Linus."

"Yeah, I guess you're relieved that these kidnappers have made themselves known. Now nobody is going to say you were in on it. But you know, you could really help Margo out by letting her interview you anyway," suggested Linus. "Think of what a coup that would be for her, how much exposure she'd get."

"You don't give up, do you?"

"I'm just saying . . ."

"How about this?" Eliza suggested. "As soon as I have Janie back, I promise that the first interview I give will be to Margo and *KTA.*"

"Not just the first interview," said Linus. "The only interview."

When Linus hung up the phone, he called Annabelle over. "I want you and B.J. to go up to Kinko's and get the manager to talk, see what you can find out."

Annabelle looked at him quizzically. "I thought we weren't going to report on this yet," she said.

"Yeah," said Linus. "But I want us to have the goods for when we do."

CHAPTER 79

At 9:15 A.M., Kathy Joyal called to say that the money was ready to be picked up whenever it was needed. By 9:30, the FBI had a description of the man who had used the fax machine at Kinko's the night before. According to the store manager, the guy was a fairly regular customer, usually using the all-night photocopying facilities.

"As a matter of fact," said the manager, "I think he's used his credit card to pay those other times."

CHAPTER 80

It was her turn to open up and bring in the doughnuts. Ruth Wilson balanced her coffee on top of the Krispy Kreme box she held with one hand while she locked the door of her Escort with the other. She noted with surprise the other car in the parking lot. Carol wasn't supposed to come until this afternoon since she had worked last night.

When she got to the front door of the Urgentcare, it was already unlocked. She went inside. The lights were on.

"Carol?" she called.

Ruth put the doughnut box down on

the reception desk and called out again. "Anybody here?"

She took the plastic top off the paper cup and took a sip of coffee. Ruth noticed Carol's bag, placed on a chair.

"Carol? Are you here?"

As she rounded the reception desk, Ruth slipped but caught herself from falling. She looked down and saw the large pool of blood that covered the linoleum floor.

CHAPTER 81

Passing through the reporters still camped out in front of the house, Stephanie Quick made her way to the front door and was granted entry.

"I had another dream last night," she told Eliza, Mack, and the FBI agents.

"Oh, yeah?" said Agent Gebhardt. "What was it *this* time?"

Stephanie ignored Gebhardt's tone. "In the dream Janie was near water."

"Now, that's specific, isn't it?" asked Gebhardt. "River, stream, lake, reservoir, ocean, swimming pool, or bathtub?"

"It was some sort of natural body of water," said Stephanie, ignoring the agent's sarcasm again. "And the water was moving. Rushing, really."

"Anything else?" asked Gebhardt with impatience.

"Yes," said Stephanie. "I'm getting a feeling about the letter *M*."

Agent Gebhardt bit her lip to keep herself from making another disparaging comment.

"Do you see kidnappers asking for ransom?" Eliza asked quietly.

Stephanie shook her head. "Not yet. No."

"Well, that's strange, because they have," Gebhardt said smugly.

The psychic looked puzzled. "No, I don't see that. I only get a feeling about the letter *M* and Janie near rushing water."

As Eliza escorted Stephanie to the door, she said, "You caught me totally off-guard yesterday when you said my husband was glad I still wore the same perfume."

Stephanie nodded. "I don't know how I know these things, Eliza, but I do."

CHAPTER 82

The cluttered apartment above a delicatessen on Ninth Avenue was not where he had imagined being at this point in his life. But so many things had not gone as planned.

He looked at the stacks of books and papers scattered around the floor and sighed heavily. He had tried so hard over the years, suffered so many rejections, worked so many miserable jobs just to pay the rent, all the while holding on to his dream. It was a dream that he had slowly come to realize wasn't going to come true.

In the solitary life he led, he had too

much time to think. That was a writer's blessing and his curse. The time to daydream led to the concoction of all sorts of fictional scenarios that, when transferred to the page, could entertain, enlighten, and delight. But in the downtime, when the mind had time to ruminate on the disappointments and unfairness of life—that's when he got into trouble.

The piles of rejected manuscripts showed how hard he had tried. He'd put every ounce of himself into his stories but no literary agent wanted to take him on as a client. He'd e-mailed pitch letters, sometimes even attaching his manuscript, directly to the publishing houses but his proposals were all met with letters of rejection. Nobody was interested, nobody wanted to take a chance on him.

It wasn't fair. No matter how hard he tried, he hadn't been able to catch a break. But in the past few days, an opportunity had presented itself and, in his desperation and anger, he had used his fertile imagination to come up with a plan to capitalize on that opportunity.

When he turned on the television, the

news at noon led with the Janie Blake story, but no mention was made of any ransom demand.

Was it possible they hadn't gotten his fax?

CHAPTER 83

The taxi stopped at the corner of Seventy-second Street. Annabelle paid the driver and got out. While B.J. unloaded his gear from the trunk, she looked in the direction of the Kinko's store. There were three dark SUVs double-parked out front, unmarked vehicles that Annabelle instantly recognized as belonging to law enforcement.

When B.J. joined her on the sidewalk, Annabelle motioned in the direction of the SUVs.

"Feds," said B.J.

"Uh-huh," said Annabelle. "Better get the exterior shots now."

B.J. made the necessary adjustments, lifted the camera to his shoulder and began recording, taking close-ups of the Kinko's signs, long shots of the building, and pans of the sidewalk and street out front, capturing images of pedestrians and the FBI vehicles.

"I don't think we should go inside until we see the agents leave," said Annabelle. "I doubt they'd welcome us questioning the Kinko's staff. We don't want to risk being thrown out and told to stay out."

They positioned themselves in the alcove of a building across the street and waited until they saw several men and one woman, dressed in conservative business attire, come hurriedly out of the building and get into the SUVs.

"Let's go," said Annabelle. She crossed the sidewalk, stepped into the street, and lifted her arm to hail a cab.

"What are you doing?" B.J. called after her. "I thought we were supposed to get the interview with the manager."

"We are," said Annabelle as a cab glided to a stop in front of them. "But I have a feeling we should follow those FBI guys instead."

CHAPTER 84

"We have the name and address of the person who sent the fax," said Agent Gebhardt. "Our people are on their way to the apartment right now."

Eliza closed her eyes and prayed with an intensity more powerful than she had at any other time in her life. She thought of the stolen minutes she'd spent in the hospital chapel when John was dying. She realized now that, though her initial prayers then had begged God not to let her husband die, those prayers had evolved as she became resigned to the fact that John wasn't going to make it. In the end, she prayed for him to be free from pain, she prayed for him to have a peaceful death, and she prayed for the strength to go on, have their baby, and live without him.

This time was different. Janie was her only child. Janie didn't have a cruel and vicious disease. Janie had been taken from her, and if the kidnappers simply let her go, or the FBI rescued her, all could be well again. If the strength of her prayers might actually determine her daughter's and Mrs. Garcia's fate, Eliza felt she had to focus with every fiber of her being.

It was all she could do.

Agent Gebhardt signaled to Agent Laggie. He followed her out to the kitchen.

"This is too easy," she said in a low voice as she poured some coffee.

Laggie took the cup she offered him. "I've been thinking the same thing myself," he said.

CHAPTER 85

Feeling her way in the darkness, Mrs. Garcia inched toward the steps. She jumped in fright as something lightly grazed her forehead.

What was that?

She stood for a minute and composed herself. Then, slowly, she raised her arms and groped tentatively through the black air. Her fingers touched a string. When she pulled on it, a bald, low-watt bulb barely lit the underground room.

Unaccustomed to any light, Mrs. Garcia momentarily squeezed her eyes shut, but she gradually adjusted and was able to see the place where she was held captive. There was not much to the space, a square, windowless room with walls made of two-by-fours spaced about two feet apart. In between the wooden struts were sandbags piled from floor to ceiling. The shelves that lined the walls were mostly bare save for a few empty baskets and the mason jars she had felt earlier. Ravenous, she considered opening one of them now to savor its contents but, not knowing how long they had been stored down there, she thought better of it. Hunger was preferable to food poisoning.

She noticed there were two pipes, one at the ceiling and the other down near the floor, probably designed to afford ventilation of the gases given off by the fruits and vegetables once stored in the baskets. Mrs. Garcia was relieved to realize she'd have enough oxygen.

Certain the only way to get out was through the trapdoor at the top of the stairs, Mrs. Garcia climbed the first few wooden steps. She positioned herself beneath the door, crouched down, and then sprang up, ramming her shoulder upward. She winced with pain but the door did not budge.

Mrs. Garcia forced herself to try again, but this time one of the rotted steps gave way beneath her and she crashed to the cement floor.

CHAPTER 86

The smell of corned beef and vinegar permeated the hot air in the narrow stairwell as the FBI agents carefully climbed upward. When they got to the landing, they separated, some to one side of the door, some to the other. A few positioned themselves across the hall and on the stairs. All were determined that no one inside the apartment would escape.

He was sitting at his desk, preparing his next letter, a list of instructions on where and how the ransom money should be delivered. He went through several drafts, not happy with any of them.

He sat back in his chair and stared at the computer screen. There was so much riding on this, his future, really. He had to get it right. Two million dollars would enable him to get out of this dump, leave his lousy job, and devote himself full-time to his writing. After a while he might even be able to use this experience in his fiction. What a story that would be. Hollywood would surely come calling on that one. He would finally live his dream.

The persistent banging at the door wrenched him from his reverie.

CHAPTER 87

The people who passed by on Ninth Avenue scarcely glanced at the television cameraman and his female companion staked out on the sidewalk in front of the delicatessen.

"That's one of the things I love most about New York," said B.J. "Nobody's all that impressed with anything. They couldn't give a damn what we're doing."

"They'd be impressed if they thought that Janie Blake was inside and the FBI were in there trying to rescue her," said Annabelle.

B.J. smiled. "God, I hope I'll be getting pictures of her any second," he said.

"And it'll be exclusive video to boot. Nobody else is out here. I can picture Linus jumping up and down with glee."

"When they start coming out, you're on your own," said Annabelle. "Because, as soon as I see Janie, I'm going to get on the phone and call Eliza."

The door opened. An FBI agent came out of the building, walked to one of the SUVs, and opened the back door. He was followed by a cluster of agents who surrounded a disheveled-looking man, holding his arms as they escorted him to the vehicle.

B.J.'s camera recorded their movements.

Annabelle moved closer to the doorway, eager to view the child being carried safely out of the building. She strained to see if there were more people coming down the stairwell.

There weren't.

CHAPTER 88

Phil Doyle needed a mental health day or, at least, a mental health afternoon. He deserved one. He worked hard, made a good living, took care of his wife and two sons. But sometimes, he just needed to get away by himself and have some fun.

After lunch, he got his car out of the company garage and started up the West Side Highway. As he drove over the George Washington Bridge, he listened to the radio and heard the latest news on the kidnapping. The FBI had raided the apartment of some guy who had sent a ransom demand. The feds had the guy in custody, but there was no child in the apartment and the authorities were convinced Janie had never been there at all.

An hour and a half later, Phil was in the Poconos, parking his car outside the lodge. He left his cell phone in the car, knowing from experience that there was no service where he was going. He went inside, paid, registered, and signed a waiver that he wouldn't sue anyone if he got hurt.

"Want walkie-talkies?" asked the man at the desk.

"Nah," said Phil. "I'd get them if one of my sons was with me, but I'm by myself. I don't really need one."

Phil went outside again and boarded the bus that took him up to the meeting post. Once there, Phil had his air tank filled, got his ammunition, and took possession of his rented gun, a Tippmann 98. Though, even in the woods, it was a hot day, Phil pulled the camouflage jumpsuit over his shorts and T-shirt. He'd have a better chance of survival if he blended in with the environment.

Phil was introduced to the man who was going to referee the fight and shook hands with his opponents, the other guys who had come for the same thrill as Phil. Together, they all hiked up to the field.

It wasn't a field in the agricultural sense, open and uncovered, with no place to hide. Instead, it was an expansive, seemingly boundless area of mountainous terrain covered with tall trees and thick underbrush, full of rocks, caves, and streams. It was in the middle of nowhere and it was a field of war.

Adjusting his safety mask and the baseball cap that covered his head, Phil waited for the horn to blow.

Everybody scrambled, running to find the best position. Phil looked for a spot where he would be hidden, a place where he'd be able to pick off his opponents without their ever knowing what had hit them. He moved from cover to cover, from tree to tree, from rock to ditch to cave, crouching to make himself as small as possible. At each place, he stared through the plastic shield that covered his eyes and managed to get off several shots. But Phil didn't shoot just for the sake of shooting. He conserved his ammunition, hoping that, when the time was right, he would let loose with a barrage that would annihilate his enemies.

CHAPTER 89

"I shouldn't be surprised that some mis-guided individual would actually try to take advantage of this nightmare," Eliza said softly, "but, at the same time, I just can't believe it."

No one else in the kitchen said a word. Mack reached out and put his hand on Eliza's shoulder. Katharine and Paul stared down at the table, desolate with disappointment. The FBI agents trained their eyes on the view through the French doors out to the yard. Even Daisy seemed to understand the anguish that permeated the atmosphere in the room. The dog walked up to Eliza and rubbed gently against her mistress's leg to comfort her.

Eliza bent over and stroked the dog's golden coat. "You're a good girl, Daisy," she whispered. "A good girl."

The dog looked up at her and Eliza remembered how excited Janie had been when the yellow Lab puppy had arrived in their lives. Eliza had been skeptical about the idea of having a pet at first, but Janie had won her over with her enthusiasm and love for the sweet little dog. As Daisy grew ever larger over the next two years, Janie played with her, cuddled with her, and learned early lessons of responsibility as the child made sure there was water in the dog's bowl and that she brushed Daisy's soft coat. Daisy, in turn, allowed herself to be hugged, hard and often. She fetched the plastic toys that Janie threw, followed her young owner around, and watched over her.

"Are you feeling that you didn't protect our girl, Daisy?" asked Eliza plaintively. "I feel that way, too."

The dog nuzzled Eliza's thigh.

"It's all right, Daisy. It's got to be all right," said Eliza, her voice breaking.

"But we have to get Janie and Mrs. Garcia back. How are we going to get them back?"

"Do you want to take a call from Annabelle?" Mack asked.

Eliza nodded and accepted the phone from him. She walked into the bathroom and shut the door behind her.

"I'm so sorry, Eliza. To have your hopes raised like that is really terrible."

"You have no idea."

"You're right, I don't."

Leaning against the wall, Eliza slid down to the floor and pulled her knees to her chest. She pounded her fist on the tile floor. "Damn it, who are these people and why have they invaded my life like this? How are we going to find them?"

"Let the FBI and the police do their jobs, Eliza. That's what they're trained to do."

"They aren't infallible, Annabelle. And honestly, I don't think I should leave it entirely in their hands."

"What do you mean?" asked Annabelle.

"You know the psychic I told you about?"

"Yeah, what about her?"

"She was back this morning and she told me that the kidnappers had *not* sent a ransom demand. When Stephanie said that, I thought it showed she really wasn't tuned in to anything, because we *had* gotten a ransom note. But, now, I'm thinking she was right because the ransom demand *wasn't* from the real kidnappers."

"Oh, Eliza." Annabelle's voice was soothing. "I don't think you should be putting faith in that woman, I really don't."

"She said she dreamed that Janie was near water," said Eliza.

"That's a pretty broad category," said Annabelle. "Pretty much everybody is near some kind of water. I'm holding a bottle of it in my hand right now."

"Moving or rushing water, Annabelle."

"Still a wide category. Near a beach, near a river, near a waterfall, near a fountain?"

"And the letter *M*," Eliza continued, ignoring Annabelle's skepticism. "Stephanie sees the letter *M* figuring prominently."

"Manhattan?" asked Annabelle. "That's where you work every day. It could be Musquapsink—after all, that's where Janie was taken. Or maybe it's Mackinac, Michigan. That has *two M*s and it has *water,* too."

"I see what you mean," said Eliza, suddenly embarrassed to mention Stephanie's bridal veil vision. "Still, I just have a feeling that Stephanie knows what she's talking about." Eliza felt for the zodiac medallion in her pocket and hoped that Stephanie could somehow lead them to Janie and Mrs. Garcia.

CHAPTER 90

In the early afternoon, the figure in the Olive Oyl mask came in with a tray and laid it on the table. She leaned forward and shook Janie's arm.

"Come on. You've got to get up and eat something," she said. "You've been sleeping since you got home from the Urgentcare last night."

Janie opened her eyes, looked at the grotesque mask, and closed them tight again.

The woman put her hand on the child's forehead. "You're still hot," she said. "Wait here while I go get the thermometer."

Janie waited until she heard the footsteps leave the room, then she opened her eyes. She got up and went to the television and switched it on, keeping the sound low. She hoped she would see Mommy again, like she had early this morning before the bad people woke up. She had turned on the television and had seen her mommy talking to her, telling her she was coming to get her. Mommy said it again and again as Janie changed channels on all the morning news shows.

Yet as much as she was relieved to see Mommy, Janie was worried more than ever. The people on the television said that Mommy and the police weren't having any luck in finding her and Mrs. Garcia. Why did they look in Kentucky? They should be looking here. But Janie didn't even know where *here* was.

Maybe Daisy can help Mommy. Maybe Daisy can use her nose and follow the trail to find me and Mrs. Garcia.

CHAPTER 91

Throughout the morning, people wandered into the community room at St. Luke's Catholic Church in Ho-Ho-Kus, New Jersey, as word spread about the volunteer center being set up there. By lunchtime, the crowd was so large that the pastor of the church offered the use of the gymnasium at the neighboring school as well. He also lent a fax machine and a copier and gave his permission for coffee and doughnuts to be served in the school cafeteria.

Susan Feeney stood in the middle of the community room, clipboard in hand, taking names, addresses, and phone numbers and gradually giving the volunteers assignments. Several offered to bring in their laptop computers. Many agreed to put up flyers. Others said that, when the time came, they wanted to be part of any search party.

Having spent much of the night on the Internet, reading about missing children and suggestions on what should be done to recover them, Susan had learned that it could do some good to have the media aware of a volunteer center. She sent one of the volunteers over to Saddle Ridge Road to alert the news people staked out in front of Eliza's house. Within the hour, five news crews, eager for any fresh video elements, showed up to record what was happening.

Susan found microphones being thrust in her face. She answered the questions about what the volunteer center planned to do the best she could and assured them that she would make the flyers available to them. She also announced that a candlelight vigil was going to be held that night.

As the news people began to straggle out, one of them lingered to introduce herself. "I'm Annabelle Murphy, a producer at KEY News and a good friend of Eliza's. I just wanted to thank you for all you are doing."

Susan extended her hand. "No reason to thank me," she said. "I wish I could do more, but this is all I can think of. I still feel so guilty that I didn't make it a point to get that license plate."

Annabelle made the connection. "Ah, so you're the neighbor who saw the van."

"Guilty," said Susan. "Every time anyone from the media has rung my doorbell over the last few days, I've either not answered or I've made my husband get it. I just couldn't face them. I'm only talking about it to you now because you're a friend of Eliza's."

"And you live across the street from her?" asked Annabelle.

"Across the street and down a ways," said Susan.

"You wouldn't want to talk about what you saw that morning now, for the camera, would you?"

Susan looked uncomfortable. "No. Not really."

"It might be helpful to other people," Annabelle urged. "Make them realize that they should pay attention to anything that seems out of the ordinary in their neighborhoods."

"Well," Susan said, wavering. "Maybe something positive could come out of my mistake."

"Great," said Annabelle, waving at B.J. to come over. As the cameraman attached a small microphone to Susan's shirt, Annabelle knew that they were going to win kudos back at the Broadcast Center. She was scoring an exclusive interview with the only person who had seen the alleged kidnapping vehicle.

The interview itself didn't provide any new information, but having Susan Feeney on camera, talking about what she had seen, was a valuable element to have. Annabelle was certain the video would be used on the *Evening Headlines* and tomorrow morning on *KEY to America.*

As B.J. removed the microphone and began to pack up his gear, the women continued to chat.

"You know, if positions had been reversed, and my child had been taken and Eliza hadn't paid attention when she could have, I'm afraid I would have been angry with her," said Susan. "But, instead, when I talked about it with her yesterday, Eliza was very understanding. The only thing she asked me to do was go over and check on Mrs. Garcia's family."

"Have you done that yet?" asked Annabelle.

"Not yet, but I'm going over there soon."

Annabelle immediately saw the opportunity. "Mind if we tag along?" she asked.

The KEY News car followed the late-model BMW the few miles into Westwood. As they pulled up, Annabelle and B.J. saw police cars parked in front of the rundown two-story house. A cluster of people who looked Hispanic were gathered in the driveway.

B.J. immediately got out of the car, unloaded his camera gear from the back, and started shooting. Annabelle went over to one of the cops.

"What's going on?" she asked.

"And you are?" asked the officer.

"Sorry," said Annabelle as she pulled out her press pass and held it up for his inspection. "This is the house where the family of the woman who disappeared with Eliza Blake's child live, right?"

"Used to live," answered the policeman. "It looks like they've taken off."

"Why do you think they would do that?" Annabelle asked.

The officer shrugged. "Look around," he said. "See these people? Not one of them is in this country legally. Maria and Vicente Rochas are no different."

Annabelle looked at the quiet people standing in the driveway. Their expressions were solemn, worried even, but none of them was running away.

"For the most part, we turn a blind eye," the policeman continued. "We know they live here, dozens of them sometimes packed into one house. But most of the time they stay quiet and don't bother anybody. They do the jobs that nobody else wants to do anymore, and they do those jobs for very little pay. So even though some people resent it if they're taking advantage of social services, others like having them around for the cheap labor."

Annabelle nodded. "But they all know they could be sent back at any time, right?"

"Yep. And they've seen it happen, too. So most of them try to stay under the radar. But this week, with the abduction of the Blake kid and her nanny, the Rochas couple were under our scrutiny. That's what made them run."

Annabelle called Eliza and told her that the Rochas family had fled.

"I don't understand," said Eliza.

"The cops were breathing down their necks," said Annabelle, "and they were scared." Annabelle paused. "You don't think . . . ?" Her voice trailed off.

"I don't think *what*?" asked Eliza.

"That they have something to do with the abductions and that's why they left?"

"No, I do not," Eliza said firmly. "Maria

and Vicente Rochas are honest, hard-working people who want to stay in America rather than go back to a poor and dangerous country that holds little future for them. They thought the authorities were going to arrest them—and, at the very least, deport them. I'm certain that's why they ran."

Driving back to the Broadcast Center, Annabelle voiced her frustration. "We're spending all our time gathering video elements and interviews for the day-of-air story and we aren't doing enough to find Janie."

B.J. slowed as they approached the E-ZPass toll lane to the George Washington Bridge. "It's pretty hard to investigate when you have specific assignments on what you have to get for the piece," he said. "They're paying us to get what they want for their coverage of what's happening today."

"There just aren't enough hours," Annabelle said as she looked out the car window to the Hudson River and the New York City skyline. "You know, it's terrible.

Eliza is so desperate, she's clinging to anything that psychic says. The latest is, Janie is near water and something with the letter *M*."

"Minnesota, Mississippi, Massachusetts, Maine?" said B.J., smiling in spite of himself.

"Ridiculous, huh?" said Annabelle.

"Sure," said B.J. "You need something a lot more specific than that to go on."

It had been nagging at her since her conversation with Eliza, and now Annabelle remembered. The cookies with the disturbing note written to Eliza. The cookies from the Marzipan Bakery.

She had looked the town up on the map but hadn't gone any further than that because she hadn't had the time. They'd been busy with what turned out to be the bogus ransom demand and then shooting at the volunteer center and at the Guatemalan family's home. Tomorrow, Linus would surely have more ideas about what he wanted them to do and, again, the day wouldn't be their own.

"I have an idea," said Annabelle. "How would you like to pick me up at three A.M.?"

"I'd rather stick pins in my eyes," said B.J.

"Seriously, Beej." She told him about the Marzipan Bakery.

"And you want to go there because of the letter *M*?" B.J. asked incredulously.

"No, I want to go there because of the creepy letter sent to Eliza," said Annabelle, "but I guess the *M* thing is the icing on top. Come on. It's only about an hour's drive."

"Yeah? And what do you think we're going to get at four o'clock in the morning?"

"Baking is done overnight, so somebody will be there," said Annabelle. "We can ask our questions, see what we can find out, see what video you can shoot, and be back in New York before our paid workday is scheduled to start."

CHAPTER 92

She was a prisoner in her own house. She couldn't go outside for some fresh air, couldn't take a walk to clear her head, couldn't take a ride in the car to get away for a while because the press was out there, ready to ambush her.

Eliza got up from her chair. "I'm going upstairs to take a shower," she announced.

She stood beneath the soothing spray and let the warm water cover her, washing the tears from her cheeks and easing the stiffness in her neck and shoulders. It was a relief to get away from the tension downstairs, if only for a little while.

As Eliza dried herself, she remembered again what Stephanie Quick had said that morning, remarks that Eliza hadn't paid much attention to, her mind focused on the ransom note and the possibility of Janie's imminent return. Stephanie had said that the kidnappers hadn't sent a ransom demand yet. As soon as Stephanie had said that, Eliza had tuned her out—but it turned out that the psychic had been right.

Since Stephanie was right about that, and she had been right about the green face paint and her vision about John and the perfume, she could be right about the letter *M* and Janie's being near moving water. *Please God,* thought Eliza, *let Janie be near the water, not in it.*

She dressed in fresh clothes, went downstairs, and marched in to talk to Agent Gebhardt. "What's being done with the lead that Stephanie Quick gave us about the water?" Eliza asked forcefully.

Agent Gebhardt looked up, her facial expression perplexed. "That's not a lead,

Eliza. That's just a general statement, from a psychic, no less. And even if we were to treat it as a lead, where would you suggest we start? Where would you look for moving water?"

"Well, we could let the public know about it at least," said Eliza. "Then people all around the country, around the world for that matter, would know and could be paying attention."

The FBI agent didn't comment.

Eliza's despair turned to anger. "All right," she announced. "If you guys won't, I will. I'm doing the interview for *KEY to America* and I'm going to tell the world what the psychic saw."

CHAPTER 93

The Internet, and volunteers all around the country, made it possible for flyers featuring the faces of Janie Blake and Carmen Garcia to be displayed in post offices and hospitals throughout the United States. Flyers were stapled to trees and telephone poles and taped in the windows of convenience stores, fast-food restaurants, gas stations, and low-rent motels, all in the hope that someone would recognize the faces and have an idea of who was holding one child and her caretaker, or where to find them.

Nell studied a yellow flyer tacked to a fence that surrounded the grocery store parking lot. She looked around to make sure no one was watching her. Then she reached up and pulled the flyer down, ripping it. She crumpled the paper in her hand and stuffed it in her bag.

She went inside the store and saw another flyer, blue this time, on the bulletin board. But there were too many people who could spot her if she took it, so she left it where it was. All around town, she found multicolored flyers identifying the missing pair and urging anyone with any knowledge or suspicion to contact the police.

Nell took down as many flyers as she could.

CHAPTER 94

Linus Nazareth was thrilled when Eliza called and told him she was going to do the interview.

"You want to do it live in the morning, or do you want us to tape it?" he asked. "Either way, we could come out and do it at your house if you'd rather not come into the Broadcast Center."

"Let's tape it tonight," said Eliza. "That way, if I forget to say something important, we can go back and edit it in. And I think I'd rather come in to do it. I've got to get out of this house for a couple of hours."

"Perfect," said Linus. "I'm wondering,

would you be willing to bring in a video-tape of Janie, too?"

Eliza considered the request. She hated sharing her personal home videos with the world, but her public exposure had gotten them into this horror, so more public exposure might get them out of it.

"All right, Linus. I'll bring one with me."

"Yes!" said Linus with enthusiasm.

Eliza could picture him pumping the air with his fist.

"Linus, do me a favor and don't be so damn happy."

His tone changed immediately. "You're right. I apologize. I'm sorry that the ransom demand turned out to be bogus, Eliza," he said. "I really am."

Yeah, thought Eliza, *but I bet you're not so sorry that the story is continuing. I bet you're not sorry you are going to be exclusive with the interview and I bet you're not sorry you can tease the hell out of it so tomorrow morning's ratings are through the roof.*

The videotapes and discs were kept in a cabinet in the den. All of them were marked by subject but not filed in any particular chronological order.

Eliza picked one marked JANIE SWIMMING and put it into the machine. She watched, with an increasing tightness in her chest, the images of Janie wearing inflatable water wings and paddling in a swimming pool. Eliza recognized it as one of the pools at the Grand Floridian in Walt Disney World. *Janie was three years old when we went there,* she thought. *We need something more current than that.*

JANIE AND NASTY SANTA. *That should do it.* Last Christmas, Janie had begun asking questions about the existence of Santa Claus, but she had still wanted to cover her bets and alert him to what she hoped to find under the tree. Eliza had suggested they go into New York City to find Santa, but Janie had insisted they go to the local mall, where her school friends were going. The outing turned into a disaster.

They'd been there when the mall opened because Eliza hoped to avoid a long line and the curious stares that inevitably followed her. When they got to Santa Claus, there were already two other children in line.

Eliza fought to control herself as she watched the pictures of Janie waiting her turn. The child's face glowed with excitement, her cheeks pink, her eyes sparkling blue. *That will certainly be the shot they'll use on the broadcast,* thought Eliza. *Let the world see the vibrance and innocence of my precious girl.*

She kept watching as Janie walked up to Santa's chair and stood beside him. He offered her his knee, but Janie shook her head. Santa might have been miffed, or just miscast for the job, but he definitely wasn't very friendly after that.

Eliza had gotten closer so the camera would pick up the audio.

"And what can I bring you for Christmas, little girl?" he asked.

"A new bike," said Janie. "A pink one."

"You don't already have a bike?" asked Santa.

"I do," said Janie, "but it's too little for me now and it's red. I want a pink one."

"Do you think you deserve a new bike?" he asked her rather pointedly.

Janie looked at him with uncertainty.

"Have you been a good girl and done what your mommy and daddy told you to do?"

Janie nodded.

"Are you sure about that?" he asked.

Janie's bottom lip began to quiver. "Well, I've been good for my mommy."

"What about your daddy?" he asked. "Haven't you been good for him?"

Janie started to hiccup.

Eliza intervened. "She's been very good, Santa," she called out.

But the damage had been done. Janie pulled back from the man in the red suit and ran to Eliza. The camera had been turned off after that.

Eliza's heart had ached. A simple trip to see Santa had turned into a painful reminder for the child that her father wasn't with her. Janie had hiccupped, as she often did when she was upset or nervous, the whole ride home.

It occurred to Eliza that Janie was probably suffering with the hiccups now, while she was going through this ordeal. She wondered if the hiccups were worth mentioning to the FBI.

CHAPTER 95

Janie lay blindfolded on the mattress, staring into the darkness. She could hear the man in the next room. He was grunting loudly. Every so often Janie heard something hit the floor. Then the noises stopped.

The door opened. She knew the man was checking on her. She didn't move.

"After I finish lifting my weights, I'll bring you something to eat," said the man.

Janie didn't answer.

"Suit yourself, you little brat." He slammed the door closed again.

Janie whimpered quietly as she turned over and tried to fall asleep. The lady at the Urgentcare had been nice but her legs still hurt. The lady reminded her of her mother and Mrs. Garcia trying to make her all better. Janie wished that she had been able to tell the lady at the Urgentcare to call Mommy, but if she had, the man had said he would kill Mommy. Besides, the lady never came back after she went to get the medicine.

Her small body shuddered as she hiccupped.

She wished so much she was with Mommy now. Mrs. Garcia promised Mommy would be coming.

Where is she?

CHAPTER 96

When six-year-old Melissa Bushell got home from Camp Musquapsink, she ate some grapes and drank some milk. Then she asked her mother if she could watch the video from the swimming race the day before.

Glad to have something to occupy the child while she started dinner, her mother cued up the video. But as the images appeared on the screen, Karen Bushell found herself sitting down to watch alongside her daughter.

"There I am!" shouted Melissa.

"You did a great job in that race,

sweetie," said her mother as she reached out and stroked the child's hair.

"I know I did," Melissa said, smiling happily. "Let's watch it again."

"*You* can watch it again," said Karen. "*I* have to start making dinner." She rewound the video, hit the PLAY button, and left the room. She was just opening the refrigerator door when she heard Melissa call out. Karen ran back to the family room.

"Come back and look, Mommy." Melissa pointed at the screen. "There's a man watching the race through the fence."

CHAPTER 97

Crouched behind a giant hemlock, Phil waited and regrouped. Air came in from the vents at the bottom of his safety mask as he breathed heavily from exertion and excitement.

One by one, many of his opponents had been picked off, either by him or by the other guys. He estimated that there were only a half dozen of them still left out here.

Phil listened intently for some sound of movement, but it was quiet. He had two choices. He could stay where he was and hope that his enemies would come to him, or he could go out there and try to hunt them down.

Slowly, he rose and walked out from behind the tree. He had ventured out only a few steps when he felt the stinging pain in his chest. White paint exploded across his jumpsuit and splattered over his plastic eye shield.

They got me, he thought with disappointment. *Man, that's going to leave a big black and blue.*

Knowing he'd been killed, Phil threw his hands up in the air and walked off the paintball battlefield.

Phil started back, following what he thought was the trail to the post. After half an hour, he knew he was lost. His chest was sore and his legs were tired. He sat on the trunk of a fallen hemlock to rest.

In the stillness of the forest, the silence was broken by chirping birds. Phil also thought he heard the sound of moving water. He ached for a drink of cool water, but he would have to wait until he got back to the post and bought a bottle of the pure stuff. *The sooner the better.*

As Phil stood up to begin retracing his steps, he thought he heard the noise of a passing car. *There must be a road over there,* he thought.

He could either turn around and hike all the way back or he could follow the sound of the car and find the road that must be nearby.

A deer darted across Phil's path. He made his way with care, climbing over termite-ridden fallen trees and rotted stumps and through the ferns that covered the forest floor. Just when he thought he had made another mistake by choosing this way, the dusty road appeared before him.

He stood for a moment trying to decide which direction would be best. His eyes were drawn downward by the movement of a chipmunk that scurried across the dirt. The rodent scampered into the greenery at the side of the path and was gone from sight.

Phil spotted something else at the side of the road and he moved closer to see what it was. He bent down and picked up a cluster of multicolored beads strung together to form a necklace.

Some of the plastic beads had letters on them, letters that spelled out a name.

J-A-N-I-E.

CHAPTER 98

She was in her room getting dressed to go into the city for the interview when Agent Gebhardt knocked. Eliza pulled on a robe and opened the door.

"We think we have something, Eliza."

Eliza stood back and indicated that the FBI agent should come into the bedroom. "What?" she asked. "What is it?"

"A body was found this morning at an Urgentcare in Milford, Pennsylvania."

Eliza's knees buckled. "Oh my God," she cried out.

Agent Gebhardt reached out to her. "No, it wasn't Janie or Mrs. Garcia,

Eliza. I'm so sorry for scaring you like that."

Eliza sat on the edge of the bed. "Milford," she repeated. "The letter *M*. Stephanie Quick said she saw the letter *M*."

"It was the body of a young woman, a nursing student," Agent Gebhardt continued, ignoring the reference to the psychic. "She was murdered. The coworker who found her said she had volunteered to close the place last night." The agent neglected to fill Eliza in on the gory details of how the murder had been committed.

Eliza tried to control her breathing while she waited for Gebhardt to continue.

"The thing that has us interested is the fact that a woman called into the hotline from that same Urgentcare last night. The person who took the call said the woman was speaking very softly, whispering, but he's positive he heard the woman say 'Janie Blake' before the connection was broken."

"And you think that the woman who called the hotline was the nursing student who was killed?" asked Eliza, her pulse quickening again. "That she had some information about Janie she was trying to tell us before she died?"

Agent Gebhardt shrugged. "We can't say that for certain. But it sure seems like more than a coincidence that a call comes from that Urgentcare just after closing time last night, a call that's cut off, and then this morning the last person known to be at the place turns up dead."

"What do we do now?" asked Eliza.

"Our guys are up there and they will let us know as soon as they have anything," said Agent Gebhardt. "In the meantime, you should go ahead and do your interview. Get your message across, get some more publicity. Somebody might be listening out there who can lead us to Janie and Mrs. Garcia."

CHAPTER 99

"This will probably be a wild-goose chase," the police officer said to his partner. "If those kids saw a black van on Monday afternoon, it's long gone by now."

"Yeah, you're right," said the other patrolman, "but we've got to check anyway." As they rounded the corner of the dry-cleaning plant, they saw a white Volvo station wagon parked on the cracked and otherwise deserted macadam.

"Eureka."

They called the find into headquarters.

"You search around the perimeter of the building. I'll go over the parking lot."

The men got out of the police vehicle and began pacing the area.

"Hey, Barry. Come over here."

"What have you got?"

The policeman pointed to the strip of green construction paper stapled together to form a circle. A dirty yellow feather dangled from the band.

"Somebody's been playing cowboys and Indians."

"You thinking what I'm thinking?"

The other cop nodded. "Janie Blake was last seen with paint on her face. The kid was decorated for Indian day at camp. What's an Indian without a headdress?"

He reached down to pick up the paper headpiece.

"Careful, Arnie," warned his partner. "If there are prints on that thing, you don't want to screw them up."

CHAPTER 100

Margo couldn't remember the last time she had been this tense. The kidnapping had shaken her deeply, and so far she had felt utterly powerless to help her friend. With the interview, Margo felt she was being given the opportunity to help get out further news of the kidnapping investigation and to present Eliza to the audience as the devoted mother she was. Margo was intent on being prepared and doing it right.

In the years of medical school, internship, residency, and hospital and private practice, Margo had seen countless examples of people who had been pushed to their limits and finally had broken. Afterward, it took years of nurturing to build them back. Some were never whole again.

Margo was glad she would be the one questioning Eliza, primarily because she wanted to ensure that the interview would be handled with the delicacy it deserved. Eliza was under extreme pressure as she waited for word on the fate of her child and Margo didn't want this interview to add to an already almost unbearable load. Despite Linus's urging, Margo had already decided she would not ask Eliza to respond to the ridiculous reports that she herself was a suspect.

Margo looked at her watch. Ten minutes until the hour. This would be the time to reach him, while he was between patients.

She made the call.

She waited for her colleague to pick up the phone.

"Margo. Good to hear from you. I caught you on television this morning. Nice going."

"Thanks," said Margo. "But I'm afraid I'm a duck out of water there. And that leads to the reason I'm calling. I need your help, need your opinion."

"Shoot."

"I'm about to interview Eliza Blake."

"That's a terrible situation. Terrible."

"It is and I don't want to make it worse with this interview. I don't want to screw it up."

"You won't, Margo, I'm sure you won't. What exactly are you concerned about?"

"That I'll ask her something that might hurt her."

"She's not going to be hurt by anything you ask her. The hurt comes from what's happened to her child. Whoever took her daughter is the one who has hurt her. Unless you plan on attacking her, I don't think you're going to damage her. I don't know the woman, Margo, but I know some of the things she's been through. She's survived them, and she's not only survived but she's thrived in a pretty high-anxiety professional world."

"Losing a child is different," said Margo.

"But she hasn't lost the child, not yet anyway. And let's hope she doesn't." Her colleague paused momentarily before continuing. "But I suppose we should acknowledge, Margo, that there's also the horrific possibility that Janie will never be found or won't make it through this alive."

"Eliza would blame herself for the rest of her life," Margo whispered. "Whatever kind of life would she have after that?"

"Look, Margo, it's not a therapy session. It's a television interview. You don't have to probe, you don't have to get into Eliza's innermost feelings, just ask the questions you think you should, the questions the audience would ask if they were in your place. Trust your instincts. And trust Eliza's strength."

Trust your instincts.
Trust your instincts.

The words filled Margo's head. She just had to go with her gut, question Eliza and see where the interview went.

As she went over the questions she had planned to ask, Margo's thoughts turned to the psychic who had been sharing her premonitions with Eliza. She hoped Stephanie Quick's instincts were wrong and that Janie wasn't hurt, or worse.

CHAPTER 101

He wasn't sure which way to go, but Phil Doyle started walking along the dirt road. He didn't realize he was going deeper into the forest and farther away from civilization. Instead, he was thrilled when he spotted the small house and separate shed set back from the road.

Phil noted that there were telephone lines coming from the house, lines that draped from pole to pole as far as he could see in both directions. It was getting late and it would be dark soon. There was no way he wanted to spend the night in these woods. He needed to call for help and let the police know about the necklace he'd found.

Approaching the house, he considered the possibility that Janie Blake and her kidnapper could be inside. If that were the case, he would be risking his life. Phil decided he would try to see in the window before knocking on the door.

As he crept around the foundation of the small house, Phil saw that some of the windows at the rear were covered with planking, allowing no view in or out. He positioned himself near one that he supposed would be an opening from a bedroom. The walls of the cabin were thin and Phil could hear the sound of a television. It sounded like cartoons were playing inside.

Was Janie Blake in there? Why would these windows be boarded up when none of the others were?

He took out his pocketknife and began prying out the nails that attached the plywood to the window frame. Trying to be as quiet as possible, he was able to remove four nails from the corner of the board. Phil slid his hand beneath the plywood and pulled back enough of it to be able to see inside.

A little girl was sitting on a bed, watching television. Her back was to him, so he couldn't be absolutely sure it was Janie but, because of the necklace he had found on the dirt road, Phil was convinced the girl was Eliza Blake's kidnapped daughter.

Should he try to get the child's attention? Or should he run and try to find someone who could help him?

Before he could decide what to do, Phil felt himself being pulled backward by a strong hand grasping him under his chin. Another hand grabbed the back of his head. Both hands twisted and pulled in opposite directions at the very same time, snapping Phil's neck and silently killing him.

CHAPTER 102

The studio was cleared except for only the most necessary personnel. Margo fiddled with the microphone battery pack that was attached to the rear of her waistband, invisible from the camera, while Doris Brice finished brushing powder on Eliza's cheeks.

"We don't want you looking all shiny," Doris said soothingly in her throaty voice.

"It's hard to care a whit about how I look," said Eliza. "But thanks, Doris." Eliza rubbed the zodiac medallion Stephanie had given her.

"Good-luck charm?" asked Doris.

"Something like that," answered Eliza.

The makeup woman patted Eliza's arm before retreating to her post behind the cameras.

Eliza and Margo sat in chairs facing each other on a raised, carpeted platform. Spotlights were trained on the two women, but the rest of the studio was dark.

"Ready when you are." The announcement came over the speaker from the director in the control room.

Margo cleared her throat and began.

"Thank you for coming in to do this, Eliza."

"You're welcome," Eliza answered.

"First of all, is there any new information you can share with us?" asked Margo.

"Actually, there *is* something. Just before I left my house, I was told that there's a new lead up in Milford, Pennsylvania. An employee at an Urgentcare was found murdered this morning and investigators think she might have been trying to make a phone call last night to the Find Janie hotline."

"And she was killed because of *that*?" asked Margo.

"That's what they're trying to find out," said Eliza. "But if the woman did have information about Janie and was killed because of it, that lets you know what we're dealing with here, doesn't it?"

"You must be terrified," said Margo.

"That doesn't even begin to describe how I feel." Eliza took a deep breath. "But it doesn't matter how I feel. What matters is finding Janie and Mrs. Garcia, our housekeeper."

"There's been speculation that Mrs. Garcia might be involved in the plot to take Janie," said Margo.

"I know there has been," said Eliza. "But that women is totally trustworthy and gentle and good. When this thing is over, everyone will see that Mrs. Garcia had absolutely nothing to do with it. I'm sure of that."

"What do *you* think happened, Eliza?"

The camera lens closed in on Eliza's face. "I'm not sure what happened," she said. "Someone took my daughter, that much is apparent. I don't know why. So far, it doesn't look like money is the motive because there hasn't been a legitimate ransom demand. But whoever has Janie . . ."

Her voice trailed off. She bent her head and looked down at her hands, in her lap. Margo waited while Eliza composed herself. After a few moments, Eliza raised her head again.

"I'm sorry," she said.

"There's nothing to apologize for," said Margo. "Do you want to continue?"

In that instant, Eliza had a mental flash of Linus praying out loud in the control room, praying that she would keep talking so he would have lots of tape to use on his show in the morning. But satisfying Linus wasn't the reason she forced herself to go on.

"Yes," she said. "Let's keep going."

Margo glanced at her notes. "You said it doesn't look like money is the motive for this kidnapping," she said. "Do you have any suspicions about what the motive might be?"

Eliza shook her head. "No, I don't," she said. "Of course, your mind wanders and goes where it shouldn't. You think of all sorts of things that could be happening to your child. You're scared to death that some sick person has taken her and is doing God knows what with her." Eliza's voice cracked. She grabbed hold of the arms of the chair to steady herself. "I was watching some videotape of Janie before I came here, tape you could show on the air. There is such a happy shot of Janie waiting to talk to Santa Claus last Christmas and a little while later there's video of her upset and hiccupping when the visit didn't go so well. I hope you'll use that shot, too. Because that picture of Janie is the one that is far more likely to look like she does now. Whenever Janie is scared or really worried, she gets the hiccups."

Margo watched and listened, marveling that her friend could speak as eloquently as she was. She decided to change the subject to something more productive than speculation about what hell Janie was going through.

"Law enforcement is all over this case, Eliza. But what can *we* do?" Margo asked. "What can somebody sitting at home do to help?"

"They can download our missing-persons posters from the Find Janie Web site and put the flyers up wherever they can. They can keep an eye out for Janie, and if they see her or Mrs. Garcia or anything at all that seems suspicious, call into the hotline." Eliza paused. "And we can all pray."

"Is there anything else you'd like to say, Eliza?"

"Yes, there is. I'm reaching out to anyone who might be able to help. If you'd told me before that I'd be consulting a psychic, I would have said you were crazy. But that's how desperate I am to find my daughter. So, even though many people will think I'm nuts, I want to let the audience know what the psychic says she has seen, in case it might help find my daughter. She thinks Janie is near moving, or rushing, water and is hurt, and she thinks the letter *M* and a bridal veil are involved in some way. So I ask anyone listening to keep those things in mind as well as we try to find Janie and Mrs. Garcia."

CHAPTER 103

The stack of multicolored flyers sat on the kitchen table.

"Where did you get all those?" Nell's uncle asked as he took another beer from the refrigerator.

"I went around town and pulled them down," Nell answered, not particularly concerned. She had witnessed her uncle help himself to fistfuls of mints at the diner and take piles of the free community newspaper so he could get the coupons inside. If something didn't have a price tag on it, Nell figured it was up for grabs. "I thought it would be a good idea since they were about Janie."

His fist came crashing down on the table. "Damn Janie and damn you," he shouted. "What the dickens were you thinking?" demanded Lloyd. "People in town already think you don't belong up here alone with me. If some busybody saw you tearing down those flyers, they'll send the cops for sure. We don't need that kind of attention."

Uncle Lloyd will get over it. He always does. His blowups were always followed by more beers. Sometimes he would drive off and leave her there, not coming back until the next morning. So far, tonight he was staying home.

After Uncle Lloyd went outside to the porch to clean his gun, Nell spread the flyers out. She arranged them according to shade. Yellow, orange, red, blue, green. She pasted them, one by one, in her scrapbook, thinking all the time what a good mother Eliza was. She had everybody, everywhere looking for her daughter. Nell suspected her own mother would never have made such an effort. Uncle Lloyd wouldn't have, either.

She was jealous of Janie Blake.

CHAPTER 104

Word that Eliza was in the house had spread through the Broadcast Center. Scores of employees were waiting for her outside the studio when she finished the interview. Some offered verbal encouragement, some hugged her, some squeezed her hand. All of them were eager to express their support.

"Thanks so very much, all of you," said Eliza to the group. "I know you've all been working hard on covering this story. Keep praying, will you? Keep Janie and Mrs. Garcia in your thoughts and make those thoughts positive ones. All right?"

Annabelle, B.J., and Margo waited as

the crowd slowly dispersed. When they were finally alone with Eliza, Annabelle suggested they go upstairs together. Once in the anchorwoman's office, she told Eliza where she and B.J. were thinking of going in the morning.

"What do you think, Eliza?" Annabelle asked. "Does it sound like a good idea?"

"It couldn't hurt," said Eliza. "The thing that intrigues me most about the idea is the *M* part of this—that the anonymous letter came from the Marzipan Bakery."

Annabelle exchanged glances with B.J. and Margo. "I hate to admit it, but that's what pushed me over the top in favor of going, too," she said.

"Even though the FBI agents blow me off any time I bring it up, they have to admit that Stephanie was right about the green paint on Janie's face," said Eliza. "And, honestly, I don't care what anybody says: When she told me that John is glad I still use the same perfume I wore before he died, she was telling me something that nobody else would know. Nobody could know that was one of the last things we talked about." Eliza paused.

"We'll see if she's right about Janie and the blood. I have the sinking feeling that she is and that Janie is hurt."

It was quiet in the room for a few moments until Margo broke the silence.

"Okay," she said. "The FBI and the police are doing their thing, investigating in ways we can't, with a network and technology we don't have. But, since they aren't paying any attention to Stephanie, what do we have to lose in going over the things she says she's seen?"

"Well, besides thinking the letter *M* is involved," said Eliza, "Stephanie said she dreamed about Janie being near moving water."

"God, that's so general," said B.J. "Where do we even start?"

"I know it is," said Eliza. "She also said she dreamed about a bridal veil in connection with Janie."

"A bridal veil," mused Margo. "All little girls like to dress up as brides. Could that have something to do with anything?"

Annabelle shook her head as she considered the clue. "I know Tara is obsessed with her Barbie doll, and the bride's costume is her favorite one of all."

Eliza bit her lower lip, determined not to cry. "Janie loves dressing up her Barbie in that white dress and veil, too."

"But how could a bridal veil translate into where Janie is, or what she's doing?" asked B.J.

"I don't know," said Eliza. "I don't know."

"All right," said Margo. "What else?"

"That's all really," said Eliza. "But Stephanie did give me this." She took the silver zodiac medallion from her pocket. One by one, the others examined it.

"She told me to keep it with me and keep concentrating on Janie."

"As if you could do anything else," said Annabelle.

"Look," said B.J., wanting their meeting to end on a hopeful note. "We'll go up to the Marzipan Bakery early in the morning and see what we can find out there. And we'll keep on thinking about the water and the bridal veil."

CHAPTER 105

At the end of the day, one of the paint-ball guns had not been returned. The manager scanned his records and saw that it was the gun rented by Phil Doyle. The manager wasn't terribly concerned. Doyle was a regular and he could simply have forgotten to return it. The manager was sure he'd be getting a call from Phil tomorrow, apologizing for the oversight and promising to bring the gun with him the next time he came up to play.

The manager finished locking up the lodge. As he walked to his car, he noticed that there was still one other vehicle left in the parking lot. He recognized it as Phil's old GMC Jimmy.

God, is he still up there in the field? Is he hurt? Or is he just lost?

The manager called the police, knowing full well that no search was going to start until the morning light. As long as he wasn't hurt, Phil Doyle was the kind of guy who would have no problem surviving a night in the woods.

CHAPTER 106

Beneath the window, the kidnapper crouched over the body. He examined the gun the man had carried and realized it had not posed a threat after all.

Some of the white paint that covered the front of the man's jumpsuit had not dried completely. He carefully zipped open the jumpsuit and found a wallet in the pocket of the guy's shorts. Inside was a driver's license and eighty-three dollars. He took the bills and put them in his own pocket before throwing the wallet back in the jumpsuit and zipping it up again.

Next, he checked the pockets of the

jumpsuit itself and found the plastic necklace that spelled out Janie's name. *How had this guy gotten that?*

As he looked at the beads, he realized that he hadn't seen the necklace since earlier in the week. *Was Janie wearing it on the day she tried to run away? Had she dropped it on the road on purpose? If she had, she was a clever little thing.*

He decided it didn't really matter how the necklace had ended up in Phil Doyle's pocket. What mattered was, if he hadn't killed this guy the whole operation could have failed.

Now, what to do with the body?

CHAPTER 107

With her head bowed, Mrs. Garcia sat on the cold floor. Her lips moved as she silently prayed the rosary, counting the Hail Marys and Our Fathers off on her fingers.

The dim bulb had started flickering several hours before. Mrs. Garcia had turned it off, afraid that it would burn out completely. But as she heard the noise coming from above, she pulled the string to light the root cellar.

Her muscles ached as she stood up but she wanted her ears to be closer to the ceiling so she could hear better. Her ankle throbbed from the twisting it had taken when the rotted step collapsed beneath her. She shifted her weight to one side as she listened. It sounded like something was being dragged across the ground overhead.

Someone was up there!

Mrs. Garcia positioned herself beneath the ventilation pipe and started screaming. She yelled and yelled, thinking of Janie, thinking of her precious family. She called for help until her voice grew hoarse.

Finally, she sank back down on the cement floor and wept.

CHAPTER 108

Rhonda watched as her husband went to the living room and turned on the television, clicking the remote repeatedly until he settled on CNN. While she straightened up the kitchen, Rhonda heard the reporter's words.

"It's been another frustrating day in the search for Janie Blake and her caretaker, Carmen Garcia. This morning FBI agents raided the apartment of a New York City man who had sent a fax demanding two million dollars in exchange for the child's safe return. The ransom demand turned out to be a hoax, with no evidence what-

soever that the man had anything to do with the child's abduction."

She put down her dish towel, walked into the living room, and sat next to Dave on the sofa.

"If they only knew that Janie was safe with us, there wouldn't be all this hoopla," she said.

Dave clicked off the television and stalked into the kitchen. Rhonda could feel her husband's anger as he went to the refrigerator, took out a can of beer, and slammed the door shut.

"Janie, Janie, Janie. How many times do I have to tell you that I don't want to hear you talking about that child?" he yelled. "I'm sick and tired of her."

"First of all, please keep your voice down, Dave. She'll hear you. Second of all, the whole world is talking about Janie," said Rhonda. "You can listen to them talking about her on TV, but you can't listen to me talking about her?"

"It's different," said Dave. "You know, I have a breaking point, too, Rhonda. I've had it with this Janie thing. She's not Allison and she's never going to be Allison." He lowered his voice. "Allison is dead,

Rhonda. She was hit by a car and she died. Nobody can take Allison's place."

"I know that," Rhonda said softly. "Janie is her own person. Why can't you love her like I do?"

He looked at the expression of hurt and bewilderment on his wife's face. "Forget it, I'm going in to take a shower."

She listened to the sound of the water running and decided what she should do. Rhonda went to the child's bedroom.

"Come, Janie. Daddy's very upset. We're going to go out for a while and let Daddy cool down and relax."

Rhonda picked up the stuffed monkey sitting on the bed. "Come on, sweetheart," she said. "We'll take Zippy with us."

On the way out of the house, Rhonda stopped in the kitchen and took a large knife out of the drawer. If things got bad enough, she might need it.

CHAPTER 109

Investigators know that perpetrators often come back to the scene of their crimes. Because the amateur video had been taken at Camp Musquapsink, it got priority over the other leads that were streaming in.

Picture enhancement showed a man wearing a black jacket, peering from behind a separation in the fence. His complexion was ruddy, his eyes glistened, and there was a rapt expression on his face.

As a start, comparisons were made with the mug shots culled from a list of child predators and other criminals known to be living within a fifty-mile radius of the camp and Eliza Blake's home.

CHAPTER 110

The grounds of the historic Ho-Ho-Kus estate that had been used by George Washington as one of his many headquarters during the Revolutionary War became the place where the crowd met to pray for Janie Blake and Carmen Garcia. Hundreds picked up candles as they streamed through the gates of the Hermitage property. The media were represented as well. Reporters and camera crews mingled with the crowd, getting video and conducting interviews.

The Town Car dropped Eliza off after the interview. Mack and Katharine and Paul were already there. Many neighbors and other people in town she had never even met came up and offered support. Among the well-wishers was Stephanie Quick.

"I wanted to be where there were so many individuals joining in the common hope of finding Janie," she said as she held on to Eliza's hand. "I hope all their energies help me see things better."

"I hope so, too," Eliza whispered. She was about to turn away when she remembered. "I should tell you I just talked about you in an interview that will air in the morning."

"Oh?"

"Yes, I shared the visions you shared with me, hoping that it might help. But, don't worry, I didn't give your name."

"I'm not worried," said Stephanie. "It's fine if people find out that I'm helping you. The more people know, the better, I think."

A hush came over the crowd as Eliza took the podium. She looked out over the audience, their faces illuminated by the glow of candlelight. She was touched by the sight of young children being held by their parents, the teenagers, the middle-aged, and the elderly citizens of the town, united by the common goal of finding Janie and Mrs. Garcia and bolstering their family.

"Thank you all for coming tonight," Eliza began, wishing that Maria and Vicente Rochas were there. "I can't tell you how much our family appreciates your keeping Janie and Carmen Garcia in your thoughts and prayers and how much you are encouraging us by standing along with us here. Knowing that all of you are supporting Janie and Mrs. Garcia, and are determined that we find them, somehow makes things a bit more bearable and a lot less lonely. So thank you for that and please, continue praying that we find Janie and Mrs. Garcia."

Music played and songs were sung. When the vigil was over, Eliza turned to Katharine and Paul and insisted that her in-laws go home to their apartment in Manhattan.

"Get a good night's sleep," she urged. "Mack's with me. I'll be fine."

"Are you sure, dear?" asked Katharine.

"Absolutely," said Eliza. "I'll talk to you in the morning."

Eliza shook hands and accepted people's warm greetings for almost an hour. Before she left to go home, she sought out Stephanie.

"Well, did you get any feelings?" asked Eliza.

Stephanie cracked a smile. "It doesn't work like that," she said. "It's not immediate. But since you said you'd spoken about the things I've seen regarding Janie, I told a couple of reporters here tonight, too. Maybe that will help. Maybe somebody will be spurred by my visions."

FRIDAY
JULY 25

CHAPTER 111

At precisely 3:15 A.M., the KEY News car pulled up at the curb in front of the Greenwich Village apartment house. Annabelle was already waiting in the lobby.

"You're late," she said as she climbed into the sedan.

"Give me a break," said B.J. "I could barely get out of bed. Plus, I stopped to get us some coffee. There won't be anybody on the road this early. I'll make up the time."

"I want to live," said Annabelle as she took a paper cup from the cardboard container on the seat. "Take it easy."

"You have directions?"

"Of course," said Annabelle, pointing to the MapQuest pages sticking out of her bag. "Start off by taking the George Washington Bridge."

What traffic there was, was headed into Manhattan, not out of it. In just under an hour, they were in front of the Marzipan Bakery. The windows were dark. Annabelle and B.J. got out of the car and rapped on the glass door. Nobody came to answer.

"I guarantee there's something going on in there. Somebody's got to be getting the stuff ready for today," said Annabelle.

"Let's go around back," said B.J.

They walked to the rear of the building. A car was parked near the heavy iron door that led into the bakery.

"See?" said Annabelle. "Somebody *is* in there."

B.J. knocked, then banged on the door until it was opened by a middle-aged man wearing white cotton pants and a white T-shirt. His face was flushed and his forehead was covered with perspiration.

"Yeah?"

Annabelle handed the man her business card. "We're with KEY News," she said. "And we're hoping you'll be able to help us."

"With what?" asked the man.

"We're trying to track down something," she said. "A package of cookies and other goods from this bakery was sent to KEY News for Eliza Blake. We were hoping to find out who sent them."

A bell rang and the baker looked over his shoulder. "Hold on a minute," he said. "I have to get the crumb cakes out."

Annabelle and B.J. followed him into the kitchen and watched while he pulled the trays out of the industrial-type oven.

"God, that smells great," said B.J.

"Thanks," said the baker as he slid a tray onto the cooling rack. "Now why do you want to know about the cookies? You didn't come out here in the middle of the night just to thank whoever sent them."

"You're right," said Annabelle. "There was a note inside the box and we want to find out who wrote it."

"Would whoever wrote the note be in any kind of trouble?" asked the baker.

"Not necessarily," said Annabelle. "But I'm sure you can understand that, with Janie Blake's kidnapping, we want to check out anything that seems strange."

"What? You think whoever sent the cookies kidnapped Janie Blake and that babysitter of hers?" asked the baker. "You've got to be kidding me."

"Look," said B.J. "Nobody knows *who's* responsible, but that little girl and the housekeeper have been missing for almost four days now."

The baker looked over at the pictures that were tacked on the wall over his worktable. "I have kids myself," he said.

"So you have an inkling of what Eliza Blake is going through," said Annabelle. "Whatever you know that could possibly help find Janie, you should tell us."

"All right," said the baker. "I know who sent the cookies."

The baker offered them some crumb cake and coffee. "I'm going to have to keep on working while we talk," he said.

He sprinkled flour over the surface

of the marble worktable. "Rhonda Billings is a tortured soul," he began. "Her daughter was killed in a car accident a few years ago. The kid had just gotten a new bicycle and wasn't really that steady on it yet. She was riding close to the curb and all of a sudden a car was coming and Allison lost control. Rhonda saw the whole thing."

"God, how horrible," said Annabelle, thinking of the twins and the New York City traffic they dealt with every day on their way to school or the park. Standing and watching as a car plowed into them and killed them would be beyond anything she could endure.

"It was," said the baker. "Brutal." His strong hands kneaded the dough. "Rhonda hasn't been the same since. She and her husband tried to have another baby, and she did get pregnant, but she miscarried. I don't know all the details, but afterward she was told she wouldn't be able to have another child." He lowered his voice to a whisper. "I even heard something about a suicide attempt."

Annabelle digested this information.

"Do you think there is any possibility that she would take someone else's little girl?" she asked.

"Possible?" Forming the dough into loaves, the baker considered the question. "Almost anything's possible, isn't it? To tell you the truth, there have been times I've been creeped out having her here in the kitchen with me, thinking maybe she would completely wig out and hurt herself or, worse yet, me. But she *has* seemed happier lately." He looked up from the dough in his hands and said, "I know Rhonda was seeing a shrink—he'd be able to make a call about her taking somebody's kid better than I could."

"But do you have a gut feeling about it?" pressed B.J.

"I can tell you that Rhonda Billings is a very troubled woman who still longs to have a child. Her husband has stuck with her through all this, though Lord knows how. He must be at the end of his rope at this point. I keep her on here because she's a good employee and gets her work done, plus I feel sorry for her. But sometimes, when she goes on and on about Allison, I think I'll go crazy myself. I don't know how he's stood it."

"Was Rhonda here at work on Monday morning?" asked B.J.

"No," said the baker. "We're closed on Mondays."

CHAPTER 112

Overflowing baskets and tall vases of flowers lined the dimly lit room and people with grim faces stood watching as she approached the small casket. The little coffin was covered with a spray of roses and lilies of the valley arranged in the shape of an angel.

With every bit of strength she had, Eliza forced herself to go forward. She knelt before the casket, her fists clenched, her eyes shut tight. She felt excruciating pressure. Everyone was looking at her, waiting for her reaction, relieved that they were watching *her* life and not theirs. Nothing would go forward without her doing what she had to do.

You have to look. You have to look. You have to see what's inside.

Eliza bent her head down and opened her eyes. The first thing she saw was a cascading shower of white tulle spilling from the casket walls. Her hand shook violently as she reached out to pull back the bridal veil.

Eliza bolted upright, her nightgown clinging to her body with cold perspiration.

CHAPTER 113

Will Jorgenson ate his cereal as he watched the exclusive interview with Eliza Blake air on *KEY to America*. His heart went out to the poor woman.

He sat up straighter when she mentioned that there was a new lead in Milford. His pharmacy was in the town. He'd heard all about the young woman who'd been found with her throat slit at the Urgentcare Center down the road. That was all anybody could talk about yesterday. A killer in their own quiet town.

Watching the video of Janie Blake, smiling with excitement and pleasure, Will's mouth turned down at the corners and he felt his eyes begin to tear up. *What a lovely child she was. So innocent, so young.*

"There is such a happy shot of Janie waiting to talk to Santa Claus last Christmas," Eliza was saying, "and a little while later there's video of her upset and hiccupping when the visit didn't go so well."

Pictures appeared on the screen of the child trying to catch her breath, her facial expression downcast.

". . . that picture of Janie is the one that is far more likely to look like she does now. Whenever Janie is scared or really worried, she gets the hiccups."

Hiccups.

That surly guy who came into the pharmacy the other day had been asking about hiccup medicine. That was a fairly rare request. Will tried to remember what the guy had actually purchased. He seemed to recall that children's aspirin had been in the basket. He did remember that the guy paid cash.

Should he call the police? he wondered.

He listened to the rest of the interview.

Eliza implored anyone with any information at all to call the Find Janie hotline and announced that a psychic had told her Janie was near moving water and that the letter *M* was also involved in some way and that a bridal veil was part of the case.

Poppycock, thought the druggist. *But the poor woman is so desperate she's resorted to consulting a psychic.*

He made up his mind. It was better to call with his information even if it turned out to be nothing than to not call and have it turn out that the kidnapper had been in his store. He imagined that, after the interview, the hotline would get thousands of calls from the public and his call would get lost among all the tips. He figured he'd be better off just calling the Milford police.

CHAPTER 114

The FBI agents laid the evidence envelope on the desk. The sheriff inspected
the contents through the clear wrapping.
The handwritten letter was decorated
with colorful stickers.

"The postmark sent us here, but, as you
see, it's not signed. Got any ideas?"

The sheriff stroked his chin. "I'd bet
my badge I know who sent that letter,"
he said.

The agents waited expectantly.

"You don't think that whoever wrote
this has something to do with the Blake
abduction, do you?" asked the sheriff.

"That's what we're trying to find out."

"Well, I think that letter was sent by Nell," said the sheriff.

"Nell?"

"Yep. She's had a tough life, that one."

"How so?"

"Father deserted her, mother didn't really want her. After her mother died, Nell got stuck living with her no-good uncle. He's got a heck of a temper."

"Any reason why Nell would write a letter like this to Eliza Blake?"

The sheriff shrugged. "I'm no expert, but I think that girl needs a mother figure to look up to. After all, she's only nine years old."

CHAPTER 115

The computers of the Integrated Automated Fingerprint Identification System came up with a match to an index finger and thumbprint found on the construction paper headpiece discarded in the dry-cleaning plant parking lot. There were also prints from two other people. It was going to take a while longer to see if the smaller ones belonged to Janie Blake because her prints were not on file with IAFIS. The other print was also not in the system.

CHAPTER 116

Calling into the *KEY to America* office, Annabelle let Linus's assistant know that she and B.J. were going to be delayed in getting back to the Broadcast Center. They waited at the bakery for Rhonda, but she didn't show up for work.

"Let's go over to her house," said B.J. He turned to the baker. "Would you give us her address?" he asked.

"Might as well," said the baker. "You could just go look it up in the phone book."

They found the brick dwelling at the end of a road, several miles from the downtown area. There were no cars in the driveway. Several attempts at ringing the bell and knocking at the door brought no response.

"Now what do we do?" asked B.J.

"Let's see what we can see," said Annabelle. She cupped her hands over her brow to shield her eyes from the glare as she looked through the window. She could see a small pair of flip-flops on the living room floor.

"Either Rhonda has the tiniest feet of any woman in America," said Annabelle, "or those are a child's shoes in the home of a woman who doesn't have any children."

B.J. took a look. "Maybe she babysits or has a niece or something."

"Well, we can't hang around any longer; we have to head back," said Annabelle. "But at least we should tell somebody what we found out about Rhonda's history of losing her child."

"Maybe we should let Joe Connelly know," said B.J. as they climbed back into the car. "He's the head of security, and Rhonda's package came in on his watch."

"Yeah, but if we tell him, he's going to wonder how I found out about the cookies and the letter to begin with. That could get my source in trouble."

"Who's your source? Paige?" asked B.J.

"You know I'm not going to tell you," said Annabelle.

"Yeah, yeah," said B.J. "All right, if not Joe, then who?"

"Eliza," said Annabelle. "And she can tell the FBI agents sitting right alongside her."

CHAPTER 117

Eliza went directly to Agent Gebhardt after Annabelle called with the information about Rhonda Billings.

"Do you have any idea how many leads we have?" asked the agent. "Thousands. It takes time to track them all."

"Well, this one sounds promising," said Eliza. "The disturbing package and letter from the woman, her horrible personal history, and honestly, the fact that she works at the Marzipan Bakery adds to my interest in her."

Agent Gebhardt closed her eyes for a moment, fighting to keep her temper in check. "Not that psychic's 'letter *M*' nonsense again."

Eliza stood firm. "I'm telling you, somebody's got to go up there to check on this woman. If it turns out she has my daughter, how will the FBI look if they had the information but didn't follow through quickly enough?"

Agent Gebhardt said nothing, knowing that, if the child molester they were picking up led them to Janie, Eliza's demand would be moot.

CHAPTER 118

A line of unmarked cars and police vehicles waited at the end of the street. When the command was given, the armed occupants got out and started toward the house, trying to stay out of sight, finding hiding spots as they drew progressively closer to their target.

When everyone was in place around the house, a cluster of FBI agents, guns drawn, crept up to the front stoop. One of them knocked on the door and yelled, "FBI. Open up!"

The agents were fully prepared to force the door down, but it opened almost immediately.

Isabelle stood in the doorway, taking in the scene in front of her. It didn't upset her as much as it did the first time she had encountered a situation like this. But there were definitely more cops now than there had ever been.

"We have a warrant to search the premises and for the arrest of Hugh Pollock."

She stood back and let them enter, knowing she had no other choice.

It didn't take long to search the house and to ascertain that Janie Blake was not inside. But they did find Hugh. He was sitting cross-legged in front of the dollhouse in his bedroom. The agents informed him of his rights, handcuffed him, and led him out of the house.

"Don't worry, Hughie," his sister called after him. "I'll take care of everything."

"Do you believe this crap?" said an agent, looking around the room.

"Sickening," said his partner. "He's got the room decorated like a little girl's."

The room was painted pink. Disney posters decorated the walls. The single bed in the corner was covered with a Hannah Montana comforter. A collection of American Girl dolls was arranged on top, their skirts fanned out artfully. On the floor beside the bed, a stuffed animal slept, carefully covered with a miniature blanket. But the closet contained men's clothes.

"He actually sleeps in here?"

"I think I'm going to puke." The agent shook his head as he walked over and opened a dresser drawer. With his latex-gloved hand, he reached in and pulled out a small white tube sock. He held it up.

"Think this fits our big pervert?" he asked.

CHAPTER 119

Mack had the morning papers spread out on the kitchen table.

"I'm not going to hide it from you, Eliza," he said, handing her the *Daily News* and the *New York Post.*

Eliza scanned the headlines.
ELIZA'S IN ANOTHER WORLD
ELIZA'S GONE PSYCHIC
She shrugged. "My credibility may be shot, which means I won't have a job to go back to, but I don't really care. Let them think I'm crazy. All that matters is finding Janie and Mrs. Garcia."

Mack took the papers back and finished reading the articles. "They've got quotes from Stephanie Quick in these," he said.

Eliza nodded. "I know. She told me she talked to reporters at the vigil last night."

"Linus is going to be ripping that he didn't have her on the show," said Mack.

"Yeah," agreed Eliza. "And that the papers had her name before he did. I should call him."

Mack couldn't resist. "But I thought you didn't care about your job . . ."

"I guess I lied," said Eliza.

As she took out her cell phone to soothe Linus, another call came in.

"Eliza? It's Stephanie. I had another dream last night." Eliza could feel the excitement in the psychic's voice.

"A waterfall. The moving water I saw around Janie is a waterfall."

CHAPTER 120

"Where is she, Hughie?"

"I've told you again and again, I don't know where she is."

"If you don't tell us, Hughie, it's only going to be harder on you when we do find her," said the interrogator. "Where is Janie Blake?"

"How should I know where that little darling is? If she were my child, I'd never let her out of my sight. I'd keep her tied to me."

"I bet you would."

Hugh squirmed in his chair. "I'm hot," he said. "Can I take off my jacket?"

The interrogator nodded. Hugh peeled off the nylon jacket.

"What's with the tube sock, Hughie?" asked the interrogator, averting his eyes from the sight of Hugh's soft white arms.

"What sock?"

"The child's sock we found in your dresser drawer."

"Oh, that," said Hugh dismissively. "I like to make little hand puppets with those socks. That's not a crime, is it?"

The questioning went on, the interrogator increasingly frustrated and repulsed. Just as he was going to ask for another agent to relieve him, a call came in telling him to come out into the hallway. He left Hughie tapping his fingers on the table and singing nervously to himself.

"What's up?" asked the interrogator.

"The fingerprint results are back on the construction paper found behind that dry-cleaning plant."

"And?"

"The little ones are Janie Blake's."

"And the adult prints?"

"One still hasn't been ID'd, but we think it might belong to a counselor at the camp who helped the kid with the headpiece."

"And the other? Please, tell me it's that slob in there."

"No dice. It belongs to a guy named Carl Yates."

"And what's *his* story?"

"Dishonorably discharged from the navy twelve years ago."

"For what?"

"Assaulting another officer and 'conduct unbecoming.'"

"So we have to let Hughie in there go?" asked the interrogator.

"It looks that way. We have no real evidence at this point to hold him."

CHAPTER 121

Eliza got off the phone with Stephanie Quick and went directly to talk with Agents Gebhardt and Laggie, telling them about Stephanie's vision of the waterfall.

"Look, Eliza," said Agent Laggie. "We haven't wanted to get your hopes up again for nothing. But we do have a match on fingerprints found on a piece of construction paper in a parking lot north of Camp Musquapsink."

"What kind of a match?" asked Eliza.

"A match to Janie. We think the paper is part of a headpiece Janie was wearing for Native American Day at camp."

"Oh my God," Eliza said excitedly. "This is the first direct link we've had so far."

"Right," said Agent Laggie. "And we've also identified another print on the paper."

Eliza waited.

"It belongs to a guy in Manhattan. Know anyone by the name of Carl Yates?"

Eliza thought, then shook her head solemnly.

"Well, we have agents on the way to his apartment now."

Eliza found Mack and told him the news. Together, they went to the computer and Googled "Carl Yates." Over three thousand entries appeared.

"We just have to wait and let the FBI do their job, honey," said Mack as he reached out and took her hand.

"I know," said Eliza, "but I feel like I'm coming out of my skin."

She went back to find Agent Laggie.

"Where is the parking lot where the headband was found?" she asked.

He showed her on the map.

The parking lot was situated in a spot that could be on a route taken from Camp Musquapsink to Milford, Pennsylvania.

As Eliza waited to hear about the raid on Carl Yates's apartment, she told Mack about her dream.

"It was the worst," said Eliza, leaning her head on his shoulder. "It felt so real, as if I were really kneeling at her casket. I was about to pull back that bridal veil and I knew I was going to see Janie's face beneath it. Thank God I woke up."

Mack put his arm around her and held her close. "Let's hope that's going to be the last nightmare you have, sweetheart. Let's hope the FBI is on their way to Janie and Mrs. Garcia right now and that they'll be back home soon."

CHAPTER 122

Janie Blake and Carmen Garcia were not at Carl Yates's apartment nor was there any sign that they ever had been. Carl Yates was not in the apartment, either.

When FBI agents searched the premises, they found knives, rope, diving gear, Navy SEAL training manuals, and a catalog of Halloween masks. They also found a map on the kitchen table with a big red circle drawn around the area of Milford, Pennsylvania.

CHAPTER 123

Eliza could tell by the expression on Agent Gebhardt's face that the news wasn't good.

"Janie wasn't there," she said. "But try not to worry. We'll find Carl Yates and we'll find Janie." Agent Gebhardt didn't tell Eliza about the map.

She withheld the information for two reasons. First, she didn't want the news to get out that the FBI was now increasing its investigation in the Milford area. Secrecy was of the essence. If word got out, Yates, if he was up there, would flee. Second, she didn't want Eliza harping about the psychic and her damned letter *M.*

Try not to worry. That was the same as saying try not to breathe. The same as telling Janie to try not to hiccup when she was scared.

Eliza walked to the back of the house and looked out the French doors to the yard. She loved Mack and knew that Mack cared deeply about Janie. But Mack wasn't Janie's father. Eliza wished that John was with her now. Would John think she was handling all this in the right way? Was there something else she could be doing to make sure their little girl came home safely?

Please, John. If you have any pull up there, make sure Janie is all right and that we get her back.

As she watched the sunlight playing on the water of the swimming pool, their honeymoon came to her mind. It had been short. She hadn't been able to get much time off from work and neither had he. Instead of a trip to Europe or Hawaii, they had settled for three days at Niagara Falls.

She had never regretted it, never felt that she had missed out on some sort of grander wedding trip. Those three days had been magical. They had stayed at a charming bed-and-breakfast in a lovely Victorian house where the owners were thrilled to have the newlyweds and made sure they were afforded the utmost privacy. They had taken the boat rides to see the majestic cascades of pounding, falling water, toured a winery where samples were handed out freely, and strolled hand in hand, laughing about the wedding and talking about the life they hoped for together.

It had been all ahead of them then, with no thoughts of fatal diseases or kidnappings. It had been the sweetest three days of her life.

Eliza closed her eyes and tried to keep focused on that time. She didn't want to snap out of her reverie and face the present cruel reality. She wanted to stay with John, if only in her mind, and feel like she was back there, hiking in Niagara Falls State Park to the point beneath Bridal

Veil Falls, where he had told her again and again how much he loved her.

Her eyes snapped open.

Bridal Veil Falls.

Bridal Veil!

She remembered that the name came from the effect caused by the strong winds blowing against the water falling from the sheer cliff, making it look like a bride's white veil and train. There were waterfalls known as "bridal veils" all around the world.

Eliza ran up the stairs and searched the Internet for waterfalls near Milford, Pennsylvania. There were several listed in that mountainous region near the Delaware River. She searched further and found the image of a vintage postcard that showed frothy white waterfalls cascading down a steep rock cliff.

The caption read: LOWER FALLS ON RAYMONDSKILL AND BRIDAL VEIL.

It was located three miles outside the center of town.

CHAPTER 124

In the county park, Rhonda sat in her car, looking through the front window. A mother duck and three ducklings were gliding through the pond's smooth water. Rhonda smiled as she ran her fingers over the knife's smooth blade.

"Look, Janie," she said. "Do you see the ducks, honey?"

Rhonda's pleasure was cut short when she thought of her husband. Dave had had to leave for the night shift not knowing where his wife and child were—or if they were coming back. He should be very worried about her and Janie by now.

When he'd come out of the shower last night, after their fight, she'd been gone. If he'd searched the house and found that she had taken Zippy with her, he must have realized that she hadn't just run out to the store with Janie. They meant to be gone for quite a while.

Dave had to accept that she was serious about her commitment to Janie, that she would never let anyone or anything take her daughter from her, and that nobody could stop her from talking about her precious girl. Janie was part of their lives to stay—and Dave just had to get used to it.

Thinking about all this was exhausting. Rhonda laid her head back against the seat and fell asleep.

A patrolling county police officer rapped on the glass until Rhonda opened her eyes. She rolled down the window.

"License and registration, ma'am."

As she leaned over to rifle through the glove compartment, Rhonda realized that the knife had fallen to the floor. She didn't think the policeman had seen it.

She found the documents and handed them over. The officer inspected the paperwork.

After a conversation with her, the officer insisted that he escort Rhonda home. Meekly, Rhonda got out of her car and into the police cruiser, leaving the knife behind.

Dave had called in sick and spent the night cruising around town looking for his wife. Exhausted and discouraged, he headed home. He would call Dr. Karas and see what he thought would help Rhonda. Things couldn't go on this way.

Dave's heart sank when he turned into his street. He hadn't wanted to get the police involved. But now, he saw it was too late. A police vehicle was parked outside their house. A cop was escorting Rhonda up the walk.

Resigned now, Dave knew that Rhonda needed to be hospitalized. Her delusion of having Janie Blake as her daughter had gotten completely out of hand.

CHAPTER 125

News vans, satellite trucks, and camera crews continued to line the street in front of Eliza's home.

Mack told the FBI agents that Eliza needed to get out of the house for a while to clear her head and that he was going to take her for a ride.

"We'll both have our cells," he said, "so you can reach us. But we're going to need some help getting out of here without the news people following us."

A car pulled slowly out of the driveway. Reporters and cameramen strained to see inside, recognizing Mack McBride in the driver's seat. The passenger side was empty, as was the backseat.

"Stop a minute, Mack."

"Give us something, will you, Mack?"

"Come on, Mack. You know what it's like. How 'bout a sound bite?"

Mack resolutely ignored the pleas of his colleagues and drove away.

After traveling a few miles, he found a secluded place at the side of the road and pulled over. He popped the trunk and Eliza got out.

When they were on the New York State Thruway, Eliza called Annabelle and told her where they were going and explained why.

"Of course I can't be completely sure," she said. "But every time I mention anything that comes from the psychic, the FBI brushes me off. If they aren't going to pay attention to Stephanie's visions, I will. My gut tells me to go to Raymondskill Falls. If you and B.J. can figure out a way to meet us there without telling anyone, you might end up with some award-winning coverage, or else you'll simply have footage that makes me look like a crazy woman. Either way, Linus will be thrilled."

CHAPTER 126

"This was never supposed to play out this way!" she cried as she paced the living room floor. "Nobody was ever supposed to get hurt and now two people are dead."

"It couldn't be helped and I'm glad I did it. That guy who was snooping around had the brat's necklace in his pocket, for God's sake. And keep your voice down, would you? She's sleeping in there."

"Yeah? Well, I don't like *that,* either," she said. "A child doesn't sleep as much as she does unless something's wrong. If it turns out that we end up killing Janie Blake, you can rest assured that we will end up dead ourselves. We have to wrap this thing up and we have to wrap it up *now.*"

"I guess you're right," he said grudgingly. "But I'm not the only one who didn't follow the plan. You were supposed to send that ransom demand but you never did. When this is all over, the FBI's going to wonder why the kid was taken if it wasn't for the money."

As he went to the bedroom to get the child, she went to the Jeep and took the gun from the glove compartment. He wouldn't need it if all he was doing was dropping off Janie—and she didn't want him to have an opportunity to use it.

A half hour after the kidnapper left the house, an anonymous call, giving detailed directions on where Eliza Blake's daughter could be found, came in to the Find Janie hotline.

CHAPTER 127

Eliza and Mack traveled along the quaint downtown street, passing Ann's Candy Kitchen and the Milford Diner. Eliza rocked in her seat, willing the car to move forward. She reached into her pocket for the zodiac medallion Stephanie had given her and focused all her mental attention on Janie.

"Make a left on Route Six," the electronic voice instructed. The GPS tracking system told them they were just about three miles from their destination.

Three miles until they got to the Bridal Veil at Raymondskill Falls.

CHAPTER 128

He parked the Jeep in front of the cinder-block building that housed the restrooms and waited inside the vehicle until the only other car in the lot drove away. He reached into the glove compartment, but his gun wasn't there. Cursing, he got out and lifted Janie from her seat. He carried her down the trail that led to the waterfall.

The roar of rushing water blocked out the sound of the approaching car.

As the rental car pulled into the restroom parking lot, Eliza's cell phone rang. It was

Agent Gebhardt with the details of the anonymous hotline call, as well as the call from the pharmacist in Milford about a man asking for hiccup medication.

"We've got agents on the way to Raymondskill Falls now," said Gebhardt.

"That's where we are!" cried Eliza.

"What?" shouted Gebhardt. "You said you were just going for a ride. Stay right where you are. Wait for our agents to get there."

Eliza had snapped her phone closed.

At first, Mack tried to hold her back, but Eliza made her way as quickly as she could down the fern- and moss-covered trail. Large rocks, exposed tree roots, and rotted stumps sabotaged the descent. Along the path there were warning signs.

STAY ON THE TRAIL. STAY OFF THE ROCKS. STAY AWAY FROM THE EDGE.

As she heard the sound of the rushing water grow more intense, Eliza was filled with apprehension for her child.

Wet rocks are slippery. A fall could in-

*jure you. A sudden dunking could drown
you.*

Janie heard the sound of rushing water
over the words of the kidnapper. "Now
wait here," he said. "Somebody will be
here to get you soon."

"My mommy?" asked Janie as he
steered her, blindfolded, into a crevice
near the pool at the top of the waterfall.

The kidnapper's attention was di-
verted by a movement in the distance.
He pushed Janie to the ground, turned,
and ran as the child struggled to free
herself from her bonds.

"Look," cried Eliza, pointing to the figure scrambling up the rocks on the other
side of the waterfall.

She started running, Mack right behind her.

"He's alone," Eliza called over her
shoulder.

"I'll follow him," Mack panted. "You
see if you can find Janie."

At the top of the trail, agents wearing FBI Windbreakers sprang from their cars and began sprinting toward the waterfall.

"Janie! Janie!" Eliza's voice reverberated through the mountain air.

She picked her way across the rocks, losing her balance and then righting herself, her eyes searching the area. She looked down and there it was. The white cascade of frothy, rushing water, falling inevitably to the rock formation below. The Bridal Veil.

Could he have pushed Janie? Was that what the vision in her dream meant? Janie in death, swallowed up by a bride's snowy veil? Was Janie down there under the pounding water?

Mack's fingers grasped at vegetation as he climbed. He tucked his head as rocks tumbled from above him, the falling stones a sign that the kidnapper was overhead.

Turning his head for just an instant, Mack looked down. *A fall from this height would kill a man or, at the very least, paralyze him for life.*

He kept climbing, trying to keep his mind focused on the task at hand. The man who had taken Janie was up there and he was determined not to let him get away.

Mack heard the booming call.

"FBI. Stop or we'll shoot!"

Dear God, did they think *he* was the kidnapper? From where they stood down there, they wouldn't be able to tell who he was.

A shot rang out. And then another.

The kidnapper reached the top and began running across the ridge. He ducked as the first shot was fired, losing his footing. He tried to right himself. The second shot rang out. Still, they had missed him.

The feds didn't know who they were

up against. He had received better training than even they had.

Full of his final hubris, his feet skidded across the slippery rocks. He struggled to keep his balance but slipped, falling through the air, his body ending up splayed across the rocks at the bottom of the waterfall.

Eliza watched the man's body sailing downward, but averted her eyes before he crashed.

"Janie. Janie?" she called out desperately. "Janie, it's Mommy. Where are you, sweetheart?"

"Here she is."

Eliza swung around in the direction of the voice. She saw an FBI agent, coming from the trees, carrying her little girl in his arms.

CHAPTER 129

Eliza held on to the child so tightly and for so long that eventually she could feel Janie squirming to get free.

"Oh my angel, I'm so relieved that you're okay," Eliza breathed, her eyes closed. "Everything is going to be all right now, Janie."

"Where were you, Mommy? Mrs. Garcia said you were coming but you took so long."

Eliza released her grip on her daughter. "I'm sorry, Janie," she said, looking directly in her child's eyes. "I'm so sorry. I came as soon as I could. I didn't know where you were."

"Did you find Mrs. Garcia?" Janie asked.

"No, we haven't found Mrs. Garcia yet. Do you know where she is, Janie?"

The little girl shook her head. "The man took her away. I don't know where. He covered my eyes so I couldn't see."

Annabelle and B.J. arrived in time to see Eliza and Janie getting into the car with Mack. Tears ran down Annabelle's cheeks as she sprang out of the news vehicle. She rushed to Eliza and hugged her.

"Thank God," she whispered.

"I know," said Eliza, hugging her back. "I know."

Annabelle pulled away and looked over at the child. "She's all right?"

"She seems to be," Eliza answered. "They want to question her more, but she's been through enough for now. I want to get her to a doctor right away and have her checked out, have those legs looked at. Then I'm going to ask Margo about therapy for her."

"Right," said Annabelle. She looked around for B.J. and saw him hoisting up his camera. She noticed he stopped to wipe his eyes.

CHAPTER 130

Records showed that Carl Yates owned a piece of property fifteen miles outside of Milford. The FBI searched it.

There was no one in the house, but inside, among other things, they found a paintball gun, Janie's plastic necklace, and a scalpel.

"I bet the Urgentcare victim's blood is on this," said the agent who carefully placed the instrument in an evidence container.

"I'm going to go out and see what's in that shed," said his partner.

Buried in the root cellar, Mrs. Garcia drifted in and out of sleep. Every time she woke up, she willed herself to go back to sleep again. Only in sleep did she find any respite from the pain, fright, and hopelessness that enveloped her.

The agents pulled back the door of the shed and found a black van with a dented rear door parked inside.

In the van's cargo hold was the body of a man dressed in a camouflage jump-suit.

Mrs. Garcia opened her eyes, not sure what had awakened her. The bulb had burned out, so she couldn't see her surroundings. She lay on the cement floor and listened.

She heard something coming from above.

"We should leave the body where it is until the coroner comes," said the agent.

"Let's close the door again, so no bugs get on him," said the other.

He slammed the van door shut.

Sí! There *was* a noise above her. Somebody was up there.

Mrs. Garcia struggled to raise herself and get to the ventilation pipe, but her swollen ankle collapsed beneath her and she fell to the floor.

The agents walked out of the shed.

"Leave it open to air the place out."

They started back to the house.

Leaning against the wall, Mrs. Garcia inched her way up again. With no light, she couldn't be sure where the air vent was. She reached up and groped along the two-by-fours and bags of sand, her heart beating faster, knowing that she had to be heard to be rescued.

Where was the pipe? Where was it?

Her hand hit a round metal tube jutting out from the wall, just below the ceiling.

"Help!" she cried. "I'm down here. Help!"

"Did you hear something?" asked the agent.

They stood still and listened. Following the direction of the sound, they went back to the shed and found a pipe jutting out of the floor. They knelt down beside it.

"Hello," called the agent into the pipe. "Somebody there?"

"Ay, Dios mio. Yes, I am here. Please help me."

The agent found a wood panel in the ground, hidden at the back of the shed. It was secured with a heavy padlock. They broke it, opened the door, and pointed flashlights down into the dark.

A middle-aged woman, her hair disheveled, her face covered with dirt, squinted up at them from the bottom of the root cellar.

CHAPTER 131

The Ho-Ho-Kus police held back the throng of newspeople who surged around the car carrying Eliza, Janie, and Mack. Blocked by the aggressive, competing journalists, Mack inched the vehicle up the driveway.

"We should give them their photo op," said Eliza as she held Janie in the backseat. "They deserve it."

Mack got out of the car and opened the rear door. Eliza emerged with Janie to a frenzy of shouted questions and flashing camera lights. Microphones were thrust at all of them.

Eliza held out her hands and smiled.

"Okay, everybody," she shouted. "We have our happy ending. Janie is home, and we just got a call from the FBI that Mrs. Garcia has been found as well."

The reporters pounced.

"What do you know about the kidnapper, Eliza?"

"Do you know why he abducted your daughter?"

"Janie, what did the kidnapper do to you?"

Eliza felt her daughter snuggle closer against her for protection.

"We have to get inside now," said Eliza, responding to her daughter's vulnerability. "Janie needs to rest. I'll be out later, everybody."

Surprisingly, the reporters parted to let mother and child pass. As they made their way up the walk, Eliza spotted Stephanie Quick standing on the lawn. She motioned to the woman to come over. Eliza kissed Stephanie on the cheek before turning to the reporters again.

"The FBI has worked hard and has done a wonderful job, but if it wasn't for this woman, we wouldn't have gotten to Janie in time. Stephanie Quick is the psychic who helped us. I know some have treated my consultations with her as a joke, something not to be taken seriously. Perhaps if I were in your places, I would have called it all mumbo jumbo, too. But Stephanie's visions are the reason we have Janie back. And my family and I will be forever in her debt."

Questions were shouted again, demanding more details. Eliza whispered in Stephanie's ear and the woman nodded. "Come inside so I can thank you properly when you're done out here," Eliza whispered before turning around to address the reporters.

"Stephanie is going to stay out here and answer your questions," said Eliza. She and Mack flanked Janie and, hand in hand, the three of them walked inside the house.

CHAPTER 132

Eliza refused to let Janie be questioned right away.

"Janie's been through enough," Eliza told Agents Gebhardt and Laggie. "There will be time for that later."

She took Janie upstairs and gave her a warm bath, taking care as she washed around the cuts on the child's legs. Eliza could tell that the child had lost some weight, and her suntan had a gray pallor to it.

"Dr. Burke will be coming over in a little while, sweetheart," she said, preparing her daughter. "He's going to make sure your legs heal up all better. Kay Kay and Poppy are on their way over, too."

"What about Mrs. Garcia, Mommy? When will she be back?"

"Soon, sweetheart." Eliza kissed the child's forehead. "Soon."

Dressed in a fresh pair of summer pajamas, Janie made no protest about getting into bed. She climbed in between the clean sheets and lay her head down on the pillow. One small arm cradled Zippy, the other reached out to stroke the dog's head that rested on top of the comforter.

"Good girl, Daisy. I missed you so much," Janie murmured as she fell asleep.

Eliza looked down at her daughter, her heart filled with love, relief, and profound gratitude. As she tiptoed out of the room, she realized that Janie wasn't hiccupping anymore.

CHAPTER 133

Mrs. Garcia was admitted to Bon Secours Community Hospital in Port Jervis, New York, suffering from dehydration and a broken ankle. She refused pain or sleep medication.

Her skin was ashen against the crisp white pillowcase. "Janie. Is she all right?"

"Yes," said the FBI agent. "She's safe and home already with her mother."

"That is good," said Mrs. Garcia. "*Gracias a Dios.* And I would like to call my family and let them know I am all right," she said.

The FBI agent looked uncomfortable.

"What is wrong?" asked Mrs. Garcia.

"Your family is gone. We don't know where they are."

She smiled for the first time. "I think I know where they might be." Mrs. Garcia had one more question. "And the people who took us? Did you catch them?"

"*People?*" asked the FBI agent. "There was more than one person?"

"*Sí,*" said Mrs. Garcia. "There was a man and a woman."

CHAPTER 134

The Maryknoll fathers, brothers, and sisters have worked as missionaries in Guatemala longer than in any other country, witnessing the massacre of the Indian population there. It was well known among the Guatemalan immigrants who found their way to the United States that the Maryknollers provided refuge for those in trouble and opened their doors to those fleeing political repression. Though their story was a unique one, Maria and Vicente Rochas and their baby hadn't been turned away when they arrived at the Maryknoll sanctuary in Ossining, New York.

Vicente had already been put to work on the grounds and was mowing the grass when Maria, with Rosario in her arms, ran out onto the lawn and beckoned excitedly.

"They found them, Vicente!" Maria cried. "They found Mamá and Janie. It's on the television right now."

CHAPTER 135

Eliza came downstairs to wait for Dr. Burke. She went to the kitchen and put a kettle of water on the stove. As the whistle sounded, Agent Gebhardt came in from the garage.

"Thank you, Barbara," said Eliza, going over and hugging the woman. "Thank you for everything."

"That's our job," said the agent. "It's so good when everything turns out all right. Getting Janie back safely is the only thing that matters."

"Thank God it's over now," said Eliza. "When I think what *could* have happened, how this could have ended . . ." Eliza didn't finish the sentence.

"Yes, we were lucky," said Agent Gebhardt. "I wish they all turned out this way."

Eliza nodded. "Would you like some tea?" she asked.

"Actually, I'd love a good strong scotch," said Agent Gebhardt.

"You got it," said Eliza, heading for the liquor cabinet.

Gebhardt held up her hand and smiled. "Stop. I was only kidding. I'm on duty, so I'll settle for that tea."

As she poured the hot water over the tea leaves to steep, Eliza couldn't resist asking a question. "What do you think of psychics now?"

Agent Gebhardt shrugged. "I'm still not convinced, but I don't think I'll be ignoring those kinds of leads in the future. Quick's bridal veil vision was especially impressive. How could she ever have known that?"

"I know," Eliza agreed. "She's remarkable. I'm glad she's outside getting the attention she deserves."

The two women sat at the kitchen table and talked.

Agent Gebhardt took a sip of tea. "The case isn't over yet, Eliza. When they searched the kidnapper's property, they found another dead body. A male this time. It looks like the guy had been out paintballing and stumbled into something horrible."

Eliza groaned. "That poor soul—and the young woman who was murdered at the Urgentcare. I'd like to be able to contact their families."

Barbara Gebhardt nodded. "And our agents with Mrs. Garcia up in Milford just called."

"How is she? Is she all right?"

"She's going to be fine, but she says there was somebody else involved. Two people abducted her and Janie."

Eliza digested the information. "So the other one is out there still," she said quietly.

"A woman," said Agent Gebhardt.

"What do you know about the male kidnapper?" asked Eliza.

"Not enough," said Agent Gebhardt. "Even though there was no identification on the body, we feel confident that fingerprints will confirm he is Carl Yates, a guy who was dishonorably discharged from the Navy SEALs about a decade ago for assaulting another officer. The only thing our agents found on him was a medal in his pocket with the name Skip engraved on the back. We think that's a nickname he got when he commanded his unit."

Eliza was puzzled. "A medal? You just said he was dishonorably discharged. Last time I checked, they weren't giving out medals for that."

"It wasn't a military medal," said Agent Gebhardt. "It had a circle of the zodiac stamped on it."

Eliza put her hand in her pocket and wrapped her fingers around the medallion Stephanie had given her on the first day she'd come to the house.

Hold on to this and keep concentrating on Janie.

She had kept the medallion with her all through this awful week, knowing in her head that it wasn't going to help bring her child back but hoping against hope that it would. She'd wanted to believe in its power and she had been determined not to abandon any good-luck charm that might lead to Janie's safe return.

What an utter fool she had been.

Eliza was about to show the medallion to Agent Gebhardt when the bell rang and she thought better of it. Eliza wanted to confront Stephanie Quick herself.

Stephanie was smiling broadly when Eliza opened the door and invited her inside.

"My phone will be ringing off the hook with requests from police departments around the country," said Stephanie breathlessly. "I've been waiting my whole life for this moment."

"Come into the den with me, Stephanie," Eliza said softly. "So we can have some privacy."

The moment the door was closed, Eliza turned and stared directly into Stephanie's eyes.

"Is that why you kidnapped my daughter?" she asked. "For the publicity?"

"What are you talking about, Eliza?" Stephanie sputtered. "Of course I didn't have anything to do with Janie's abduction. I only helped to find her."

Eliza pressed the zodiac medallion into Stephanie's hand. "I guess it's only a coincidence then that the kidnapper had a medal with the zodiac on it in his pocket. I guess when the FBI compares the medallion you gave me to that one, they won't see they are the same."

Stephanie sank down on the sofa. "It wasn't supposed to go the way it did," said Stephanie. "Nobody was supposed to get hurt. Skip and I just wanted to get major media attention. I have gifts, Eliza. You saw that when I told you about John being pleased you still wore the perfume he liked. But not enough people would take my gifts seriously. Skip said Janie's kidnapping would be national news. Everybody would follow it. And if my visions led to Janie's recovery, the whole world would know about that and respect me for it."

"Not to mention that you stood to make a quarter of a million dollars in reward money and too much to count in future earnings. Just think of the book deals and television shows and the fees you could charge any pathetic soul who

was desperate for help in finding somebody they loved."

"It really wasn't about the money, Eliza.
It wasn't."

Eliza ignored Stephanie's protestations.
Still in disbelief at the audacity and cruelty
of the plan, Eliza studied the woman's face.

"So, you took Janie and Mrs. Garcia,
knowing all along that you were going to
drop my child off at the Bridal Veil waterfall in Milford?"

Stephanie hung her head.

"Now two innocent people are dead
and so is your Skip. What was he, your
boyfriend?"

"Yes."

"You know, my heart goes out to those
families, the families of the people you
killed," said Eliza.

Stephanie protested. "I didn't kill them."

"You might as well have," said Eliza.
"And you are going to spend the rest of
your life paying for that, and for the kidnapping of Janie and Mrs. Garcia—even
though prison is too good for you."

Eliza turned and stalked out of the
den to tell the FBI agents and to brief the
press.

ACKNOWLEDGMENTS

It Only Takes a Moment is the story I've wanted to tell but was afraid to write because it deals with kidnapping, a subject that has frightened me since I was young, for reasons beyond the normal ones.

My father was a special agent with the Federal Bureau of Investigation, assigned to high-profile kidnapping and extortion cases. While my father would never, at the time, tell us about his cases, it was easy enough to read about them in the newspaper or hear about them on the radio and television. And because I knew my father was working on solving these crimes, I paid a lot of attention to the details at an impressionable age . . . details which fascinated me while at the same time terrified me and led to a shivering dread that has followed me throughout my life.

Until now, it's always felt as though writing about a kidnapping might somehow tempt fate. But today my children are grown and I don't worry (as much) about anyone stealing them. My father is eighty-one years old, and there was no time like the present to harvest his memories . . . memories which fed my imagination and led to this story. So, first of all, let me thank Frederick V. Behrends, my dad; and my mother, Doris Boland Behrends, who met and married while working at the FBI.

My parents had two daughters, so I suppose if there was no FBI there would have been no me. The FBI also went on to assist me by training Margot Dennedy and Cathy Begley, special agents past and present, who generously lent their expertise for this story. I appreciate their considerable knowledge; I treasure their loyal friendship.

Another law enforcement pro, Stan Romaine, former director of CBS Corporate Security, came through for me yet again, this time providing the background on what a television network would do if the child of one of its stars was kidnapped. Thank you, Stan, for consistently answering my questions and sharing your wealth of experience.

In just another instance of the support he has given me over almost twenty years, Dr. Steve Simring offered his prescription for the best drugs to accomplish what I needed to get done in the story.

Phil Doyle gave me a tutorial on paintball warfare. Thank you for that, Phil, and for being such a good sport when your character had to die.

Beth Tindall and Colleen Kenny continue to inject their skill and creativity into www.maryjaneclark.com. Nice work, ladies.

Through the marvels of the Internet, Father Paul Holmes was able to provide his invaluable help all the way from Italy, where he was on sabbatical trying to get his own book written. *Tante, tante grazie, Paolo.*

Editor Carrie Feron, a mother herself, understood my terror of kidnapping. She shepherded the book through its stages, asking the right questions and contributing her smart thoughts to make the story better. Tessa Woodward paid exacting attention to so many, many details. Sharyn Rosenblum is the most enthusiastic and savvy publicist any author could want. There are so many talented and dedicated people at William Morrow/HarperCollins and I worry that I will leave someone out when thanking them for what they've done. Apologizing in advance for overlooking anyone, I'm grateful to Lisa Gallagher, Michael Morrison, Jane Friedman, Lynn Grady, Liate Stehlik, Adrienne Pietro, Debbie Stier, Tavia Kawalchuk, Lauren Naefe, and Kristie Macrides. Josh Marwell, Carla Parker, Brian Grogan, Mike Brennan, and Mike Spradlin constitute a powerful sales force.

Special thanks to Victoria Mathews, who did a fine job of copyediting, and

Thomas Egner, who designed such a haunting cover.

Much gratitude as well to Rachel Brenner, Mark Gustafson, Michael Morris, Rhonda Rose, Jeff Rogart, Dale Schmidt, and Donna Waitkus for placing those important orders.

Peggy Gould, I thank God every day for you and the other devoted and extraordinary people at SHS. Without you, I couldn't write the book.

Finally, some things may only take a moment, but building a publishing career isn't one of them. My deep appreciation to Jennifer Rudolph Walsh and Joni Evans, who continue to guide mine.